Flirting
WITH
40

All My Best,
K. Bromberg

NEW YORK TIMES BESTSELLING AUTHOR
K. BROMBERG

All My Best,

K. Bombard

PRAISE FOR K. BROMBERG

"K. Bromberg always delivers intelligently written, emotionally intense, sensual romance . . ."

—*USA Today*

"K. Bromberg makes you believe in the power of true love."

—#1 *New York Times* bestselling author Audrey Carlan

"A poignant and hauntingly beautiful story of survival, second chances, and the healing power of love. An absolute must-read."

—*New York Times* bestselling author Helena Hunting

"A home run! *The Player* is riveting, sexy, and pulsing with energy. And I can't wait for *The Catch*!"

—#1 *New York Times* bestselling author Lauren Blakely

"An irresistibly hot romance that stays with you long after you finish the book."

—#1 *New York Times* bestselling author Jennifer L. Armentrout

"Bromberg is a master at turning up the heat!"

—*New York Times* bestselling author Katy Evans

"Supercharged heat and full of heart. Bromberg aces it from the first page to the last."

—*New York Times* bestselling author Kylie Scott

"Captivating, emotional, and sizzling hot!"

—*New York Times* bestselling author S. C. Stephens

ALSO WRITTEN BY K. BROMBERG

Published by JKB Publishing, LLC

ISBN: 978-1-942832-27-0

Cover design by Helen Williams
Cover Image by Wong Sim
Cover Model: Amadeo Leandro
Editing by AW Editing
Formatting by Champagne Book Design

Printed in the United States of America

Everything begins and ends with the heart . . .

Flirting
WITH
40

One

Blakely

don't get what the big deal is.

Glancing around the trendy bar, which was dubbed the *go-to* place by all of my co-workers, I simply don't get it.

The atmosphere is nice if you're into rose gold and mirrors everywhere so you can see yourself in every reflection possible, save for the bottles of alcohol lining the walls in front of me. And those bottles? The bartenders use them to pour designer cocktails for customers who view the drinks as badges of maturity. EDM music is piped softly through the speakers much like jazz in an elevator, playing background to the chatter of the mostly twenty-something crowd. They flit from table to table with loud screeches when they find their next best friend for the night. Cell phone cameras flash just as frequently as the screeches.

You're stepping outside your comfort zone, Blakely. Isn't that what this is? Seeing how the other side lives so you can relate better?

Isn't that what Heather said? If I want to relate to my demographic, I need to understand them. Go out, visit the spaces they frequent, and become familiar with what they see as cool. She said that my ideas on this campaign felt old. Stale. As if I still thought wearing nylons was still all the rage or something.

The bartender sets my drink on the marble bar top in front of me just as my left shoulder is bumped from someone sliding onto the stool beside me.

"Excuse me. I'm sorry," a deep tenor apologizes, but my irritation at having to come here is already through the roof, so I just nod without glancing his way.

What a fucking day.

That's all I focus on as I lift the glass of amber liquid to my lips. I hum and welcome the burn as it slides down my throat in a useless attempt to wash away the shitty afternoon I've had.

"Now that's a drink," the man says. "I would have pegged you for a red wine type of girl."

Not used to random men approaching me in bars, I open my eyes and keep them focused on where my hands are wrapped around my glass.

There's no way he's talking to me.

There just isn't.

"What is that? Whiskey?"

Now I know he's definitely talking to me. Can't a girl sit in a bar in peace and enjoy a drink before heading home to her quiet house and empty bed?

"Brandy then?" He keeps at it.

Doesn't he get the hint that I'm not interested?

Doesn't he get the vibe that I'm in a crappy mood, and no, I won't go home and have a drunken one-night stand with him? No, I'm not going to stroke his ego and giggle like an airhead while flipping my hair either. I've been there, done that, and frankly, got screwed in the process.

And, no, not the good kind of screwed either.

"Rough day, then?" he continues.

He has no idea. First it was my boss, Heather, and the digs she took at me throughout our creative brainstorming meeting earlier. Then it was the text from my ex, letting me know he'd gotten the promotion I'd spent years helping him maneuver into, *and* oh, she said yes. As if I wanted to know just how quickly he replaced me and threw away the seventeen years we had been married.

Seven months to be exact.

I shouldn't care. I shouldn't. But it was still a blow.

"I'm sure it wasn't that bad," he says as if I'm actually listening.

"Nothing's ever as bad as it seems. So tell me, what it is you're trying to drink away with a stiff one?"

A stiff one? Jesus. Does he really get women with lines like that?

"Sometimes it's good to talk about it."

He wants to know?

I'll let him know.

"And sometimes it is as bad as it seems," I say, eyes still fixed on the drink in front of me. "I have a brand-new boss, who doesn't know what the hell she's doing. And it's not just an I-need-a-few-weeks-to-remember-the-details type of incompetency. It's more of an I-don't-really-care-so-long-as-no-one-else-notices type of ineptness. To top it off, I swear she's out to get rid of anyone who calls her on it. For example, *me*. Add to that, she's suddenly determined to make our office feel more *youthful*," I say, adding a healthy dose of sarcasm to the last word. "Then there's the fact that I'm up for a promotion that I'm sure I won't get despite being the most qualified person on her staff because she's trying to make me look bad at every freaking turn. What else? My ex-husband of a whole seven months informed me today that he did, in fact, get his new promotion to partner—*as if I care*—and oh, newsflash, he's engaged to a woman I'm sure is young enough to be my daughter. Add to that, my car is making some kind of ticking noise, so it's in the shop, and I'm sure that'll be nice and cheap . . . and the loaner car they gave me broke down on my way to work this morning. Horrible Heather wasn't too thrilled with that excuse, so she gave me some bullshit task as punishment that wasted a whole workday. And more than anything," I say as I turn to face him for the first time, "I hate when . . ." *guys don't get the hint that a woman just wants to be left alone.*

The thought going unspoken because, *of course*, the man I'm currently being a bitch to with my sarcastic, long-winded diatribe is stunningly handsome.

Like word-forgetting, thought-voiding gorgeous.

And young.

Like ten years younger than I am type of young.

But *damn.*

My smile is automatic, but it's hard to look intelligent after berating someone and then having your words fail you.

But this is me, feeling like a fish out of water in a trendy bar I was told to stop by as a homework assignment of sorts.

But there's him, fitting in perfectly with the crowd and angling his gorgeous smile my way and rendering me stupid when I know I'm a strong woman. One who doesn't get weak in the knees or fall for stupid lines.

I've done that before. Look where that got me—discarded and divorced.

But my god. I stare at him like a doe-eyed idiot, wondering how I back out of the trouble my words put me in.

I'm a woman whose career is built on paying attention to details, and believe me, I'm noticing every single detail about him.

The dark hair that's a little mussed even though it's styled. The tanned skin and broad shoulders beneath his plain black shirt. He's casual when no one else in here is casual, and yet, he totally fits in.

His eyes are unrelenting as they meet mine. They could be green or blue or even gray. The dim light of the bar makes it hard to decipher their color, and on the off chance that I'm coming off like a freak with a staring problem, I avert my eyes.

Right to his hands clasped around his glass. To his whiskey. To the cuffs of his dress shirt and how they're rolled up to reveal sculpted forearms. Major arm porn. Sexy hand porn.

Even thinking that makes me feel old.

Aren't I supposed to be focusing? On this? On why I'm here? On how I was a total bitch to a guy who seems to be as nice as he looks? Instead I'm sitting here skeptical of him simply because he's talking to me.

Focus, Blakely.

Easier said than done when he's sitting beside me.

It's definitely been too long since a man has paid me attention.

"You hate when, what?" he asks, pulling me back from my way-too-many thoughts about him and garnering a quick glance from me.

Yep. He's still there. His brows are narrowed some, and those lips of his are fighting back a smile.

"You didn't finish what you were saying." He lifts a lone eyebrow.

"Um . . . nothing. Never mind. I didn't mean—I thought you were someone else." I shake my head and wish I had five more of these drinks or a hole to climb into. "I'm sorry."

"Don't be. It's good to get it out sometimes."

I slide another glance at him, trying to figure out why, in a bar full of attractive, obviously available women, he's talking to me. "I think I got enough out. Again, I'm sorry. I didn't mean to be a bitch—"

"Yes, you did." My eyes whip over to him and catch the dimples that accompany his devastating grin as he turns on his stool to face me. "And I get it. You're in a bar. You either want to be left the hell alone, or you're waiting for someone else and don't want them to think you're chatting it up with some incredibly handsome man such as myself." He winks, and I hate that I'm charmed by it.

By him.

I laugh and shake my head. I can't help that I do, but the man beside me is the last thing, person—whatever—in the world I expected to find when I took a seat at this bar. "I'm not waiting for anyone," I say and return his smile.

Was that a flirt?

Did I actually just flirt with this guy who is definitely younger than I am and is positively more handsome than my ex, Paul, when everyone thinks Paul is the bee's knees.

Bee's knees?

Jesus. Definitely don't say that aloud.

"Tell me about her."

"About who?"

Why is he still talking to me?

"Your boss."

He's just being nice.

"My boss?"

Or lost.

"Yes. Horrible Heather I believe is what you called her. You said you were up for a promotion, but you don't fit the mold or something to that effect. What do you do?"

Or anything other than the type of guy he's coming off as because nice guys don't talk to women like me.

Or rather, from what I've learned after half-heartedly entering the dating pool again, nice, young, attractive guys like him don't talk to divorcées who are knocking on forty.

I stare at him, blinking for a few seconds as my thoughts run wild. "I'm in advertising. I work for a cosmetics company."

"Which one?"

"Glam."

"Nice." He draws the word out with a nod while he takes a sip of his drink. I don't think Paul bothered to remember what company I worked for most days. "And your boss. This Heather. She's new?"

"By a few months. Yes."

He rests his hand on the back of my chair in a casual pose, his fingers slightly touching my back.

"What's the promotion?"

"Vice president of marketing," I muse.

"Big time." He raises his eyebrows and glances down the bar where a gorgeous brunette meets his eyes for a beat before he looks back my way unfazed. "Why do you think you won't get the promotion?"

I part snort, part laugh. "Because she's determined to bring a new, youthful vibe to the office. Easy for her, not so easy for me."

"And how exactly does one make their employees have a youthful vibe and more importantly, how is she qualified to be the judge of that?"

"The youthful vibe will be demonstrated at the upcoming company retreat in the mountains where we're to experience team bonding at its finest so that we leave feeling like a family." I emphasize the last sentence in a singsong voice. "And she designated herself queen ruler of youthfulness."

"Oh. One of those." He snorts.

"Exactly." Why does it feel so good to have someone seem to genuinely understand?

"Do you have something against the mountains?" he asks, his eyes alight with humor.

"What do you mean?"

"Well, you said the word *mountains* with a healthy dose of disdain."

"I did, didn't I? I'm a city girl, so unless being in the mountains involves sitting on a porch swing sipping wine, then it holds no appeal to me."

"You're missing out big time." He gives a subtle shake of his head as the bartender slides fresh drinks in front of us. "But what does not liking the mountains have to do with hating your boss? Is it simply because she's making you go on the group bonding session?"

"I can stomach the team bonding because it's my job, and I think it's best I form closer connections with my coworkers. It's more that I think she'd love nothing more than if I didn't show up. She'd have a perfectly good reason to say I'm not a team player and make sure the world knows so it would be a ding against my possible promotion evaluation."

"So, you're going then, right?"

What does he care?

It doesn't matter because it feels good to talk to someone who actually listens.

"It's a catch-22. I miss the event and validate what they think of me—that I'm the matron of the group who's no fun—or I actually go and look like the matron of the group who doesn't have a significant other so I'm singled out without a partner in all the activities. I don't know, I get the feeling that my being over the cute late-twenties, let's-go-and-get-wasted vibe is a detriment in her eyes."

"And that's why you don't like her? Because she's younger?" He angles his head to the side and doesn't back down on his stare.

Of course, I just probably described him.

And then offended him.

That hole I'm digging keeps getting deeper and deeper.

"No. Yes. I mean . . . no."

"That's more than clear." He laughs and holds out a hand to me. "Slade Henderson. Younger than you. Has an affinity for the mountains, the outdoors, and can tolerate team bonding even if I don't always play by the rules. I'm also amused by long diatribes that I have to decipher from the random, beautiful woman sitting beside me in the bar."

Slade.

His name is Slade.

Isn't that so damn typical of a twenty-something-year-old? To have a name that proves his mom tried too hard to make him unique in that cute, I'm-an-awesome-mom kind of way?

She is probably a Pinterest perfectionist who always brings the right dessert to a party, makes crafty homemade gifts that everyone coos over, and who never loses her temper at her kids.

And then there's me. Not a mom because I was too focused on work and then, once I was ready to have kids, Paul told me it would cramp the lifestyle we had built. And Pinterest? Let's just say I'm the queen of failing anything I've attempted. So much so that I've given up even trying.

My inadequacies in the stereotypical female department are shining bright.

Only in my own head of course.

Wait? Did he just call me beautiful?

"And you are?" Slade asks.

"Blakely." I roll my eyes playfully but reach my hand out to shake his. "I'm Blakely Foxx. Older than you, thankful you are being nice to me instead of asking for me to be removed from the premises—"

"You say that like a woman who's been removed before."

"—and obviously having a shitty day."

"You forgot the part about having an absolute dick of an ex-husband."

I just look at him and shake my head as I chuckle. "Sorry. TMI."

"No, really," he says, "it'll make you feel better to say it and get it out in the open."

I eye him and wonder what the catch is. Is this some television show with a hidden camera and I'm the unsuspecting person being pranked?

When he nods in encouragement, I chuckle and look at my glass as if I can't believe I'm really going to. "Fine. He's an absolute dick of an ex-husband."

"See?" He nudges me. "Feels better, doesn't it?"

I laugh. "Yes. Sure."

"C'mon. You know it does."

He's right. It does. Even if it's catty and childish, it does.

"So, tell me something, Blakely, do you have something against youthful vibes?" he asks innocently enough, and for the briefest of seconds, I forget that's the term I used—youthful vibes—and almost choke on my drink.

"No. It's more than that. It's hard to explain." I think back to the meeting I had this afternoon. How Heather shot down every one of my ideas—calling them *dated* despite their high-performance track record, while touting ideas that any high school student could think up as brilliant when the younger members of the team proposed them. Her disapproving looks and loud sighs every time I gave input tell me my concerns are warranted. She looks at me and sees a dinosaur she wants extinct.

"Do you like your job?"

"What?" I ask.

"Do you like it? Are you good at it?" There's a nonchalance to the way he asks that doesn't put me on the defensive like it may have had if my boss asked me that same question.

"I'm damn good at it. It's my passion."

He purses his lips and nods. "Then what's the problem?"

"The problem is I've worked my ass off for almost twenty years to be where I am. I started with Glam when they were nothing and helped them grow to be the well-known brand they are today. And when other, bigger companies, tried to woo me away, I didn't stray. I'm a hard worker. I contribute. I deserve my position and the promotion . . ."

"But?" he prompts.

I hesitate because he doesn't know me from Eve, and I'm definitely not his type, but what does it hurt to use the ear someone offers?

"I'm petrified of losing my position because I'm not who they—who *Heather*—wants me to be."

"And who do *they* want you to be?"

"Hipper. Trendier. Without baggage." I take a sip of my whiskey. "Whatever it is, I know I'm not it . . ."

He doesn't respond, and when I glance his way, his lips are pursed and he's nodding ever so subtly. He slides those mysterious colored eyes my way. "Know or feel?"

"What's the difference?"

"Feeling is something that is fed by insecurities, knowing is something that is backed by facts."

"Aren't we full of wisdom?" I say and earn an adorable shrug and a lift of one of his eyebrows.

"It's a rarity, but it peeks its head up every once in a while." He looks to his left where someone has slid beside him and then turns back to me. "How is it you know Heather wants you gone?"

"It's present here and there. It's in how she talks to all of us in the meetings. The new people she's brought on." I chuckle, but it's more to myself than him. "They hear how long I've been there, and instead of thinking *wow, she has a breadth of knowledge that we can benefit from*, they think, *wow, she's so old she can't possibly know what's trending now*." I add a smile to hide my defensiveness and pretend that I'm not bothered by it, but I'm not fooling anyone.

"You're assuming though. There's no way for you to know what they're thinking." He shrugs as if telling me my insecurity is what's fueling my opinions is something I shouldn't be offended by. "Flip it around. You think they're judging you, but maybe you look at them as teenagers with acne and braces and judge them for not being old enough instead of giving them the benefit of the doubt that they're qualified. It's all a matter of perspective."

"I can't hide my age." I snort, the effects of the whiskey starting to kick in and relaxing me a bit.

"I wouldn't say that," he murmurs and has no shame as his eyes stroll lazily up and down the length of my body. They stutter over my legs, which are crossed at the knee, and take in my nude heels before they crawl their way back up to meet my eyes.

I can't recall the last time I was objectified so blatantly. I open my mouth to say something—to object out of principle—but why ruin the moment when I'm silently pumping my fist?

When the heat that's left in the wake of his gaze is still warming my skin.

Then reality hits me.

Slade, with his perfectly trendy name and the sexy arm porn, is only doing this to throw a middle-aged woman like me a bone because he's gay.

He has to be.

It would be a detriment to women everywhere if I was right, but why else would he be sitting in a bar like this on a Thursday night talking to me when he could be hitting on the gorgeous brunette a few seats down who keeps eyeing him.

No longer flustered by his too-long stare, I turn the conversation to him. "What about you, Slade? Why are you here tonight? Killing time until your girlfriend gets off work?"

The roll of his eyes and lightning flash of his grin shouldn't affect me the way they do, but they do.

"More like avoiding my mom who's visiting from out of town and who is currently invading my house." He tips his drink back and emits an audible sigh.

"That bad?"

"Ever had a meddling Italian mother who asks too many questions, berates you because all the women you've dated aren't good enough, and blames you for her not having any grandchildren when she has three other children who are just as capable?"

He isn't gay.

"Can't say that I have." I smile in sympathy.

"If you'd love to experience it, be my guest. She's probably making some kind of incredible dinner to lower your defenses and win you over before she goes for the jugular," he says and laughs.

"At least she feeds you before unleashing her full-fledged mother guilt on you."

"True." The ice in his glass clinks as he swirls his tumbler, eyes focused on it. "But it's been quite the adjustment having her stay with me for a bit."

"Cramping your style."

"Something like that," he murmurs and then looks my way again. "Why here?"

"Why where?" I ask.

"This bar of all bars. I've never seen you in here before."

"You frequent it often?" I ask, which earns a low rumble of a laugh from him.

"Now and then when I'm not working, but you . . . you don't seem like someone who cares about hitting the trendy spots to be seen."

"What do I seem like?" I ask and then wish I could take the words back because I fear the answer.

His eyes sparkle as they shamelessly take me in, and I want to squirm under their scrutiny. "Cautious but curious. Beautiful but doesn't acknowledge it. Here but not sure why. And definitely interested in the man she's talking to but isn't exactly sure how to let him know. But those are just observations. Give me a bit, and I'll let you know if I'm right or not."

Oh. Okay. Um . . . thoughts. String them together. I know I'm out of touch with this dating, flirting, whatever this is type of thing, but I shouldn't be this addled.

Usually, if a guy fed me lines like that, I'd tell him he was trying too hard and it would never work . . . but there is something about Slade—the candid, unassuming way that he delivers the lines—that makes me blush instead of cringe.

"So . . ." He lets the word float between us until I meet his eyes. "Why here?"

"I could ask you the same thing. Why here? Are you here to be seen at the trendy spot?"

He chuckles. "I couldn't give a rat's ass about being trendy. I'm meeting a friend in a bit and decided to stop in and have a drink beforehand. What about you? Why here?"

"I don't know," I murmur, knowing I can't exactly explain I'm here for reconnaissance so I can understand someone his age. "I've heard a buzz about it, so after the day I had . . . I thought, why not?"

"Well, I am glad that, for whatever reason, you stopped in here tonight."

Our eyes hold, that smile of his unwavering as my cheeks flush with heat. I do my best to push away all of my insecurities threatening to derail my thoughts.

I jump when the cell phone on the bar top between us rings. Slade groans when he picks it up and sees the number on the screen.

"Excuse me a second. I've been waiting for this call. Do you mind?"

"No. Of course not," I say as he slides from his barstool.

"Another round, please," he says to the bartender before he steps away and puts the phone to his ear. "Hello? Hi. Yes . . ." His voice is drowned out by the chatter of the bar, but I continue to watch him as he meanders through the tables and closer to the exit.

He's taller than I thought, and I take the moment to admire him and his nice ass. The women who notice him don't do it because his laugh is ringing out. They're watching him because he's all around hot.

He runs a hand through his hair as he laughs again, and just before he heads out the side door of the bar onto the patio, he looks back at me and flashes a grin.

"Well, I am glad that, for whatever reason it was, you stopped in here tonight."

His words replay in my head and inflate my ego more than it's been boosted in what feels like forever. I'm not ashamed to admit it feels good.

And I do believe he was flirting with me.

Me.

A thirty-nine-year-old divorcée who usually goes straight home after work and has her bra off and threaded through one sleeve before the door to her house even shuts behind her.

And I didn't panic.

Well, I did. I mean I'm doing it right now since I have a minute to, but this is all uncharted territory to me. I can't remember the last time I flirted with someone.

Is this real?

Do I want it to be real?

Of course, I do. Even if I'm nowhere near interested, what does it hurt to have a handsome man make me feel desired and good about myself?

I smooth my hands down my dress and shake my head. I'm just going to go with it and have a little fun flirting back. What'll it cost me?

With a sip of my drink and a glance over to the door Slade disappeared through, I nod, and realize this is what life after divorce feels like. Muddling my way through and taking the little victories as they come. Trying to gain confidence by scraping together the bright spots in my day. Trying to remember the woman I was—the one I want to be—after letting Paul get the best of me for so many years.

"Excuse me."

"I'm sorry. This seat's taken," I say to the gorgeous brunette who has been eyeing Slade since he sat.

"Oh. I know. I just . . ."

"Yes?" I ask as she shifts and plays with the business card in her hand.

"I'm shy . . . and don't want to be too forward, but I was wondering if you could give your son my phone number?" She holds the business card out to me and gives me what I think is a shy smile but is probably a you-are-out-of-your-league type of smile. "I don't have the guts to give it to him myself, but he's really cute."

Cue my rapid blinking and the opening and closing of my mouth as if I'm a guppy out of water while I register what she's saying, while I let the weight of her request hit me.

"My son?" I laugh, my brows narrowing and my head shaking in disbelief.

"Yes. I just assumed since he was talking to you, and you—"

"He isn't my—"

"Oh my god." Her face goes blank and jaw falls slack. "I'm so sorry." She takes a step back, her card still firmly between my fingers. "I just assumed because he's my age and you look like you're my mom's age that—"

"You should probably stop talking and walk away," I murmur as I turn my back to her and face the bar.

His mom?

Jesus.

Do I look that old?

I gulp down the rest of my whiskey as the panic I was fighting back earlier—the good kind of panic because an attractive man was talking to me—morphs into the kind of anxiety that has me wondering what in the hell was I thinking?

Do I look that desperate?

"Christ, Blake," I mutter as I rise from my stool, flustered and suddenly dying to get out of here before I make more of an ass out of myself than I already have.

There's no way Slade is interested in a woman like me.

I push some cash across the bar to pay for the drinks.

He has to be waiting for someone.

Then I slide her business card under his drink for him.

Or maybe he has mommy issues.

I glance over my shoulder to where he went one more time, and then I walk out of the bar.

Is it a coward move?

Hell, yes.

But what am I doing thinking a young guy like him would actually be flirting with an older woman like me?

TWO

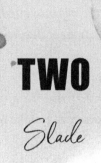

Slade

I stare at the business card in my hand. The one with the name Hillary on it and tattered edges from where I've toyed with its corners while listening to my team's bullshit rambling.

One had a crazy lady who refused to keep her gown on.

Another got to scrub-in on a heart transplant.

A third got into a tiff with an attending and was put on a genital warts case as retribution.

They are all gripes that come with the territory but are things I miss dearly and can't wait to get back to.

"What's up, Henderson? You off in la-la land?"

"Nah. Sorry," I say as four pairs of eyes turn my way and I drop the useless card into Leigh's empty water glass, letting the ice cubes darken its edges. "Just thinking how much I miss this"—I flick my hand to the people sitting around the table—"but don't miss the lack of sleep that comes with it."

"Fucker," John mutters but smiles.

"You missed our last bonfire," Leigh says. "For a man who has nothing to do, you sure seem busy."

I smile and shrug, too damn stubborn to admit it was too hard to hang with them. Sure, they're my best friends, but being with them also reminds me of what I'm missing. "My mom's been in town."

"Ohhhh," John says. "Nothing like a little nagging from Momma Henderson to make you antisocial. She still on you about dating all the wrong women? About needing grandchildren?"

"Something like that." I push the business card farther down into the glass.

"You'll be at the next one though?" Sarah asks.

"Sure. Yeah."

"By the way you keep looking at that card, it must be important," Prisha says and nudges me.

"No. Yes. Not anymore." I half laugh.

"A woman?" Her smile is wide, and her eyes glint with amusement.

"It's always a woman when it comes to Henderson," John says with a quick smirk and a shake of his head.

My mind flashes back to last night. To the green eyes peppered with temper and a full mouth not afraid to speak her mind. To a pair of sexy heels and long legs that I'm sure were even more impressive when she stood. To a woman who was stunning in a classic, sophisticated way that intrigued me. She was confidence laced with insecurity, defiance edged by doubt, and a captivating nature that shined through every so often when she let her guard down and forgot she was supposed to be angry.

"A woman? What woman?" Leigh adds.

"You actually have time to have a healthy relationship and then you went and turned down whatever offer came with that card?" Prisha asks. "Or did you get stood up?"

"My man here does not get stood up," John says, having my back, in a conversation about me they obviously are fine having completely without my participation. "We all know better than that."

"That's what it is, isn't it?" Prisha asks, but before I can respond, she turns to the rest of our friends. "He was stood up."

"Definitely," Leigh chimes in as if I'm not sitting between them. "He never sulks and he's definitely sulking."

"Since when do I get dumped?" I say and throw my hands up with a shrug, but the phone call I made earlier proved I'd been wrong-numbered.

"Hello?" the female voice came through the line as I looked around the diner, waiting for everyone to show up.

"Hi. I'm not sure who I should be asking for." I chuckled. "You said your name was Blakely, but your card says it's Hillary. Was this one of those situations where you gave me the wrong name until you were sure you actually liked me?"

"Blakely? I'm not sure who that is," she said, the confusion in her voice about as clear as my own confusion. "This is Hillary with Edge Pharmaceuticals, can I help you?"

"The other night. You were drinking whiskey. I asked you about it?" I said to the silence on the other end of the connection. "The mountain retreat with your work. Your jerk of an ex-husband. All of that?"

"I'm sorry. I don't—"

"The Bitter End?"

"Oh my god. *You.* You were the one with the dark hair, black shirt."

Hallelujah.

"Yes. That was me."

"I can't believe she actually gave you my card."

"Huh? What are you talking about?" I asked.

"I was too shy to approach you and let you know I was interested. I had on the pink dress and was sitting at the end of the bar? I gave the woman you were sitting with—your mom or sister or whoever—my card to give to you."

My hand stopped my beer when it was halfway to my mouth.

My mom or sister or whoever. What the hell?

"Wait. So you're telling me that we didn't meet?"

"No. I was too shy to hand it to you myself." Her laugh was throaty, sexy, and nothing like the shy woman she was claiming to be . . . and yet, I remembered her. The stunning brunette at the bar. The come-fuck-me eyes she kept trying to catch me with.

This woman was not shy.

No. She was trying to cut down any competition. Fucking females.

"Are you there?" she asked.

I didn't have time for games.

"Thanks. I thought you were someone else."

"But—"

"Maybe some other time."

"Earth to Slade," John says, snapping his fingers in front of my face.

"Definitely a woman," Leigh says as she plucks the business card from her drink. Taking it from her hand would be a dick move, and frankly, I've lived, breathed, and suffered with these four, it isn't as if they won't get it out of me at some point. "Who's Hillary? She the one who dumped you?"

"Nah." I shake my head with a shy smile. "But she might just be the reason someone I wanted to get to know better walked away."

I'd assumed Blakely had to leave when I'd taken the phone call. I'd figured she left me her card to let me know how to get in contact with her. I'd thought the attraction was mutual.

"C'mon, Romeo. Who is she?" Prisha asks.

"No one in particular. Just a woman in a bar."

She is someone, who for some reason, I can't seem to shake from my mind.

Maybe it's because she was nothing like I'm used to and . . . so damn intriguing.

"Isn't that how it always starts?" John teases. "Just a woman in a bar."

"Ah," Leigh coos, "did Slade find another lost puppy to fix and love before he adopts it back out?"

"Screw you." I laugh and take a sip of my beer.

"It comes with the territory, doesn't it?" John says with a shrug from across the table. He's wearing scrubs, and I realize wearing my own scrubs is one of the random things I miss more than I can express. "The need to save and fix and make whole again."

"I don't know what the hell you're talking about." I lean back, mimicking his casual posture.

"Projects. All of us residents love to have projects for the days we can't save someone, then at least we can save the project we're working on." Prisha wraps her arm around my shoulders and gives me a quick squeeze.

Projects?

She's crazy.

"I talked to the lady for like twenty minutes. She wasn't a project. She was . . . I don't know what she was."

"The lady?" Prisha laughs. "Why so formal? That's what you do when you're hiding something from us."

"Ohhh," Leigh draws the sound out, "I think there was legitimate interest there with *the lady*, guys." She clinks her glass of wine to the tip of John's beer bottle. "Henderson doesn't get like this over a booty call in the on-call room. I should know." She raises her hand, and we all laugh, drawing the looks of those around us.

"Why you gotta bring up things that happened years ago?" I tease. Our fling was short, more than hot, but definitely magnified by the fact that we were merely two exhausted first-year residents who needed someone who understood them.

"It's okay. We know how you roll, Henderson." John chuckles. "*In*—make them get hooked on you. *Out*—oh crap, they're hooked on you. *Done*—next, please."

"You guys make me sound like a man whore," I say and lean my head against the back of the booth with a shake of my head.

"But you do it in such a nice way," Prisha says. "Never have I ever met a man who has so many exes—"

"Not really exes," I try to explain.

"—who still love him after the fact."

I lift my beer and ignore their razzing. I'm used to it with this group. "You guys are messed up."

"And you miss the hell out of us," John says, and the table quiets some, Prisha's smile softens, and Leigh's fingers play with the stem of her glass.

"I do." I half snort, half laugh as my tone sobers. "More than you know."

"How much longer?" Prisha asks.

"Your guess is as good as mine." I shrug. "They want to hear from Ivy herself. She's the victim, and until she can make a statement, it's 'my suspicions and overreactions'—*their words, not mine*—against his statements."

"And so, what? You're in limbo until then?" John asks.

"Basically. I'm waiting for the review board to reconvene in the next week or so, but I know nothing's going to be decided until they hear from her. I'm sure that, at some point, I'll have to do some dog and pony show to get the powers that be to accept me back into the program without prejudice." I take a sip of my beer, acting as if it's no big deal when they know it's exactly the opposite. It's my whole damn world. "But it is what it is."

"How is she?" Leigh asks gently, and I meet each of their eyes, knowing I technically shouldn't know the answer considering I'm not supposed to be anywhere near the hospital.

"Still in a coma. Still . . . hanging on. I'm not really allowed to check in on her, so that's all I know."

"The whole thing is fucked up." John sighs. Each one of them has told me that they would have done the same thing had they been in my shoes. Would have let emotion get the better of them and protected their patient. That they would have acted how I did.

But they didn't do it.

I did.

And I'm paying the price.

"I don't regret it. I mean, I regret the suspension and the red tape I'm going to have to possibly cut through, but I don't regret what I did when it comes to him . . . just don't tell the board that."

"Not a chance, brother," John says.

"Not a chance," Prisha reiterates.

THREE

Blakely

"I can do one better," I say and take a bite of pizza before settling back against the couch.

"Nothing can be worse than walking into your very hot boss's office with your skirt tucked into your panties. And panties is a loose term for the back-of-the-drawer ones I grabbed because I hadn't done laundry. Nothing," my best friend, Kelsie, says with a definitive nod as she empties her glass of wine and has no shame in refilling it with the bottle sitting on the coffee table between us.

"How about sitting in a bar, thinking the cute, sexy, *young* guy sitting next to you is flirting with you—"

"And the problem with that is what?"

"I'm far from finished, Kels." I take a sip of my own wine, and the ridiculousness of my thinking he was actually flirting with me hits me once again. "The guy, Slade—"

"*Slade?*"

"Yes. Just go with it."

"It's kind of sexy. Tell me what he looked like." I stare at her and shake my head. "What? I need the whole visual, and besides, you should humor me. It'll be the most action I've gotten in months."

I laugh and am so grateful that I have her in my life. "Tall. Dark hair. Super light and gorgeous eyes. Great smile. Well dressed. And his hands and arms were super sexy with the rolled-up dress shirt thing going."

"A watch?" she asks. "Watches are sexy."

"I think so. Yes. I think. It doesn't matter," I say, but her eyes tell me it does matter for her complete visual. "Sure, yes, he had a watch."

"That visual just gave me the chills." She claps.

"Yeah, well, I kind of unloaded on him when I thought he was hitting on me, and—"

"Why would you do such a thing?" she shrieks.

"Can you let me finish, please?" I ask, this stop-and-start conversation between us not unusual.

"Yes. Sure. I just don't understand why you'd tell off a hot, young guy."

I eye her above the rim of my glass. "First, I didn't tell him off. Second, I didn't know he was hot when I started my rant. And third, I had just come from a shitty meeting with Heather—"

"Don't ruin the visual by bringing her up. We don't like her, but we like Slade." She hums. "Slide-It-In-Slade."

"Oh my god. You're . . . you're—"

"Just saying the things you've thought since." She laughs in that loud, obnoxious hyena way of hers that dares me not to smile. "Finish. Slade. Hot. Sexy. Watch-wearing."

"What I was going to say is that more than him being all those things, he was super nice. And funny. And interested. I mean, how often do you meet a guy who actually asks you a question and listens to the answer?"

"Any man will listen to you if he thinks he's going to get laid."

"It wasn't like that—the half-listening, eyes-roaming, only-there-for-one-kind-of-thing attention like most guys give. He was different. I can't explain why, but he was."

"Was he gay?"

"I thought the same thing, but he mentioned how his mom doesn't like the women he dates."

"Oh." She scrunches her nose. "A momma's boy, then."

"I don't think that either." And I shake my head because I'd thought that too. "He was just nice and funny and endearing. And . . . it was so great to talk to someone for a while. To have someone talk to me."

"Shocker," she says sarcastically.

"Kelsie!"

"What? Maybe your 'Bitter Party of One' sign wasn't hanging around your neck for once, so you didn't scare him off."

"What's that supposed to mean?"

"It means you do all the things that say you're single but only because you feel like you have to. You go to a bar but seem unapproachable. You meet a nice guy but come off bitter. You put yourself out there because you're figuring out how to navigate this new world, but when you do, it's only for show."

Leave it to my best friend to call me on the carpet.

"Can you blame me?"

Her expression softens. "No. I don't blame you. I think you've been emotionally battered and bruised, and while you know that you're better off without Paul, he also took some parts of you during your marriage that you're trying to find again. That takes time and a willingness to acknowledge and accept that he did."

My sigh fills the room because she didn't say anything I didn't already know. Still, it's hard to hear.

"I'm sorry you are going through all this. Of course, you enjoyed Slade's company. Hell, you were with dickhead Paul, who only listened to himself and cared about his own needs, for so long that anyone is better than him," she says, her hatred for my ex growing exponentially with each and every passing day. "So, tell me the rest. If things were so *nice*, why are you comparing your conversation with him to me showing my ass to my boss?"

"Because, at some point, Slade had to go take a phone call so he stepped outside, and this gorgeous woman came up to me. She explained that she was super shy and asked if I could give *my son* her phone number."

"*Your son?*" Kelsie chokes on her sip of wine. "You're kidding me, right?" And before I can say anything else, she flops back into her seat and begins laughing so hard she can't speak. The sound fills the room, and I can't believe my lips are tugging up at the corners as I watch her wipe tears from beneath her eyes.

"Are you done?" I ask, making a show of crossing my arms over my chest in false annoyance.

"I just—how did she actually think you were his mother? Was he fifteen or something?"

"Funny."

"No, I'm serious," she says, setting her glass down and realizing that I don't find her theatrics as amusing as she does. "Either she had no idea how offensive she was being or she thought that making you feel insecure would get you to walk away because she was truly one catty bitch. Bet you anything that's why she did it."

"Oh, please."

"Oh, please? There is nothing more annoying than a skinny person complaining about how fat they are or a gorgeous woman acting as if she doesn't understand why men think she's attractive. Case in point," she says, pointing at me.

"Whatever." I wave a hand her way.

"You have great curves and salon-worthy hair—"

"I think you've drunk too much—"

"And you're smart and dedicated, and I could go on and on."

"Thank you, but you're my best friend—you knew me when I had frizzy hair and wore glasses—so you have to say that."

"I don't." She holds up her hand to stop my argument. "It's a fight for another day." She tops off my glass when I hold it out. "Let's get back to how Little Miss Thang reacted when you tore her card up and told her to go to hell."

I stare at my best friend of twenty-plus years and twist my lips in response. I may have replayed the scene in my head a couple of (hundred) times, and in each one of them, not once did I scamper away like a mousy female and let the gorgeous brunette get the better of me and my self-confidence.

"Please tell me you told her off." There is a pleading disbelief in her voice that has me averting my eyes. "Blake." She waits until I meet her eyes and then huffs. "Why would you not put her in her place?"

I stare at her as I fight the tears welling in my eyes and shrug, embarrassed. "I should have. I felt so good about myself for the first time in forever, and then . . . I didn't."

"What did you do?"

I cross my hands over my face as if to hide from her. "Don't ask."

"Blakely." My name is a warning. "Spill it."

"I slipped her card under his drink and snuck away while he was on his call." Shame heats my cheeks as I force myself to meet her eyes.

"Why on earth would you do that?" she asks. "Why would you let her win?"

"I've asked myself that a million times. It isn't as if anything would have come from it. He was there for whatever, and I was trying to unwind—"

"But you obviously hit it off."

"That's an exaggeration. We barely met." I say the words, refusing to acknowledge that there was a connection so I don't feel like more of an idiot than I already do.

"Did he flirt with you?"

"I don't know. I mean, he was just being nice," I deflect.

"Was there any casual touching? You know, the kind where his knee accidentally hits yours but doesn't move away?"

I think of his hand on the back of my chair, of the soft graze of his thumb against my shoulder, and don't answer.

"Was there the tingly feeling?" She waggles her eyebrows, and I laugh.

The funny thing? Kelsie and I are best friends on the level of we tell each other everything. She knows the things Paul did in bed that I hated and the ones that I loved. I know the quirks of the men she dates. And yet, I'm hesitant to admit that I really liked Slade.

Well, I am glad that, for whatever reason it was, you stopped in here tonight.

"Hey, Blake?"

"*Hmm?*"

"You should never let another woman steal your sparkle. You know that."

She's right. I do know that. "This thing with Paul—his moving on—has really done a number on me." It pains me to admit it, but there it is.

"It would do a number on anyone. Hell, you aren't made of stone, but at the same time, who the hell was she to say that to you?"

"It was probably for the best. Did I really think anything was going to come of it?"

"That's beside the point," she says resolutely as she rises and heads to the kitchen to choose another bottle of wine. "For all you know, Slade was falling massively in love with you. You were going to have a quick, torrid love affair where he made you realize that you were a wildcat in bed, that Paul was more than selfish with giving oral, and that you are a badass at work who is going to get that promotion."

"I think you've had too much to drink," I say through a laugh as the neck of the bottle clinks against the rim of her wine glass as she refills it.

"And I think a man like Slade is just what you need—a little youthfulness to remind you that you may be divorced but you aren't dead. A little reminder to you that—oh my god!" she screeches as if she just had the biggest epiphany ever.

"What?"

"Do you know how awesome it would be if he went with you on your company retreat? Some hot, sexy man who all the women would be jealous over? He would make the bitches in your office see you in a new light."

"Gee. Thanks." I roll my eyes. "Because, obviously, you have no faith that I can win them over on my own."

"No, that isn't what I mean. You know I have faith in you, but women pay attention to men. They'd all be vying for a scrap of his attention while he's too busy doting on you. Then they'll wonder what you have that he sees but they don't, and then"—she throws her hands up—"voilà. They fall in line, and you become the one everyone wants to be."

"You're forgetting one very important fact."

"What's that? That he has a huge cock—"

"Yes, that's exactly it. In the whole twenty minutes we talked, we talked about how big his dick was. You really do need help."

"Can't blame a girl for thinking large." She offers me a sarcastic smile. "And that is *one* very important trait."

"Well, the fact I was opining on"—I clear my throat—"was that you can make up this whole Blake and Slade fantasy all you want, but it isn't going to happen."

"Says who?"

"Says the fact that I left without finding out anything about him other than his name," I say. "So even if you concocted the most beautiful love story ever, it isn't going to happen."

The cogs in her brain seem to click into place as she settles back into her seat. "But if you did—if fate worked in some funny way and you had his phone number—would you call him?"

"Let's not have you make up fake scenarios and live vicariously through me, *hmm?*"

"I'm serious." She gestures dramatically. "If you had his number—no, better yet, if he told you he really wanted to take you to your company retreat, what would your answer be?"

I stare at her and her ludicrous ideas with a dumbfounded look on my face. "I'd say have another glass, er, bottle of wine."

"The answer is yes. It's always yes."

"Whatever." I wave a hand at her.

"I'm serious. If Slade was standing in front of you right now, the answer would be 'Yes, please come to my mountain retreat with me. Show everyone else up with your easy charm, nice ass, incredible smile, and huge co—'"

"You haven't even met him."

"I don't have to."

"He could be a serial killer."

"He isn't." She holds her hand up to stop me from asking her how she knows that. "He's the perfect rebound for you."

"Oh Jesus."

"What better way to get over stick-in-the-mud Paul than have a hot, young guy with all kinds of stamina who'd gladly ride you into finding your self-confidence again."

"Your imagination is tireless." The wine is hitting me, and my lips are starting to tingle.

"The answer, Blakely, would be yes."

"You're insane."

"Say it with me. Yes." She draws the single-syllable word out.

"I can say yes to you all you want, but it doesn't matter. Nothing's going to come of it. He was a chance meeting that's gone and forgotten."

"And sometimes fate works in mysterious ways."

I roll my eyes dramatically. "Since when have you ever believed in fate?" I mutter to the one woman who grabs whatever it is she wants by the balls and takes it without asking.

She's fearless.

And a whole lot more like who I'd love to be but can't find the way to do so.

"I'm not handing over more wine until you say it." Her eyes narrow in demand.

"Kels . . ."

"Say it."

"Yes," I say. "Sure."

Her laugh fills the room. "I'm not buying it. I want the whole phrase: *yes. It's always yes.*"

I slide an evil glance her way because I know she won't stop until I give in. "Yes. It's always yes," I say in my most melodramatic voice.

"Yes!" She throws her free hand up and finally walks toward me and my empty glass. "Just you remember that! Next time you see him, you'll say, '*Hi, Slade. Yes, Slade.*"

"Jesus. You're—" An alert of sorts emanates from her phone, telling her that someone has just pulled up her driveway, and she groans.

Within seconds, the front door opens and then slams. We both wait for her to call out for her mom like she used to. The single word filled with excitement that she's home and can't wait to tell Kelsie how much fun she had at her friend's house.

"Three. Two. One," Kelsie whispers, knowing the tornado of walking hormones her daughter has been as of late.

I'll just say my goddaughter and the term "bundle of joy" are as far apart as humanly possible at this point.

"Hi, honey," Kelsie says as Jenna rounds the corner to the family room.

My heart floods with love at the sight of her. I know Kelsie is struggling with how much she loves her daughter and, at the same time, has days when she wants to tear her own hair out in frustration.

"Boozing it up again?" Jenna asks when she eyes the glasses in our hands, those gorgeous lips pulled into a sneer.

"Did you have fun at Andrea's?" Kelsie asks with a timorous smile.

"Do you really care?" Teenage snark in full force.

I steal a glance at my best friend, knowing she's debating if reprimanding her daughter is worth the fallout or if letting it go is just better to preserve the peace for the rest of the night.

Kelsie takes a sip of wine and sighs before giving her daughter a warning smile. "I'm going to ignore you said that."

"I'm not," I chime in because I can get away with more than Kelsie can since I'm not her mother. "Let me guess, you were tik-snapping and chat-tocking? Can we see some of them?" I hold out my hand for her phone.

"Eeew. No way." Jenna takes a step out of the room in utter horror even though she knows damn well that I know it's TikTok and Snapchat. But there's a crack of a smile there, a hint of the sweet little girl I used to know, and for now, it's enough. "I've got homework to do."

"Good. You go do that and be responsible while your mom and I drink some more wine, talk about cute boys, and figure out how to make your life more miserable than it already is." My smirk and shrug have Jenna rolling her eyes.

"So gross." She huffs and then heads down the hallway and into her room, loudly shutting the door behind her.

"It's a phase," I say as Kelsie tips her drink to her lips.

"I know I have to pick my battles, but lately, it feels as if everything with her is an all-out war, so it's just easier to ignore the attitude and move on."

"Hormones, wondering if boys like you or not, the pressure of everything . . . it's a lot for a fourteen-year-old to handle. I understand, of course, because I feel the same way most days."

I laugh to hide behind the joke, but I know she sees what I keep hidden most days—the doubt of how I'm coping, the embarrassment and failure of not being able to make my marriage work, and more than anything, my loss of self-worth.

Her expression softens, and she looks at her wine for a beat before meeting my eyes again. "You need to let loose, B. You need to say fuck it to everything you never would have done before and just try it. What's holding you back? Sure, you're divorced, and damn straight, you're flirting with forty, but you aren't dead. You've dropped that ball and chain, and it's your turn to fly."

My raised eyebrows and heavy sigh are the only response I give her.

"Say yes. The answer is always yes."

FOUR

Blakely

"That's just an outdated way of thinking and marketing. We need to—"

"I have years of sales data to back up the success of this marketing campaign. In the past, we've made a point to run the campaign sporadically, so when we do use it, it hits with a maximum punch," I say, trying to tamp down my frustration. Heather catches it. I know she does. And the slightest smirk ghosting on her mouth says she really doesn't care.

The worst part? The fifteen other attendees sitting in the product campaign meeting can see the look and can infer she doesn't trust me.

Either that or they figure she feels threatened by me.

"We can definitely add it to our list of options, but it's an old approach when we want to be progressive. The world is moving on, and yet, you . . . you seem to like the past."

Her eyes hold mine, and the condescension in her tone has me gripping my pen so tight my fingers ache.

There is an uncomfortable silence as others shift in their seats, and all I can do is nod in appreciation that she put my idea on the list.

And then I sit there and listen as every other person pitches ideas that lack substance or really even creativity.

"Okay, let's get to it," Heather finally says with a faux fist pump, probably tiring of hearing her own voice. Then again, maybe not. "Blakely, stay a sec, will you?"

Oh, joy.

"Sure. Not a problem." I plaster a smile on my face and sit back in the seat I just stood from, my laptop and notebook still pressed against my chest. "What can I do for you?"

"Moving forward, if you can't stop showing me up at our creative meetings, then I'll have to have you sit them out."

"I'm sorry . . ." I shake my head. "Show you up?"

"Yes. We all know you've been here forever. I don't need you bringing it up constantly in front of all the new people I've hired. Frankly, it makes you look dated, and when I'm the one constantly trying to fight for you, it makes it that much harder to do."

Fight for me? Does she think I buy her bullshit when I'm incessantly afraid to turn my back to her?

My pause is simply to make sure I have a lock on my cool before I speak. I need this job. *I love this job.* I've weathered incompetent bosses before. I can do it this time too.

Or so I hope.

"Experience doesn't make me dated. My knowledge of how certain marketing campaigns and sales affect the Glam brand, which I know inside and out, should be looked upon as an added value."

She purses her lips as she stands there, arms crossed over her chest, disdain written all over her face.

"I'm not sure how we got off on the wrong foot," I say as I rise from my seat again and make my way toward the door where my boss of a whole four months is standing. I guess it's up to me to be the mature one in the room. "But somehow we did. I love my job, and the last thing I want to do is show up anyone—least of all you. Besides, if I get the promotion, we'll be sharing this responsibility so it behooves us to iron out these wrinkles."

Our eyes hold as the silence stretches, and my palms grow clammy at the disdain etched in the lines of her face. Why does she make me nervous?

Because I've spent my whole career working toward the vice president of marketing position, and now that it's just within reach, she's the only one who can take it away from me.

"Perhaps it's something we can work on at the team bonding retreat." Her smile is quick and holds even less warmth. "I look forward to seeing you and your . . . husband?" She waves a hand in my direction. "I'm sorry, I forgot. You're divorced. It's okay if you come single. We have a few who are. We can modify some of the challenges so you aren't alone the whole time."

You condescending cow.

"My boyfriend will be there." My answer is too fast, and I inwardly cringe at how pseudo desperate it sounds.

"Boyfriend?"

"Yes. Boyfriend."

I offer a catty smile and then silently freak out the entire time I walk the length of the glass walls that house the conference room, knowing she's staring at me.

I have no idea how in the hell I'm going to pull a boyfriend out of my ass for the retreat.

Maybe Kelsie was right. Maybe I'm sabotaging myself so that I have no other option but not to go.

It doesn't help that, three hours after the fact, I'm still preoccupied by my lie. When I leave my office, hobo bag under one arm and cell phone held up to my ear, I cross the street completely distracted.

So distracted that, when I look up, I stop dead in my tracks the second I see them.

The person behind me bumps smack-dab into me, and a car that wants to use the turn lane I'm standing in honks its horn. It doesn't matter, though, because all I see is them.

Paul is standing ten feet in front of me, looking as handsome as he ever did. His skin is tan, his hair is a little bit longer, and his typical white button-up shirt that I could never get him to veer from is gone. It's been replaced by a silver one with its sleeves rolled up to the elbows and the collar unbuttoned some. He looks relaxed, and the grin spreading across his lips tells me he's happy. I can't remember the last time I made him look like that.

A pang hits me low in the gut. It doesn't matter how much I hate him because I once loved him. I once adored him. I moved across the country and away from my family to start a life with him. I once put my dreams on hold—kids, the white picket fence, the whole Norman Rockwell existence—for him and his career aspirations.

All to be left with nothing.

So does it hurt to see him from afar? Hell yeah it does.

When he reaches to his left, all those pangs turn to a hand-trembling anger as he hooks his hand around the waist of the woman walking toward him. He pulls her into him and kisses her way too long. It's the kind of public display of affection that makes anyone watching uncomfortable but also screams of intimacy and still-new love.

But I can't move. I can't look away. And when she steps back, I'm stunned by the sight of her. It's the first time I've seen his new fiancée, and all I can think of is how much she looks like me . . . the me from *twenty years ago*.

As if Paul senses me the same as I sensed him, his eyes find mine. Our stares hold for a beat, his smile faltering and then widening as he presses a kiss to her cheek before pointing to me and calling out my name.

"Blakely!"

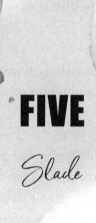

FIVE

Slade

"I love her to death . . . but, man . . ."

"What? You're a grown man who needs his space?" Lane's laugh comes through the connection.

"My own space. Silence without the constant badgering about who I'm dating, why the past chicks weren't good enough, how I need to find a good woman to settle down with but only after she approves. Shit, Lane, I miss her till she's here, but when she is, I'm ready to send her back home."

"You don't mean that," my cousin says.

And he's right. I don't. I love my parents to death, but loving them to death and having my mother take it upon herself to move in for a few weeks while I'm on suspension from work is trying my patience.

Watcha doing? Where are you going? Whatever happened with What's-Her-Name? The one with the blonde hair and crooked toes? How come you organized your kitchen drawers like this? It's against the flow of the space.

"The questions are endless, but I'm not going to complain about the home-cooked meals and laundry service."

"Bastard." He snorts. "So, other than avoiding your mom, what have you been doing?"

"I'm working on a few papers for medical publications and journals. You know me—"

"You never could sit still."

"Never. Hey . . ." I look down the sidewalk ahead of me.

I recognize the dark hair, full mouth, and subtle sophistication. Every part of me is sucker punched by the sight of her.

Blakely Foxx.

The woman who walked away the other night.

"I've gotta go. A friend's walking up," I lie to Lane, ending the call without waiting for his response.

My first instinct is to walk over to her and put her on the spot. Ask her why the fuck she left me someone else's business card before ghosting me in the bar last week.

No one's ever done that before.

No one.

I shouldn't care because, who is she anyway? A random woman amidst a million other random women in this city? Another proverbial fish in the sea?

Realizing that the confrontation isn't worth my time regardless of how intriguing I find her, just as I make the decision to walk away, I see it. The sudden slumping of her shoulders. The emotion shoved away when she looks at the man before her, and the fake smile she plasters on her face when she turns her attention to the woman beside him. A woman who could easily be her doppelganger in every sense of the word, save for age.

I stand twenty or so feet away, unable to tear my eyes away as I size up the situation. How the doppelganger makes a show of using her left hand as she speaks, ensuring the sun glints off the diamond on her ring finger. How she continually turns into the man, touching him and laughing too loud, as if to stake her newly minted claim.

It isn't my business.

No damn part of it is.

And yet, I picture the look in Blakely's eyes the other night when she went off on me. The anger mixed with frustration edged with shame and exasperation. How, when she got to the part about her ex-husband getting engaged, I could feel the hurt there.

Staring at the three of them, I can still feel it.

"Not your problem," I mutter as I close the distance, knowing I'm going to regret what I'm about to do, but know I'm going to do it anyway.

"Blakely. Sweetie," I say. Her head startles toward the sound of her name, and then her eyes grow wide as they land on me.

Yes, I'm the man from the bar.

But even better is the confusion etched in her expression when I step up beside her, slide a hand around her waist, and pull her toward me. "I thought we were meeting at the restaurant?"

Her hesitation allows me to finish the sentence and lean in and press a chaste kiss against her utterly shocked lips. I lift my eyebrows as I wait for her to respond, and then I decide to use the moment to turn to look at a very wide-eyed ex-husband.

Perfect.

"Oh, hey. I'm sorry. I didn't mean to interrupt." I keep my hand firmly where it is on Blakely's waist. "Slade Henderson. Blakely's boyfriend, man, *plaything*. I respond to all." I laugh, watching her ex's face pull tight as I offer my free hand for him to shake. My smirk is one hundred percent meant to goad. "And you are?"

He stares at my hand and then Blakely. When he finally turns back to me, he reaches out and takes my hand strictly out of manners.

"Paul Foxx. I'm Blakely's—"

"Ex-husband." I nod and squeeze my hand on the side of her waist. "Nice to meet you in that awkward, no-one-wants-to-meet-an-ex kind of way."

We hold each other's stare, size each other up, and in that brief second, I can surmise he's a smarmy, too-good-for-everyone, know-everything prick. Fucking figures.

And with perfect timing, Blakely overcomes her utter surprise and stirs to life. "Hi. Yes." She gives a subtle shake of her hand as her arm slides around my waist and she turns her body more into mine. "I was on my way to meet you when I ran into Paul here and his girl—"

"Fiancée," the doppelganger says, her eyes roaming up and down the length of me. The look tells me that the ring on her finger wouldn't stop her if I offered. She holds her fingers out to me in that debutante hand-shake—hand cupped as if she expects me to kiss the top of her hand instead of shake it.

I don't kiss knuckles, sweetheart.

"I'm Barbie soon-to-be Foxx."

"Nice to meet you," I say.

I can see it more clearly now. The similarities in the two women. The smugness on his face. How he thought the grass on the other side would be so much greener, and yet Barbie's so damn young she probably has no clue how to keep it alive.

And for fuck's sake. *Barbie?* After being married to a Blakely? Isn't he afraid he's going to say the wrong name when he's groaning a name mid-orgasm?

"Barbie," Blakely says, her face pulling tight as I gently squeeze her waist, "was telling me about how she and Paul just came back from a trip of a lifetime in Fiji."

"Fiji." I lift my brows. "How trendy."

"We got engaged there," Barbie gushes as Paul shifts his feet, definitely uncomfortable now that I'm in the mix.

"I assumed with the fiancée part." I wink at her, and she smiles coyly.

"And now we're busy planning the wedding and figuring how soon we want to have kids. I say wait a year, but Paul thinks we should start right away." Her voice squeaks as Blakely's body tenses. Clearly, that is news to her.

"Look at you, Paul, trying to get her all fat and happy so no one else snags her away from you." The dig hits its mark, and Paul winces, but my smile is all warmth like a practiced politician's. I'm not sure if Barbie is too preoccupied with making her diamond sparkle, but she sure as hell doesn't get my gist. "Good for you. They're a little more ambitious than the plans Blakely and I have made."

"Like what?" Paul asks, more than willing to get in a pissing match with me.

"When you're as in love as the two of us are, all you want to do is spend every waking minute together. In bed. Out of bed. Then back in bed."

"Oh, so this thing between you is new?" Paul asks, because of course, he's so arrogant that he can't fathom Blakely could possibly move past him like he did her.

"New?" I chuckle in disbelief because the prick deserves it. "What's it been? Four months? Or we already on five?" I meet Blakely's eyes and let her take the lead as Paul's stuttered breath tells me he's fucking livid.

Serves the fucker right.

"Almost five," Blakely says and smiles so sweetly at me that I almost believe the lie.

I pause to let it sink in before looking from Blakely to him and love that, when I do, the sudden redness to his cheeks tells me he's buying it too. Buying it and not liking it because he just realized that Blakely isn't sitting at home pining for his arrogant ass and that she moved on way before he ever assumed she did.

"Oh." He clears his throat. "I wasn't aware that—"

"No one was." I smirk. "When something is this good, sometimes you don't want any outside influences to spoil just how fucking great it is." Paul starts to talk, but I continue right over him and lay it on thick— just like Barbie and her goddamn blinding diamond ring. "But I finally explained to Blakely the other night that I'm so damn proud to have her beside me that I can't wait for the world to know. So, you may have had Fiji, and from the sound of it, you will soon have sleepless nights, diapers to change, and no social life, but we'll have The Hamptons next month for a family wedding," I say, nuzzling Blakely's neck in the least creepy way I can considering we don't really know each other. "The mountain retreat next week. Then after that—"

"Mountains? You, Blakely?" Paul laughs, grabbing on to something, anything, to stop me from rubbing salt in the wound. "You'd never step those heels of yours off a city sidewalk."

"*Those heels*," I say with a whistle and lift of my eyebrows in that boys-will-be-boys type of way, "are fantastic in so many more places than just a sidewalk." I slide my hand ever so subtly against her rib cage, mirroring his stance with Barbie, to let the insinuation hit home.

Irritation feathers in Paul's jaw while Barbie continues to smile cluelessly as he pushes back at me. "She'd never risk ruining them. Believe me. *I know.*"

Another claim made on the woman he walked away from.

"I don't think you do. It's amazing the things a fresh perspective can do. You know, out with the old, in with the new. It just brings out sides of you that you never knew you had." I say the words to Blakely, but they're a pure *fuck you* to her ex.

"And what is it you do?" Paul asks, his head angling to the side, the alpha male trying to thump his chest, ready to let me know how much money he makes or some shit like that.

Asshole.

"I'm a cardiothoracic surgeon." Blakely stills beside me as I meet his eyes. I challenge the question in his, the warring, the proverbial measuring stick that just slipped from his fingers. Yeah, I save lives. If I told him I'm also a Big Brother at the Y and that I love puppies, then his new fiancée would be walking toward me within seconds. "And you?" I ask.

"Investment banking. Mergers and acquisitions. I just made partner."

The way he says that last part, like he's staking a flag in some uncharted territory so that I'll praise him for his accomplishments, is more than pathetic.

"*Mmm.*" It's all I say. Enough to let his big prick ego wonder what it means and why I'm not congratulating him. "It isn't saving lives"—I exhale audibly as he grits his teeth—"but then again, money does seem to make the world go 'round these days."

"Is that how you met? At the hospital?" Paul asks. The five-month thing must be fucking with his head.

"Nah. I was at a bar when I looked over and saw Blakely. Talk about being sucker punched. Especially after I realized I was going to have to compete with the three other men who were trying to get her attention—"

"Blakely doesn't go to bars," he says in dismissal.

"Seems you don't know Blakely very well then—or chose not to take the time to. First high heels. Now bars. Seems you missed a lot."

He's like a voodoo doll I keep sticking pins in. Each one chipping away at that smug expression bit by bit.

And by the slight shake of his head and self-deprecating smile he gives, I can only assume he's about to say something that's going to piss me off—hell, if I were in his shoes I would—and there's no need for this to get nasty. For Blakely's sake anyway.

I've more than made my point that she moved on to bigger and better and isn't sitting at home pining away for him while he should be nailing down that new prenup. To mitigate any trouble, I turn my attention away from Paul and Barbie, who is still rubbing her hand up and down Paul's arm, and smile at Blakely. Shock still paints her expression but amusement shines in her eyes.

"Were you just coming from work?" I ask and throw a thumb over my shoulder in a random direction.

"You work?" Barbie asks as if it's a crime.

"Yep. My baby's a big wig over at Glam."

"Oh my god," Barbie says, each word overemphasized. "Paul didn't tell me you worked for Glam! My best friend, the one I tell all my secrets to"—she nudges Paul as if he has a clue who she's talking about—"she works for Glam too!" She claps like a little kid, almost giddy with excitement as she all but bounces on her toes.

"What a small world. You probably know her," I say to Blakely.

"I'm sure you do. I think she's a big deal there too . . . but probably not any bigger than you," Barbie reaches out and pats Blakely's arm as if they are best friends. "Her name is Heather. Heather Mendell."

And I see every part of Blakely's face fall. Every muscle freezes one by one.

"Oh." The way she chokes over the single syllable tells me Heather Mendell is the person Blakely was bitching about in the bar. Her boss.

"Heather?" I let my brow furrow and play the part. I press a kiss to Blakely's bare shoulder, my own way of falsely marking my territory to Paul, and look at her. "This wouldn't happen to be the same Heather who"—her eyes widen in fear—"is your new boss? The one you're so excited about?"

Relief flickers in those green eyes of hers, but her smile is so fragile it might break. "Yes." She clears her throat. "That's her."

"What a small world." Barbie clasps her hands in front of her mouth. That behemoth diamond sparkling. "Isn't this crazy, Paul? It's, like, fate that we all know each other. Some kind of cosmic intervention pulling us together."

"Something like that," Blakely mutters just as Barbie lets out a cry that startles us all.

"The mountains! I just put it together now. You two are going on the retreat then with Glam. Heather's retreat. It's all she's been talking about. So many fun things planned. How exciting." She squeals again in excitement. "I can't wait to tell her I met you and to hear about all of the bestie bonding you guys do on that trip."

"Kumbaya," Blakely says with sarcasm dripping from her words.

I smile, but I can tell Blakely has met her bandwidth in this conversation. "It was a pleasure meeting you, but we have reservations over at Metta's"—I glance at my watch—"five minutes ago."

"Get out!" Barbie holds her hand out. "That's where we were heading too!"

"Oh, Jesus," Blakely mutters as I slide my hand down to fit in hers and squeeze.

"Then we'll see you over there," I say and nod to Paul before directing Blakely toward the restaurant. "Just walk," I murmur. "I bet you twenty bucks they're watching us."

And we do. We walk hand in hand like a loving couple that is excited for a night out, but I can feel her finally realizing what just happened. It's the clamminess of her hands. The hitch of her breath. The million questions she probably wants to ask but is trying to figure out the answers to first.

The minute we turn the corner out of their sights, she yanks her hand from mine and whirls to face me.

"What the hell was that?" she demands, those emerald eyes of hers are wide and glimmer in the shade of the building.

"That was me being out running a couple of errands before heading to meet up with my cousin for drinks when, lo and behold, I looked up and there you were—the woman from the bar, who slipped me someone else's card instead of telling me she wasn't interested."

"I never said that."

Ha. Good to know.

"Your actions spoke louder. You left."

"It's a long story." The words stutter out.

"We have time." I lift my eyebrows and lean against the wall at my back.

"That isn't what I'm talking—this—right there—back there—that's what I mean." She stumbles over the words as her cheeks flush red. At least I know I wasn't crazy. The interest was mutual. Why can't she just admit to it?

"What about it?" I ask as casual as can be. I thought she was sexy when she was calm and collected the other night, but hell, she's even sexier when she's flustered and pissed.

Blakely looks back toward where we just came from and then to me. "Are you insane? You just walked up and kissed me and acted as if—"

"I think the words you're looking for are, 'Thank you for saving my ass, Slade.'"

"Saving my ass?" she sputters.

Definitely sexy.

"Yeah. From Replacement Barbie and your ex." I glance toward the small crowd that is starting to gather outside of Metta's and lift my chin toward them. "We should go so we can get a table before they do. They don't take reservations, not even for tables at the bar."

"You just told them that we had one."

"Had to think on my feet." My smile deepens. "A quick drink? We can cement your relationship status since we'll be in such close quarters with them."

"Wh-wh-what are you talking about?" she asks, her voice as scattered as her eyes moving back and forth between Metta's, me, and the direction we just came from. A woman used to being in control who can't take that she isn't.

"I mean, we can play off the fact that you didn't kiss me back as you being in shock from seeing them together for the first time . . . but I don't think Paul will buy it a second time. So, we need to get to Metta's before they do. If we aren't there, they're going to know that whole thing back there was a sham."

She just blinks. "And what exactly was it then?"

"I thought we already went over this. That was me saving your ass and letting your ex know he isn't the only one who's moved on to better."

Her smile is incredulous, but she slowly shakes her head as if she's still trying to comprehend the last ten minutes. "I don't understand. *Why?*"

There is so much confusion laced in that last word that I just stare at her and wonder when was the last time she'd been treated right.

"Because there are nice guys out there, Blakely. Guys who step in and do the right thing. Ones who treat the woman right even when she isn't theirs. Apparently, you haven't met them before, but I know for a fact they do exist."

She opens her mouth and closes it. Her cheeks flush, and her eyes well with tears that she blinks away just as quickly as they appear.

There's a moment—the briefest of seconds—when that wall of hers slips and her vulnerability surfaces. It's beautiful and fleeting and makes me want to get that smile back on her lips.

I point to the awning of the restaurant and shrug. "Go with me or leave. It's your choice. Either way, I'm going to Metta's because *one*, the appetizers are killer, and *two*, I don't know what the circumstances are between the two of you, but he's an asshole and deserves nothing less than the jealousy he'll feel when he sees you laughing despite him."

SIX

Blakely

Our drinks are served, and I'm still trying to process how in the hell I went from a shitty meeting with Heather to an unexpected run-in with Paul and his new plaything to sitting across from Slade, the man I ghosted the other night at the bar.

The man who took it upon himself to save me from that awkward conversation I probably would have walked away from, no doubt feeling shitty about myself. Instead, Paul is probably wondering what in the hell happened to his wife and who in the hell this Slade guy is.

I'm kind of wondering the same things myself.

I glance over to where Paul and Barbie are sitting across the small dining room, engrossed in their overt public display of affection, before looking back.

"She'll never stay with him if it's any consolation." Slade's words are as blunt as his stare is inquisitive.

"Why do you say that?" I ask, still trying to comprehend that our connection at the bar wasn't one-sided or made up by a hard-up older woman (*me*) desperate for attention.

"Because I know her type. She would have jumped me on the sidewalk if I'd given her an inkling I was interested."

"Such arrogance," I say teasingly because there's an ease with Slade that I can't put my finger on. A way that makes me feel comfortable when I should be mortified by everything he knows about me thus far, none of which casts me in a favorable light.

"Ah, but is it arrogance if it's true?" He takes a sip of his beer. "What's the story between the two of you anyway?"

"We met in college. Dated and got engaged. He moved out here for a job, and I followed." I shrug. "We had what I thought was a normal marriage until we didn't. He told me he was unhappy and wanted out . . . that out was sleeping with his receptionist. Apparently Barbie's job description entailed a whole lot more than just filing papers and answering phones."

"Were you devastated?"

I purse my lips in thought. "Yes and no. I thought what we had was how it was supposed to be . . . but when I was forced to sit back and look at it, I realized we were just going through the motions, too scared to admit it was over long before then."

"That doesn't make it any easier to swallow," he murmurs.

"It still hurt. I still felt like a failure. And seeing them today was like a punch in the gut." I stare at my drink, a bittersweet smile on my lips. "I had always wanted kids, but he always pushed them off . . . so to hear that he wants them now after I gave them up for him was a bit jarring."

"No one likes to see something they've put so much effort into fail."

"True, but I will say that maybe it was for the best. I lost a part of myself, and now, it's my job to find her again." I laugh softly. "Hell, I'm not sure if it's worse knowing my husband is about to marry a woman who I don't think will stick around or if I should take slight joy in the fact that, in time, Karma will most likely do her thing and return the favor."

He looks at me above the rim of his glass and holds my gaze. "Maybe a bit of both."

I shake my head, not liking that I'm sitting in a nice restaurant with a handsome man, who unexpectedly helped me have a little tit for tat moment with my ex, and all we're talking about is me and Paul and Barbie.

"I appreciate you humoring me with all of this," I say, "but what about you? I know nothing about the man who just rescued me from making an idiot out of myself." I angle my head to the side and stare at him.

"Yes, you do. You know I like the mountains, have a mom who I love madly but who needs to end her trip out here soon because she's a busybody, and . . . and I believe in second chances for women who leave bars after giving me a fake number." The lightning-quick grin he flashes me does things to my insides I haven't felt in what feels like forever. But I welcome the flutter, the spark, the whatever you want to call it.

Then I realize what he just said—that he called the number on the card thinking it was me.

Should I say something? Apologize? Explain?

That would only make me look like more of an idiot. Panic has me opting to pretend as if I didn't just have that revelation.

"But, seriously," I murmur, "you didn't have to step in. You've been more than kind. I was just a little stunned by seeing them, by you coming to the rescue—"

"Do you have a pen?" he asks.

"Uh, sure. Why?" I ask, uncertain whether I should be miffed that he isn't acknowledging what I'm saying, but by the sudden urgency in his voice, I let it go, dig through my bag, and hand my pen over to him. He takes it, and without saying a word, starts writing on the cocktail napkin in front of him. I'm trying not to read it upside down, but the curiosity is killing me.

As I wait, I glance around the restaurant. If the delicious scents coming out of the kitchen weren't enough to win someone over, the dark décor, the cozy seating, relaxed vibe would be enough to warrant the line of people waiting outside to get in.

"There," Slade says as he pushes the napkin across the table to me.

"There?"

"Yep." He leans back with a smug smile on his lips as he motions to the waitress, but I don't hear what he says to her because I'm too lost in the words on the napkin written in his chicken-scratch.

Blade's To-Do List:

Make Paul regret he ever let you go.

Figure out our history: when we met, how long your legs really are, pet peeves, etc.

Make Horrible Heather see you differently.

Win your co-workers over by being fucking awesome.

Convince everyone we are madly in love and meant to be.

Get the promotion.

Find the real Blakely again.

Fall hopelessly in love.

I read it three times, seeing what it says but trying to understand why he would write it down.

"What's this?"

"Our to-do list," he says matter-of-factly.

"*Our?*"

"Yep. Ours."

"Blade's?"

"Blakely and Slade's." He shrugs and gives me an adorable little-boy grin that makes my throat constrict and my heart race. "All awesome couples have to have a combined nickname. That's ours."

"Fall hopelessly in love?"

"There should be a reward. You know"—he shrugs—"like me." I laugh and stare at him, trying to figure out if he's for real or not. "I'm just teasing, Blakely."

He gives me that smile again.

"By the end of the retreat, this is what we need to accomplish. I always find it works better when you have something to cross off so you can see your progress."

By the end of the retreat?

"I'm sorry, am I missing something?" I ask with a laugh.

"You'll need to give me details on what to pack. Oh, and we'll have to do some prep work to sort out our history. You know Barbie's going to run straight to Heather with this gem . . ." he says before glancing toward where Barbie and Paul are sitting. "She's probably doing it right now. So, we need to get our ducks in a row."

His directness throws me, and for what feels like the hundredth time in the past thirty minutes, I fumble for words. "Ducks?"

"Yes." He smiles. "Ducks for the retreat," he carries on as if this is the most normal conversation ever. "It seems you've backed yourself into a corner since Barbie knows your boss. There's no way you can back out and not go now."

I snort and down the rest of the wine in my glass. "How did Kelsie find you?" I ask, part joking, part wondering if my best friend somehow tracked him down and put him up to this to test me.

"Kelsie?"

"Never mind." I roll my eyes, chuckle, and thank the waitress for re-filling my glass, but when I look back at Slade, he's still looking at me. "What?"

"I'm serious. I only make lists when I'm serious."

"And I think you're crazy."

"Why? Because I like to make lists and cross items off them to feel like I've accomplished something?"

"I'm not talking about the list." I'm dumbfounded that he sounds dead serious. "You'd really just pick up your life and go on a business retreat for me—a woman you don't really know?"

"You said mountains. You need help. I like you." He ticks each thing off on his fingers. "That's all I need to know." I'm so envious of his ease and surety, but I still don't understand why he would do this.

"I'm being serious," I say.

"So am I. I have time on my hands and could really use some outdoor therapy. You have to go and need a boyfriend to go with you. Seems pretty self-explanatory to me."

"I thought you said you were a doctor." I eye him and am not immune to the emotion that flickers momentarily in his eyes. Emotion that makes me want to ask more about it, but I know there's no point. "Or was that just part of the whole game we're playing?"

"Would it matter?"

His question throws me. "No. Why?"

"Just asking," he says as if I just passed a test I wasn't aware I was taking. "It's the truth. I'm in the middle of my cardiac residency, hence the shitty penmanship," he says, motioning to his handwriting on the napkin before averting his eyes to his hands for a beat. "I'm on sabbatical for the time being and am bored to tears." There is a soft tug on one corner of his mouth that clears whatever emotion it is out of his eyes.

"That bad, huh?"

"You can only stare at so many textbooks and rewrite so many articles before your eyes want to burn out of their sockets." His chuckle is soft.

"Is there a medical term for that?" I ask.

"No, but I'm serious, and we have a list to tackle. Why are you so hesitant to say yes?"

"For a lot of reasons . . . I just can't. You've already done more than enough."

Kelsie is going to kill me.

"This is coming from the same woman who's sitting in a bar with me to prove to her ex that we're a legitimate couple, right?"

"Guilty," I say and offer a shy smile.

The answer is always yes.

I study him unabashedly. I take in his easy nature and charming smile, his drop-dead gorgeous looks, and how it feels as if I've known him forever . . . and I tell myself it'll never happen.

Him. This. Pretend boyfriend. None of it.

"Just like that? You'd decide to accompany a random stranger on a company retreat for no other reason than you're bored? I mean . . . that's *odd* to me."

"Maybe to you it's odd, but where I come from, in my circle of friends, we'd do it for each other in a heartbeat."

My smile widens and then falters as I try to convince myself of all the reasons I should thank him and then leave. "You're lucky to have that, but—"

"Or maybe it's as simple as there's something about you that makes me want to get to know you better. Maybe it's that side of you that peeks through when you aren't trying to figure out who to be and you just *are*. I want to know her better . . . and maybe, maybe it's as simple as *I like you, Blake*."

After everything I went through with Paul, I should take the compliments, the kind words, and let them fill all of the dark places my divorce emptied, but it's so much easier to refute them than accept them. So much easier to hide in the depths of my insecurities than to really hear his words.

I open my mouth, and my sarcasm gets me in trouble.

"Well, I like ice cream, too, but that doesn't mean that I'd jump at a chance to go and lick every cone my mouth comes in contact with." That sounded way worse than I meant it to, and I blush fifty shades of red at how stupid I sound. "Never mind. Forget I said that."

His lopsided grin is like summer and sunshine, and where the hell did that Hallmark-card comment come from? Jesus. A man tells me he likes me, and I turn it into licking ice cream and dying of embarrassment.

"Licking is never bad, huh?" He takes a long glance at my lips before coming back to my eyes. There's desire darkening in his gaze, and of course, my brain scrambles over what to say so I can at least sound witty. "Does that mean you do or you don't like me, then?"

"No. I didn't say that." So much for trying to sound intelligent. "I like you. A lot." *For the love of God, stop talking.* "Or what I know of you." *I'm rambling.* "It's more that . . . I mean, I just don't understand." *I'm making an idiot out of myself.* "Why would you even . . . people just don't do that."

Silence falls over our table when I finally stop talking, and everything and anything is more interesting to look at than Slade. Anything.

The burgundy logo on the to-do list napkin. His fingers playing over the base of his glass . . .

The silence stretches until I look back up and meet those light bluish-gray irises of his.

"Some people do." His voice is soft, and the amusement in his eyes is taunting. "What would it hurt? You get to save face with the ex and also show the new boss you're there to play her game."

I shake my head. "I know they say never look a gift horse in the mouth, but . . ."

"Then say yes. What's the worst that can happen? You get a friend out of the process?"

A friend. Okay. So, yeah, mixed message central.

"No one will ever believe you're my boyfriend."

"They just did," he says, lifting his chin in the direction of Paul and Barbie.

"That's different. He's blinded by her."

"The way she flashes that ring around like a trophy that denotes her importance, it's easy to be blinded."

My smile is soft. "The people at my work . . . there's no way they'll think you'd date a woman like me." Talk about humiliating saying the words.

"Like you?"

I nod, my cheeks heating.

"You mean a gorgeous, well-rounded, obviously smart woman?"

"Thank you." *He's lying.* "But that isn't what I mean." *He's just being nice.*

"Then what *do* you mean?"

"There's an obvious age difference between us." The words feel so stupid coming from my mouth.

"Yeah, I'm thirty-one, and you're whatever age you are that it's bugged me so much I haven't asked you because it doesn't matter."

Thirty-one. *Jesus.*

"And no, you aren't old enough to be my mother," he says, reading my unspoken thoughts. "So *screw you, Hillary.*"

"Hillary?" I laugh, totally thrown by the name.

"The woman in the bar who chased you off the other night." I struggle with how to respond. "Because that's why you left, right? She added age to the mix because she was threatened by the fact that I was much more taken with you than by the come-fuck-me eyes she kept giving me all night long."

"You were?"

He turns so that his knees are on either side of my chair. I hold my breath as he leans into me, his lips so close I can feel the warmth of his breath. "In case you hadn't noticed"—the tip of his nose hits the shell of my ear, causing chills to dance down my spine—"I was."

He pulls back some, and for just a second, I think he's going to kiss me. I *want* him to kiss me. Our eyes hold, lock, tease.

"The way I look at it, you owe me one." His voice is just loud enough for me to hear over the din of the restaurant.

"I owe it to you?" I sputter.

"*Mm-hm.*" He nods resolutely as he puts more space between us, and my lungs find a way to breathe. "You ran out the other night without giving me a chance. I could be the best thing that ever happened to you— platonic or otherwise—and you might have missed that opportunity if we hadn't run into each other on the street this afternoon."

Or otherwise?

He's talking nonsense but is doing it so convincingly that I try to talk myself out of what he's successfully talking me in to. "I don't—"

"Does my age unnerve you?" he asks.

"Your age doesn't matter."

"Exactly." He smirks. "So, why are you making it matter?"

I walked right into that one.

"We're at different phases of our lives. You're in your residency. I'm a divorcée with baggage—"

"Everyone has baggage. It just looks different from person to person." He leans back in his chair. "What are you afraid of? Getting to know someone new? Taking a chance? Stepping outside of the box for once? Finding yourself again?"

His words root deep into me and take hold. "I appreciate you trying . . . but we'll never pull it off."

"Yes, we could."

"No one would ever believe it."

"Quit letting them—*whoever they are*—put you in a mold, Blakely. Make your own damn mold. You might surprise yourself in the process." His dimples deepen, and his eyes are as unwavering as his resolve.

"How do I know you aren't some Ted Bundy in waiting?"

His laugh is throaty and rich and draws the stares of those around us. "I'm in the business of saving lives, not taking them." He takes a sip of his beer. "Next excuse?"

"I'm . . ." I'm at a loss, and a small thrill of adrenaline shoots through me. This isn't something I'd ever do, and yet, the idea of it is invigorating, almost freeing. I chew the inside of my cheek as I contemplate agreeing to Slade's crazy scheme.

"What do you say?"

Say yes.

"It isn't a crime for a younger man to think an older woman is attractive."

I bite my bottom lip as the smile creeps around it.

He is drop-dead handsome.

"We go as friends. I help you out. No strings attached."

The answer is yes.

"When's the last time you threw caution to the wind? When's the last time you did something unexpected no matter how small?" he asks.

It's always yes.

"I can't believe I'm saying this," I mutter.

"Saying what?"

"Fine. Yes. Okay."

SEVEN

Blakely

Slade: Just making sure the number you gave me really is yours.

Me: Smartass.

Slade: Can you blame me?

Me: It's me. I promise.

Slade: Sorry I had to bail from Metta's.

Me: You had plans. No big deal.

Slade: You aren't going to back out now, are you?

Me: No.

Slade: I know where you work. If you bail, I'll just show up and cause an even bigger scene there, playing the doting boyfriend.

Me: You wouldn't dare.

Slade: Something you should know about me is that I'm a little pushy.

Me: No shit.

Slade: But only for the greater good.

Me: Lucky me.

Slade: And when I say I'm going to do something, I do it. And I love to take dares.

Me: I thought you loved making lists.

Slade: Those too. I'll touch base so we can get together.

Me: For?

Slade: Details.

Me: Details?

Slade: About our trip. If we're going to play the part, we at least have to know something about each other.

Me. Yes. Right.

Slade: That didn't sound convincing.

Me: Yay. Go team.

Slade: That's more like it.

Me: Thanks again, Slade.

Slade: Just call me Ted Bundy for short.

Me: Funny. Very funny.

EIGHT

Slade

"ICU."

"Amy Gannon, please," I say as I lean back in my desk chair and stare out the window to my backyard.

"Nurse Gannon is out sick. This is Nancy Weaverman, I'm filling in for her today, may I help you with something?"

Fuck. A new nurse, but she could possibly be a temp nurse who doesn't know Ivy's story. I try to figure out how to play this with Gannon, the only one willing to break the rules and give me updates, not there today.

"Yes, this is Doctor Henderson needing to get an update on a patient. An Ivy Keller."

The sound of fingernails clicking on a keyboard filter through the line, and I cross my fingers, hoping either she hasn't been warned not to give me information or that she won't read the notes deeper in the file. This can go either way.

"And what department are you with?"

"ER. I was on call when she came in. Her case has stuck with me, so I'm following up on her recovery."

"It has to be hard being in the ER and never knowing how things end up," she murmurs as her fingers continue to click over keys.

"That's for sure."

"You docs down there are a special kind of breed. Not everyone can handle what you guys see."

"It takes some getting used to, that's for sure."

"It's definitely refreshing to know you care about your patients enough to follow up on them."

C'mon, Chatty Cathy. Just give me the update.

"Oh, here she is. Let's see how you're doing, Miss Ivy," she murmurs to herself as she reads the computer. "I'm not seeing any change on her status in her chart. Looks to be the same."

"Okay." *Shit.* "Thanks."

"And your name again?"

I end the call without answering, fisting the cell in my hand and bringing it up to my forehead while I will Ivy to get better.

That damn little girl stole my heart.

NINE

Blakely

"So, let's talk about the state of your coochie?"

I level a glare at Kelsie, who is sitting perfectly content on my chaise lounge while I move around the family room, fluffing any and every pillow I find.

"I'd prefer if we didn't." I laugh.

"This is more than important. Did you shave it? Trim it? Or are you just full, screw-all-men beast mode down there?" she asks.

"Why do you care?"

"Because in fewer than twenty-four hours, you're leaving on a five-day retreat with your fake boyfriend. The state of your bikini line tells me all I need to know about what you expect to get out of this trip."

I stop mid-fluff and stare at her. "No. I haven't shaved it."

"Jungle bush." She lifts her eyebrows. "That'll definitely make a statement."

I laugh. "What's that supposed to mean?"

"It means I'm disappointed in you because you don't plan on getting any action."

"I've known the guy a few days. What am I supposed to do? Jump into bed with him and have wild, crazy sex?"

"Yes." She nods definitely. "That's exactly what you're supposed to do."

"I don't do one-night stands, Kels. That isn't me."

"Good thing the retreat is longer than one night." She waggles her eyebrows. "Because five-night stands are way better. You can have first-time sex. You can have skinny-dipping sex. Rebound sex. Picnic-table sex. Just think of all the fun you'll be having."

"Will you listen to yourself?"

"I am, and I'm getting all hot and bothered thinking about it."

"You have something seriously wrong with you," I say but laugh. "There will be none of that. We'll be at a campground for god's sake. Think a big communal room with bunk beds, footy pajamas, and no privacy. Besides—"

"There is no besides. There are no footy pajamas. Communal bunk beds or not, you can still get some action and walk around with the biggest, smuggest grin to let all the other ladies know just who Slade is sliding it into."

"Nothing is going to happen."

"*Shhh.* I'm not listening to you because I'm too busy making up all kinds of sexy scenarios that are going to happen—kisses against trees, blowjobs behind the dining hall . . ." She wiggles her shoulders as if she's imagining each and every one of them. "I'm going to live vicariously through you."

"Pine tree needles stuck where they shouldn't be, mosquito bites on my ass."

"Sometimes incredible sex comes with a few hazards. I'm sure you're willing to accept those if the trade-off is toe-curling orgasms."

"Whatever." I roll my eyes but will admit to myself I've thought way too much about the other night at Metta's. About his lips whispering in my ear. About the too-long stares across the table. About the bear hug and kiss on the cheek when we parted.

"Come on, the man has a to-do list for you guys. And right on top, written in invisible ink, is that he wants *to-do* you."

"He's just being nice. And organized and . . ."

"Nice, handsome, sexy, and let's not forget a freaking heart surgeon. It's perfect that he knows how to mend a broken heart."

"My heart is just fine, thank you."

"I beg to differ."

"The last thing it needs is to be involved in anything with anyone for the time being."

"That's exactly why this whole situation is perfect. He's obviously into you or else he wouldn't be doing this. You need to have some after-Paul sex to wake up your lady parts so you realize what you're missing. A rebound of epic proportions. What better way to ease your toes into the dating pool than with some sexy, hot doctor?"

"Easier said than done."

"Who cares if it's for a night or a week or a month? You played the part of the polished, pretentious wife for too long, it's about time you do what you want without caring what anyone thinks. You know for sure that I'm not going to be the one judging you."

"I know, but . . ." My sigh fills the room and smothers the excitement she just filled it with. She notices it right away and moves to sit on the coffee table in front of me so I can't avoid her stare.

"Hey." She waits until I look at her. "What's wrong? Talk to me. Tell me why you're struggling so hard with this?"

Where do I start when I feel like there is so much wrong with me?

"Why is it so hard for me to accept this? To think that Slade might actually like me?" I look down at my hands clasped on top of my lap. I think of the last line on Slade's to-do list and know that's the problem. "I swore that when the divorce was final, I was going to be this bigger and better person. That I was going to be more spontaneous. Care more about my wants and less about what others expected. But you know what, Kels? It's really hard to be this new me, and I'm not exactly sure how to wear the shoes yet."

She puts her hand on my knee and squeezes, giving me a moment to get my emotions in check. "For the record, I still like the old you."

"The old me was a pair of granny panties." I laugh. "I don't want to be granny panties anymore. I want the new me to be—"

"A G-string?"

"More like lacy, sexy, boy shorts," I say.

"Substance, coverage in all the right areas, but sexy as hell when they need to be."

I look at her and shake my head until the tightening in my throat manifests into tears welling in my eyes. "I'm sick of being the perfect ex-wife who pretends that everything is fine and then cries into her pillow at night because she failed. I'm sick of being the always-cautious, always-worried-what-others-think Blakely Foxx who is so sick of taking everyone's shit but smiles anyway."

"I don't know who you are or what you've done with my friend." She laughs, her face lighting up. "But I like where you're going with this."

"I'm here. Still the same but trying to be different . . . and as hard as it is to admit, I'm scared as hell about this week."

"What about it?"

"Just the million things that could go wrong. What if we don't get along? What if he ends up being a jerk? What if I make things worse at work? What if they find out we're not really a couple? What if—"

"What if you two hit it off and a real connection is made? What if he makes you laugh till it hurts and things go well? There are positives that could happen here, you know?"

I flop back on the couch and cover my eyes with my hands. "This has all the makings of a rom-com movie disaster. You know the kind—"

"Where the heroine is a wreck, the hero is a prick, and their whole plan goes to hell?"

"If you want to put it that way." I nod.

"Just remember that the girl always gets the guy in the end."

"This isn't fiction."

"No, but it's going to be so much better."

We sit in silence, the years of friendship between us have her giving me the space I need to process everything she's said. To finally admit what she already knows.

"I like him. A lot. And . . . maybe I'm afraid that I do. And perhaps, I'm scared that I like him simply because he's the first man to really pay attention to me—"

"Plenty have paid attention," she murmurs and holds up her hand to stop my argument. "You're just too busy not being interested to notice."

"But I am interested this time, and I'm questioning why I am and why he is, and that leads me to wonder if I would be enough for him. I mean I've only been with one man in the last twenty years. How do I know if things are done differently nowadays?"

Her grin tugs a smile out of me. "I assure you sex is done the same."

"You know what I mean."

"I do know. I know it's scary and probably exhilarating all at the same time, but I say go for it. I say be the lacy boy shorts. The kind Slade can't wait to rip off you before ravishing you."

"Ravish?"

"Ravish," she repeats with a nod. "And I have no doubt he will, and you'll do just fine with it. In fact, you'll actually enjoy it."

"We'll see about that." I chuckle.

"I believe I said you'd see him again and he'd go on the retreat with you, right?" She throws her hands up. "Then, out of the blue, it happened, so I wouldn't doubt me. I do believe I might have some kind of magical powers."

I throw a pillow at her. "I'm not going to encourage that theory for fear of your head getting so big it will never fit through the doorway."

"I have powers, so I'm sure I can manage regardless of the size of the doorway." Kelsie follows me into the kitchen where I start to clean up our leftover charcuterie board. "Your plan is to leave together in the morning?"

"*Mm-hm.*" I toss a napkin into the trash. "We'll figure out our story on the way up to the mountains. Three hours is a lot of time to kill."

"Are you sure that's enough time?" she asks as she pops an olive into her mouth.

"He had plans already. Who am I to ask for more time from him when he's already giving me five days . . . you know?"

"I do, but I know how your little planning heart is probably having a freak out over not knowing it already."

"I'm fine. It's fine. I just need to pack and then I'm set."

My phone on the counter rings, and I jump at the sound. Before I can grab it, Kelsie has it in her hand. "Speak of the devil." She holds my phone out so I can see his name on the screen. "Put him on speaker so I can hear his sexy voice."

"Give me the phone." I stick my hand out, but there is a smile stuck on my face and a giddy feeling in my stomach, which is stupid considering I'm going to be seeing him tomorrow.

In a move that's high school-ish and annoying and very much Kelsie, she hits the answer button and hits speaker at the same time. "Hello?" she says just in time for me to grab my phone from her.

"Hey." Slade's deep timbre comes through the speaker. It's sex personified, and that along with all this talk of sex and rebounds with Kelsie has me thinking thoughts and creating scenarios Kels would be proud of. "You ready for tomorrow?"

Kelsie holds the back of her hand to her forehead and mouths, *Swoon.*

"Hi. Yes. Just doing some last-minute things."

"Forget those last-minute things. Put a jacket on and come meet us."

"What?" I laugh the word as if he's crazy. "Where? Us? What are you talking about?"

"Spontaneity, Blakely. That's what I'm talking about." There is someone laughing in the background as I turn my back to Kelsie and lean my hips against the counter. "My friends and I have a monthly bonfire down at the beach. I missed the last one, but I'm here. Right now. The waves are at my back and the fire is in front of me."

"And you want me there?"

"Yes." His laugh is carefree. "I realized you might have some reservations about hopping in a car and going on a trip with a man you only know about through his own comments."

"Seems like a rational thought."

"Then come hang out with us. Come get to know me and put your mind at ease. Get a head start on that last item on the to-do list."

Say yes.

"I don't want to intrude on your time with your friends." It's a total contradiction to the *yes* my head is telling me to say.

"What better way to get to know me than through my friends? They're brutally honest even when I don't want them to be."

"Slade . . . I—"

"C'mon, Blakely." His voice is singsongy and possibly slightly buzzed, but the way he says my name makes me stand a bit taller. "Come put your toes in the sand for a bit."

"We're leaving in the morning."

"The night's still young."

"I—"

"I'm not taking no for an answer. I'm texting you directions. See you in a bit," he says before the call ends.

"Seriously?" Kelsie says at my back. "You were actually going to say no to a voice like his and a request like that? Are you insane?"

"Yes. No." I blow out an audible sigh.

But he called me.

He asked me to go.

When Kelsie moves to my line of sight, there is a stern expression on her face and her arms are crossed over her chest. The look in her eyes warns me she's going to fight the old me from turning down his offer.

And she's right.

This ends right here. Right now.

Out with the granny panties. In with the lacy boy shorts.

"I need to go get changed," I say.

Kelsie's lips stretch into a grin as a loud whoop falls from her lips. "You are soooo getting laid this week."

TEN

Blakely

The scene before me is gorgeous—moonlight over the water and fire dancing against the sand.

I don't have an excuse not to get out of my car. No barely there bikinis on drunken women. No frat boy atmosphere. Just a small group of friends, laughing and relaxing. I don't have a reason to turn around and go home.

Still, I sit and watch for a moment, getting the nerve to walk up to a group of people where I don't know anyone save for Slade.

Of the eight people sitting around the fire, there are an equal number of men and women. Some are sitting side by side, cuddled together, while others are standing with their hips swaying to the beat of music I can't hear.

Then there's Slade. He's sitting on a towel in the sand, a beer bottle is knocked on its side next to him, and the glow of the fire illuminates his hair. His expression is stoic, reflective maybe, and there is a soft smile on his lips as he stares at the embers.

In that moment, I don't know how I know that he's going to be trouble for me, but I do. That disarming grin. That easy manner. The way he gets me to do things I'd never do like going to a bonfire on the beach the night before leaving for a trip.

And I've only known him a week.

I can do this. I can be lacy boy panties. I can . . . I can let whatever happens, happen.

With a deep breath, I slide out of my car, my toes digging into the sand and the soft breeze off the ocean hitting my cheeks as I approach the group.

I stand on the outskirts of their circle for a moment, not wanting to interrupt the story being told with wild gesticulations and animated expressions from the man still wearing his scrubs. But when Slade sees me, he rises from his seat in the sand, momentarily drawing the group's attention to me.

"Hi." I hold up my hand in an awkward wave and look toward Slade.

I swear my heart drops when he angles his smile my way. Dimples and warmth and excitement are etched in the lines of his face.

I'm too old for this. Too old to have this giddy feeling when a man looks at me. Too old to allow myself to be fooled by a nice smile with dimples. Too old to believe it's a good idea to throw caution to the wind and let the cards fall where they may.

And yet . . .

"You came," he says and pulls me into him in an unexpected hug. He smells of sunshine and beer and citrus, and I feel like an idiot for just wanting to stay there and breathe him in, but I do.

"Hi."

The hug ends, but he keeps his hand on my lower back as he turns toward the group. "Blakely, meet everyone. Everyone, meet Blakely." There is a chorus of greetings that has me waving awkwardly again, but I'm met with smiles and warmth. "Do you want something to drink?"

"I'm good."

"You sure?" he asks as he takes my hand as if it's the most natural thing in the world and leads me over to where he was seated.

"Yes. Thank you though."

He stretches out the towel and motions for me to sit as the guy who was telling his animated story continues on after my interruption. Slade settles beside me so we're shoulder to shoulder, my body tensing as his breath hits my ear and he murmurs, "I'm glad you came."

I ignore the chills that chase over my skin. It's just the ocean breeze. Even I don't buy my own lie.

"Thanks for inviting me." I don't turn to face him because, if I do, our faces would be inches from each other and too close to the kiss zone.

"We do this once a month—those of us who aren't on call anyway. Just a little time to unwind and relax after all the stress of the job. It forces us to get together outside of the hospital."

"Not a bad way to relax," I say as laughter rumbles through the group.

"Nah. Not on nights as pretty as this it isn't." He leans back on his hands and looks up at the stars glimmering above before those eyes of his find mine again. "They're all pretty chill. John, Prisha, and Leigh are residents with me. Jason and Carly are in pediatrics . . ." He goes through the list of everyone. "And I don't expect you to remember any of that. In fact, it's pretty lame I invited you down here to listen to John drone on, but I thought it might be a good way for you to see who I am so you aren't worried that I'm a creep or some shit like that the whole trip."

"I'm not going to lie and say I haven't thought it a time or ten," I tease as he mocks taking offense before hitting my shoulder with his. "And I appreciate that it crossed your mind long enough to call me and invite me to come hang out with your friends."

The next hour is spent laughing at stories that are amusing to me but much funnier to those who understand the medical terminology being flung around like sight words in a kindergarten class. Slade leans in every few minutes to explain something when my expression clearly shows I don't understand or to simply make sure I'm okay.

But I'm more than fine as I sit back and listen to people who clearly understand and care for each other. There is a camaraderie between them, and they've included me in it without question. It's nice to sit out under the stars with someone who holds no expectations. When I was with Paul, every outing came with a critical eye over what I was wearing and worries about whether I would pass the test of looking like an executive's wife. Then came the list of what topics were off-limits with his clients and how I had to pretend the mistress or wife who the client was with last time didn't exist.

Too many things to keep straight. Too many lines I couldn't cross. And yet this? Watching Slade toss a football in the moonlight with his friends while being warmed by a fire? It's nothing like I expected it would be and, most likely, everything I didn't know I needed.

"So, you're the one he's been keeping tucked away from us," a voice to my right says.

I turn to find his friend, Prisha, taking a seat beside me. Her ink-black hair shimmers in the firelight, and her dark brown eyes are warm and inviting.

"No." I smile. "I'm not anything. We're . . . just friends. I mean, we've only really known each other for a week. He's helping me out with a work thing this week."

"Ah, the retreat."

"Yes," I say, surprised that he told them anything about it.

"He's almost too good to be true, isn't he?" she murmurs, and our gazes hold for a beat.

"What do you mean?"

"Guys like him—genuine, courteous, respectful—are few and far between."

"Ain't that the truth," I say, my eyes back on Slade. He runs across the sand, arms up, asking for the pass before leaping in the air to snag it one-handed with a natural athleticism.

"I was always looking for the catch when I first met him. Most people aren't as generous as he is with his time or help or . . . anything really without wanting something in return. I was always waiting for the other shoe to drop." She lifts her beer to her lips. "In five years, it never has."

We watch the men running and tackling each other on the beach, a smile on my lips as their laughter and antics carry back toward us.

There has to be a point to her telling me all of this. Maybe it's because he treats everyone like this and she doesn't want me misreading his kindness and getting my hopes up for more.

The question is, how do I ask her without coming off as a bitch when I really think she's being sincere?

"He's had a tough few months at work. Maybe your retreat will give him time away from it all."

"I'm not sure how." I laugh. "Being forced to bond with pretentious people isn't exactly what I think of as relaxing." I lean back on my hands and put my face up to the sky and close my eyes.

"Anything is better than the endless waiting for him to be reinstated from his bullshit suspension. How can you discipline a doctor for caring about his patients?"

"I completely agree," I murmur, glad my eyes are closed because it hides the surprise on my face. He told me he is on a sabbatical, not a suspension.

"He's a good guy. One of the best."

I angle my head over toward her. "Why are you telling me this?"

"Because I've watched many women come along for the ride with Slade. I've watched them go googly-eyed and fall head over heels in love with him because of who he is and how well he treats them. Then I watch them get crushed when he moves on without realizing how attached they've become."

"So, you're warning me, then?"

"Not really." She laughs when Slade tackles John. "Yes, maybe." She smiles. "I just want you to know what you're walking into, is all. I can already see it when you look at him, and us women should look out for other women."

"Thanks," I say dryly. "Warning heeded."

Her laugh is sudden. "Oh my god. I get how that just came off. That I'm interested in him and jealous." She covers her eyes with her hands and groans. "That couldn't be further from the truth. He's a brother to me. I promise. You must think I'm a total bitch."

"Not at all."

"Look." She takes a sip of her beer, and I can see her struggle with finding her words. "Slade is such a good guy that he doesn't realize why people are so taken by him. It never crosses his mind. He's generous and scattered and brilliant and caring and goddamn gorgeous, but he's just . . . *being him.* That's all he knows. He isn't reeling in women to notch a bedpost or boost his status as being a player . . . he's just that *magnetic.* So, I guess what I'm saying is—"

"Don't mistake who he is—how he is—and think he's more into me because of it?"

"I guess, but less harsh sounding," she says and laughs.

"I get what you're saying, and I appreciate the insight. He's a great guy who has brightened up my days a bit. I'm just taking it for what it is."

Her smile is soft. "If I were in your shoes, I'd still think I'm a bitch."

I laugh and then turn to find Slade and the rest of the guys walking up to us. "Nice moves," I tease.

"Pathetic is more like it." His grin tells me he knows they weren't, and he liked that I noticed. "It's closing time," he says as he plops down on the sand beside me.

"Then why are you sitting?"

"Because it's my turn to make sure the fire dies down before we leave it." Someone tosses a cup of water onto the fire, and it sizzles. "You cold?" he asks.

"I'm fine."

"Come here," he says and wraps an arm over my shoulders and pulls me against him. I freeze at first, my need to fight my attraction more ingrained than the resolve I have to go with the flow. But the heat of his body, the scent on his skin, and way his thumb keeps brushing back and forth over my shoulder makes me want to melt right into him. "Better?"

"*Mm-hmm*," I murmur as I rest my head against his shoulder.

His friends finish packing up and say their goodbyes, and moments later, an engine revs to life before it fades into the distance. Then we're left with only the crackling of the fire and the roar of waves as they land on the beach.

But there's a comfortable silence between us, an ease as we soak in the atmosphere. We don't talk about the part we have to begin to play tomorrow. We just sit and enjoy each other's company without pressure or expectations.

"You were awfully quiet tonight," Slade finally murmurs, the heat of his breath hitting the top of my head.

I shrug. "It was fun. Thank you for inviting me. They seem like a great bunch of people."

"They are. I'm lucky to call them friends. I did see Prisha talking your ear off. She wasn't spilling my deep, dark secrets now was she?"

I chuckle. "She may have told me what an awesome guy you are—"

"Clearly, I paid her to do so."

"Clearly," I say as her warning ghosts through my mind. As that charm of his pulls me under its spell and I'm left not wanting the night to end.

"Do you feel better about going on the retreat now that you know I'm not a serial killer and everything?"

"Much better," I murmur. "I'm still not convinced others will buy it."

"Why's that?"

"Because we live in two different worlds."

"And opposites attract." His sigh fills the space. "You're still hung up on the age thing, aren't you?"

I open my mouth to speak and then close it, knowing how stupid it sounds when not a single one of his friends looked at me differently because I was older than them. Not once did they make me feel awkward. "I keep telling myself to go with the flow. That no one notices the age difference, but then I think how ridiculous Paul looks with Barbie on his arm, and I get hung up on it. Is that what people are going to see when they see you and me together?"

His silence is accentuated by the crashing of waves, and he tightens his arm around me. "I think they look ridiculous because they try too hard and because she wants everyone to know she's landed what she thinks is a good catch, only we know different. I think that someone who is secure in their relationship doesn't need to keep trying to prove to everyone else that they are." He presses a kiss to the top of my head, and I tense at the connection—not because I don't want it but because I don't understand why it's so natural to accept it from him. "Am I younger than you? Yes. Does it matter to me? I wouldn't be sitting here if it did."

"I didn't mean to imply that . . . I don't know what I meant," I murmur, suddenly feeling stupid. I'm the one who's older, who should be more mature, and yet, he's the one showing me it doesn't matter. None of it does. "I'm sorry. I came down here tonight determined to have a change in attitude, not to care what people think anymore—to be more like you, but I guess old habits die hard."

"Don't be like me, Blake. Be like you. Remember our to-do list?" He knocks his knee against mine.

"Yeah."

"That doesn't sound very convincing. You're on a deserted beach with the moon above and a very handsome man at your side," he jokes. "What more could you ask for?" He rubs his hand up and down my arm. "Let it go. Take the ride. Put your toes in the sand. Howl at the moon. Do whatever it is you want to do so long as it's in pursuit of finding you again."

I blink away the tears that well in my eyes. Sure, Kelsie told me similar things, but she's my best friend, she's obligated to say stuff like that. But he said it when he didn't have to. He's cheering me on like no one ever has.

I nod resolutely. "You're absolutely right."

"You've never spoken truer words," he teases, and I hit him playfully as our laughs ring out.

And he is right.

Screw what people think.

My toes are in the sand, now I just need to find the courage to howl at the moon.

He stands, and the night chill assaults my skin again as he begins to kick sand on what's left of the fire. "We should get going before we get kicked out of here."

He reaches out his hand to me and pulls me up with a little more force than expected because, when I rise, I find myself off balance. Both of our natural responses kick in, and I brace my hands against his chest as he grabs my hips to steady me.

It leaves us chest to chest, the laugh falling from my lips dying as I look up and see his face inches from mine.

"Sorry. I'm sorry." Flustered, I try to push against the more-than-firm muscles beneath my palms and take a step back.

But his hands on my hips flex and hold me in place.

"You know you're going to have to get a lot more comfortable with me touching you if we're going to pull this off, right?"

"Yes. Sure."

"Because every time I touch you, you tense up like you're afraid I'm going to bite."

"I don't mean to."

"We're going to have to kiss, you know? To sell the lie."

"We kissed the other day on the street." I stumble for things to say because, as much as I've thought about him kissing me all night, I'm silently freaking out. "I was fine with that."

His chuckle is barely audible as he tucks an errant strand of hair behind my ear. "No one's going to buy that we're hot and heavy for each other if I kiss you like that."

He rests his hand on the curve of my shoulder so his thumb can slide back and forth over the hollow of my neck. Goose bumps blanket my skin as the waning firelight flickers and dances in his eyes. His smile is soft, seductive, and amused all at the same time.

"I guess not." My voice is barely a whisper.

"Then maybe . . ." His eyes dart down to my lips and then back up to mine. "Then maybe we should get the first one out of the way so we know what to expect."

Such a smooth line.

"Maybe we should," I murmur, my body thrumming with an anticipation that's equal parts desire and exhilaration.

Such a willing female.

When his lips meet mine, they are both soft and demanding, and I forget this is an act. I forget that we are practicing, and every part of me falls under the spell of the moment.

The briny scent of the air.

The warmth of his lips.

The taste of beer on his tongue.

The touch of his hand as it frames my face.

The soft mewl that falls from my lips.

It's the kind of kiss that you want to go on and on. The kind where you know that, once it stops, you're going to come back to yourself. Then nerves are going to hit and your sensibility is going to soar, so you decide it's so much easier to be under its pull than to slip out from beneath it.

But we do slip free with one last brush of lips, but he keeps his hands framing my face. "What do you think, Blakely? Do you think we could pass that off as being real?"

I don't trust my voice to speak, so I nod while my hands, which are still gripped in his sweatshirt, relax some and my pulse races a staccato I'm embarrassed to admit to.

"At least we know we got something right." His voice is low, laden with a desire that he isn't trying to disguise as his thumb rubs over my bottom lip.

"Good to know."

"It isn't howling at the moon . . ." A smile slides onto his lips, and it's just as devastating as his kiss.

With my bottom lip between my teeth, I take a step back. "But my toes are in the sand."

His eyes hold mine, and I swear the look in them makes it hard for me to breathe.

I can tell myself all I want that this was just practice.

But who am I fooling?

It's been years since I kissed a man like that.

Paul and I stopped french kissing years into our relationship. I'd forgotten the intimacy and romanticism of it *until now*.

Until Slade's lips and our pretend kiss that was so much more than pretend.

It was just a kiss.

It was just practice.

Prisha's advice may have been good, and as much as I want to heed it, parts of me are a lot deeper under the influence of Slade Henderson than I thought, and therefore I don't want to hear it.

I want to listen to how my body feels. How my heart is racing. How my head is swimming. How that ache in me that he created burns. And how I want . . . just simply want for the first time in what feels like forever.

He's a rebound.

That's what this is.

And that kiss just showed me he's exactly what I need.

Quick. Filthy. Devastating. A rebound romp.

My only thought as I pull out of the parking lot and head home?

I definitely need to go home and shave.

ELEVEN

Slade

I look at the stack of folded clothes on the bed before me. I think I have everything I need, including the box of condoms.

Because, fuck, that kiss last night? Was on fire.

I was interested in Blakely the first night we met. When she had dinner with me at Metta's, I might have gotten a crush on her. And last night? After she destroyed me with those soft lips and fisted hands in my sweatshirt? I'm definitely game.

What an unexpected twist.

What a risk I'm more than willing to take because . . . the woman's gotten ahold of me somehow.

There was a reserved confidence about her last night, a subtle change in her demeanor that turned me on. Quiet strength wrapped in stunning beauty.

A beauty that was effortless.

And there's no way that kiss didn't affect her either.

My dick stirs to life at the mere thought of it.

"Yep. Definitely bringing the condoms."

When my cell starts ringing and I see the name on the screen, my thoughts shift rapidly.

Talk about killing the daydream.

"It's been less than forty-eight hours and you're already calling?" I tease when I pick up the phone.

"The proper way to answer the phone is: Mom, I already miss you so much."

I snort but love the damn woman anyway. "I could, or I could ask you why you're calling."

"I just wanted to tell you to have a good trip."

"Trip?" I feign ignorance to find out just how much she snooped before leaving.

"Your duffle bag was out, I figured you were taking a little vacation to celebrate my being gone."

I cough over a laugh. "I'd never do that."

"Yes, you would." She's so matter-of-fact but the amusement in her tone is playful. "Why do you think I didn't leave you any precooked meals when I left. I figured you wouldn't be home long enough to eat them." Silence falls for the briefest of moments as I marvel at her ability to figure things out. Then, of course, she goes in for the kill. "So, who is she?"

"Who is who?" I grab my toiletry bag and add it to the pile.

"Who is the woman who is putting that smile on your face and who you are sneaking off with? I mean, if she weren't anything special, you would have said something. Your hiding her says volumes."

"And you wonder why I told you to go home."

"Deflection is not going to work," she says in her most motherly tone possible.

"There is no woman, Mom."

"Uh-huh. You sure came back all smiles the other night after meeting your cousin for drinks."

"I have to go pack now."

"Does she have three heads? Is she a celebrity?"

"You need help." I shake my head and laugh.

"Or is she *the one*?" She gasps. "That's it, isn't it?"

"Tell Dad to take your temperature."

"Was it love at first sight?"

"Or, better yet, take you to the emergency room because I think you've hit your head. There is no such thing as love at first sight."

"And that, my son, is where I've raised you all wrong."

"I know what you and Dad have is unique and one of a kind, but it just isn't like that these days."

"I don't buy it. The minute I met your father, I knew he was the one. There was a pull that made us happen to be in the right place at the right time. Could you imagine if I had resisted that nagging feeling and had not gone to the Christmas party where I met him? I had no intention of going but decided last minute I had to. Could you imagine if I'd listened to everyone who told me I was crazy when I said he was the one that first night?"

"Lucky for me you didn't."

"You're damn right," she teases.

"But I don't see how you and Dad have anything to do with my love life."

"So, there is a love life, then?" I can picture her rubbing her hands together as if she's gearing up for some juicy details.

"Goodbye, Mother."

"Have fun. When you know she's the one, you just know. I love you. Oh, and don't make me a grandma until you put a ring on it."

I sigh and shake my head. The woman is insane and incredible and exhausting all at the same time.

Right when I pull my cell away from my ear, it rings again.

Jesus Christ, it's like Grand Central Station right now. When I glance at the screen, my stomach drops.

Shit.

I take a deep breath and prepare to face the consequences of my actions. "Dr. Schultz," I say in greeting.

"Hi, Slade. How have you been holding up?"

It's a loaded question asked by the man who holds the fate of my medical career at Memorial General in his hands. I say I'm fine, and I'm not remorseful. I say I'm miserable, and I don't know what it tells him. My lawyer said to tread lightly since the hospital is in a tricky position in this case, so I muddle through a canned response. "I'm anxious to do what's asked of me, sir, so I can get back to work."

"That's good to hear. Good to hear." He sighs. "It's come to my attention that you've been following up on your patient. The one you've been expressly asked to not inquire about."

I pinch the bridge of my nose and struggle with a response, unsure of the trap I'll be walking in to. Fuck it. I might as well be honest. "In med school, we were told that there were going to be those cases that tested us. Ones that touched us so deeply we think about them years later. Ones we can't let go of until we know the outcome. Ivy is mine, sir. If you would have seen how battered and broken she was when she came in, how she held on to my hand and wouldn't let go." *How I promised her no one would ever hurt her again as she slipped into the coma.* "I'm not calling for anything other than to see if she's shown any sign of improvement."

"You put our nurses in a predicament, considering her file says you're strictly prohibited from requesting information."

"I'm sorry for that, but I'm not sorry for caring about how she's doing."

His pregnant pause feels like a knife against my throat—biting and teetering on the edge of either ending this all or letting me live.

"You're only the doctor in this case, Mr. Henderson. Not the judge, jury, or executioner, and that is why we are where we are today."

"Yes, sir."

"I have my own opinions on the matter. Personal ones that I can't express while your case is being reviewed, but maybe, in time, I'll share them with you."

"I would like to hear them, sir."

"With that said the board met yesterday, and we'd like you to come in this morning to discuss some things, if that suits you?"

Fuck.

I look at my clothes laid out, the duffle bag next to them, and the clock again, but I already know the answer before I ask the question. "At what time?"

"We can meet as soon as you get here so long as it's before rounds start. If you're unavailable, we can meet this afternoon. It won't be more than an hour or so of your time. We have a few more questions before we make our final decision."

I'm not sure if that's a good thing or a bad thing, but fuck, if it isn't one step closer to getting me out of this limbo I've been sitting in.

I do a quick mental calculation of how much time this will take and if I can still meet up with Blakely to drive together like we'd planned. It doesn't matter, I have to go in. "I'm on my way."

After I end the call, I give myself a minute to send a silent plea up to the powers that be that I can weather whatever they throw at me and finally get back to work.

And then I dial her number.

"You're bailing on me, aren't you?" she teases when she answers. Her seductive rasp doing more to me this morning now that I know what her kiss tastes like.

"Good morning." I chuckle and then sigh. "You still in bed?"

"*Mm-hmm.*" The sound conjures images of her mile-long legs wrapped around her comforter. Thoughts of other things they could wrap around fill my head. "I couldn't sleep when I got home, so I stayed up late and packed for the trip."

"I'm packing right now."

"You aren't bailing?"

"No, but I do have a slight change of plans."

"Oh." Worry threads through that simple sound, and I wince.

"I've been called into work for a quick meeting that I can't say no to. It has to do with a case I'm working on, and . . . it's complicated."

"Okay."

"But it should only take about an hour, so why don't you head up there, and I'll be right behind you. I'd say for you to wait for me, but if things run a bit longer and we end up getting on the road late, it'll just give Horrible Heather another reason to ding you."

"Okay."

Two okays in a row from a woman is never *okay*.

"I know we were supposed to go over our story on the way up . . . but I think we'll be fine. And we'll make sure to steal away tonight and sort everything out."

"Okay."

That's three.

"We'll be fine. I promise you I'll be there. I wouldn't back out on you—on this. If I'm a little late, just tell them I'm busy saving a life. No one ever argues with that excuse. Trust me."

She laughs, and if I weren't so preoccupied with thinking about what's about to happen with the board, it would've gotten me hard. There's nothing sexier than a sleep-drugged morning voice.

"Okay. I trust you."

"Besides, I like to make grand entrances."

TWELVE

Blakely

I stand in the cool mountain breeze and take in the view.

Trees upon trees upon trees.

There is a lake to my right, complete with sparkling water and a dock with canoes and paddleboards tied up.

A log cabin with the sign "Welcome to Red Mountain Lodge" above its entry is nestled in more trees and sitting straight ahead of me. It's large by any standards, and with the light reflecting off the lake and shining off the tinted windows, it looks more like a high-end resort than a summer camp.

Sixth-grade camp it is not.

Thank god for that. I might be stuck in some mosquito-ridden mountains, but at least, from what I can see, the accommodations are better than I expected.

I glance at the parking lot again, but no one else has pulled in.

Where are you, Slade?

He said he'd be here. I'm sure he's coming.

But I can't linger any longer.

With a deep breath, I pull open the door to the lodge and the scent of warm cinnamon and the excited chatter of my colleagues somewhere down the way assault my senses as I take in the rustic-yet-modern charm covering every inch of the main entrance.

"You must be Blakely Foxx," a very bubbly redhead says as she all but bounces her fairy-size frame over to me, clipboard clutched to her chest. "I'm Sue. Welcome to Red Mountain Ranch where we are excited to have you and your team."

"Hi. Thank you." Her enthusiasm scares me.

"I thought we were expecting someone else with your arrival."

"He'll be here shortly."

"Oh goody." She claps around her clipboard as her smile stretches impossibly wider. "First things first. Here is your agenda for your stay." She hands over a manila envelope with nametags paper clipped to the front for Slade and me and then starts walking, expecting me to follow. "I'll have you put your belongings over here in our bunkhouse area," she says, leading me to a huge opening on the right where bags are lying next to assigned numbers. She has me set mine down next to the number eight on the floor.

I glance into the huge room and notice numbers on all the bunks that coincide with the numbers on the floor where the luggage sits. Great. Can't wait for bunk beds and communal sleeping, said no person ever.

"This way please." She starts walking toward the voices at the far end of the complex. "We'll have all meals in the main room." She points to a dining room that is a far cry from summer camp with its large chandeliers, bar set up on the far end, and bottles of alcohol displayed in an industrial farmhouse-type cabinet. "Activities are planned every day, per your agenda. Since you're the last guest to arrive, we'll let you relax with everyone for a few minutes before we introduce our staff to your group. After we get the meet-and-greet over with, we'll give everyone some time to get settled, and then we'll meet back for a barbecue and bonfire. We like to keep the first night a little light, but we'll be up bright and early tomorrow, so be ready for some exciting activities." We turn a corner, and she gestures for me to enter.

Inside, I find a wall of windows on one side, a table with beer, wine, and cupcakes on the other, and my coworkers milling about in the center. There are a handful of people I don't recognize, so I assume they are significant others.

"You made it," Heather says as she spots me before I can get a drink to help me deal with her.

"Yes, I just got here. This place is gorgeous."

"We've been waiting for you so we could start. It isn't like you to be late, but sometimes we're forced to make exceptions, aren't we?"

"Oh, damn. My watch must be slow." I glance at it. "Nope. It's right on time. See? It says 2:55 just like the clock on the wall behind you." I point to said clock, shake my head while she looks at it, and force the smarmy smirk off my lips before she turns back to face me.

She has an audience this time. I'm curious how she'll play this.

"Well. What do you know? My watch must be fast." Her smile may reflect amusement, but her eyes tell me she's pissed I just showed her up in front of the rest of the team.

Oh. Well.

That time I did it on purpose.

"It happens." I shrug as if it's no big deal.

"Did I misunderstand?" she asks, looking over my shoulder. "Weren't you bringing your boyfriend with you?"

"He's on his way. He was called into work to consult on an emergency, so we drove separately."

"And what exactly does he do for a living?" Her eyes flick over to someone behind me, no doubt one of her minions who secretly hates her but who follows along to save themselves from her wrath.

"He's a cardiac surgeon." My smile is close-lipped and quick. "Saving lives is what he does."

"Oh." Her head startles in surprise. "That's . . . that's great."

"Are you ready to start," Sue asks from the doorway, oblivious to the tension brewing in the room.

"Yes, of course," Heather says as she steps away, and I take the chance to flee.

My colleagues smile at me in greeting as I make my way over to the refreshments table and the glass of wine calling my name. Its taste is on my tongue as Heather begins her opening speech.

"I'd like to welcome you all to the Red Mountain Retreat. My goals for us are simple over the next five days. Since we all come from different walks of life, have come together with experience from different companies—save for Blakely, our resident Glam girl, here—I'd like for us to use this time to become a team. While we should celebrate our differences, whatever those may be, we need to bond together so we know we can trust each other and learn to share our opinions without being afraid of being shot down." She pauses and takes a moment to meet each of our gazes, and I swear to God, the sickeningly sweet smile on her face is enough to make me want to roll my eyes.

She continues to drone on. Sentence after sentence while I take in her brand-new clothes and pre-scuffed boots that make her look the part of avid hiker. I would put money on the notion that she cut the tags off them this morning before she drove up here and that they're sitting in her garbage at home.

I take the moment to glance around at my colleagues—the six others who are here and their significant others. Obviously, I work with them on a daily basis, but they're all still new enough that I'm not one hundred percent sure what to make of them or know what they make of me.

Regardless, I wonder what they think of Heather. Is their job just a paycheck to them, or are they biding their time because they think she'll wear out her welcome sooner rather than later and a new boss will take her place?

I'm inclined to think the latter.

I've worked beside them, with them, and have spent late nights in the office getting pitches ready, but I still don't really *know* them. As she talks, I smile at some of them when their eyes meet mine while others listen intently.

Where are you, Slade?

"In conclusion, I was hoping that we could all come together as seven couples, have some adventures together, bond, and then leave here as one big, happy family. At least on those nights when I ask you to work late, your spouse or boyfriend will know who you're cheating on them with . . . me." Her laugh is obnoxious, but I give her credit for trying to pull this off. "So let's do a quick intro to get everyone acquainted with each other."

We take the next few minutes to go around the room, introducing our boyfriends or spouses—or rather, everyone does but me because I'm still waiting for Slade to show.

"We'll be putting on nametags later so we can get to know each other's significant others' names in case we forget them, but in the meantime," Heather glances over to Sue, who is standing against the far wall of the great room. "Sue is going to say a few things."

"Thank you, Heather," Sue says, her infectious tone filling the room. "We are so happy to have you here and to help you build your Glam family unit. I'd like to introduce you to our staff for your stay here. The activity directors, or ADs for short, are here to help facilitate the activities we have planned for you this week. Austin here," she says, pointing to a man standing at the back of the room. His blond hair curls out from beneath his Red Mountain ball cap, and he has a suntan line on his nose from his sunglasses. He's mid-twenties, and when he lifts a hand to wave in greeting, his bicep strains against the T-shirt's cuff. "Is the master of all things water related."

"Well, I do believe I might need assistance on this trip," a voice to my right murmurs in an exaggerated drawl. I glance over and find Maddie beside me.

Maddie with her vibrant red hair and loud makeup, her trendy clothes and outrageous stories, is the one person in this group who came over with Heather from her previous company. She always nods and says yes to whatever Heather says, following blindly, and her attention span with men is less than a month. She changes them like her underwear, so even though she's here with whichever of the men standing near the beverage table came with her, it doesn't mean they'll still be together when they leave this retreat.

She isn't exactly my favorite, and several things she's overheard me say have somehow ended up in Heather's ear.

"And over by the door is Leo." We all shift our attention to an equally attractive man with darker skin and a smile that would win anyone over.

"Welcome." He lifts his hand.

"Jesus. It just keeps getting better," Maddie murmurs.

"Evan is around somewhere. He's our other fixture here," Sue continues as I turn around to set my empty wine glass down.

And the minute my back is turned, Maddie murmurs, "Nope. He's the one I want. For sure."

Down girl. Talk about a bitchy thing to say when your boyfriend is within feet of you.

But, of course, I turn to see what this Evan looks like and then freeze because the person walking across the room isn't someone named Evan.

It's Slade.

And we're talking Slade looking absolutely irresistible in his dark blue jeans and plain black T-shirt.

But it isn't just what he's wearing that has my pulse racing and my teeth sinking into my bottom lip to bite back my smile, it's the attitude he has. The utter confidence and nonchalance about walking into the room and having everyone turn to watch him.

It's an ease I'd kill to have but love that he does.

It's his smile, which is genuine and happy, that's directed my way. The one that says I'm his whole world and he's been waiting all day to see me.

It's his eyes, which are more gray today than blue, that are fixed on me and sparkling with the private joke only the two of us know.

And, once again, I forget for the briefest of moments that this is all pretend and that the expression on his face is just for show.

"Sorry I'm late," Slade says to the room, not specifying anyone in particular.

"Hands down. One hundred percent fuckable," Maddie murmurs just as Slade reaches me.

"Very true," I say, glancing over to her before I turn back to Slade, "I should know."

"Hey, you," Slade says, his dimples winking as he steps forward and brushes a chaste kiss against my lips before turning to the group. I catch Maddie trying not to choke on her sip of wine when he does. "Hi. I guess I missed introductions, huh?" He runs a hand through his hair, and the aw-shucks expression he gives with it is adorable. "I'm Slade Henderson."

He laces his fingers with mine to make the statement of why he's here—as if the kiss on my lips wasn't enough. "Again, my apologies for being late."

It's petty, but the look on Heather's face is priceless—lips formed in the shape of an O, eyes blinking, surprise etched in every line of her expression. She's in complete shock that this stunner is with me.

I feel shallow for the first time in as long as I can remember, and I don't care.

"No worries." Her smile is wide, her eyes darting around the room. "Welcome."

THIRTEEN

Slade

"**H**ow was that for timing?" I whisper in Blakely's ear.

"Incredible," she murmurs, her body tensing momentarily when I put my hand on her back to guide her to the small gathering of people on the far side of the room.

We're doing some kind of pseudo informal cocktail party where everyone basically already knows each other but where no one seems to be at ease.

Fucking strange.

"Sorry again."

She stops and looks at me, concern I don't expect in her eyes. "Did everything go okay?"

Thoughts stack one upon another in my head. The nerves of sitting before the review board. The answers I had to recite—the apologies and the assurances of how it'll never happen again, that I learned my lesson, that my job is to heal instead of be the judge and jury—when they know damn well the only thing I was sorry for was not being able to protect Ivy sooner. I had to put a damper on my sarcasm and the questions I wanted to confront them with.

Was I supposed to let him be alone with her, the only witness to the crime I know deep in my bones he committed? The only one who could wake up and point the finger at him? Because wouldn't that be harming my patient too? Wouldn't that be failing her?

I sat there and nodded like a good little boy who learned his lesson when all I could think about was little Ivy five floors above me and how she needed to wake up.

I had to show that I was using my suspension wisely by handing over the journal pieces I'd written in my time off. They were supposed to help prove I was still committed to being the best doctor I could be.

I picture their stoic faces and unemotional voices as they told me they knew all they needed to know. That they were sorry that calling me in had given me the impression they were going to reach a conclusion on when my suspension would be over, but that they were in a standstill until Ivy was able to give a statement to the police.

So, instead of seeing light at the end of the tunnel, I spent the three hours driving up here replaying the entire meeting in my head, still in limbo whether I'll be dropped from the program when all is said and done.

That makes room for a lot of noise to live in your head. How my future balances on what an abused five-year-old may or may not say when she wakes up.

Because she has to wake up.

But I'm in the mountains, so there's that. A great place to quiet some of that noise for a bit. I'm also with her—the woman whose green eyes look into mine and implore me to answer.

"It went fine." Not wanting her to look too closely, I lean down and put my mouth to her ear. "You holding up okay? No backstabbing happened before I got here?"

Her smile is quick, and it lights up her eyes with a newfound confidence that looks good on her. "Nah. It's early yet. But your line worked beautifully." She laughs. "And this group doesn't need to wait for you to turn your back, they'll stab you while you're looking them in the eyes."

I glance around and laugh. "Not to me they won't." With a wink, I grab her hand and lead her over to Horrible Heather so I can introduce myself as the doting boyfriend.

This is going to be fun.

"I'll have her won over to your side in no time," I say to Blakely as we lean back on the lounge chairs on the lodge's outdoor patio.

"*Shh*," Blakely says as she looks around in a panic as if I forgot the goal here.

"What?" I say. "It's the truth."

"Not even you are that good."

"Wanna bet?" I reach over, grab her hand, and lift my free hand in a wave to the couple—Oversharing Olivia and her boy toy of the moment, Harley Hal—on the other side of the space. She's already let me know he is a temporary thing and left a mile-wide invite for me to walk into.

"Oh, please." She laughs, and it's such a good sound woven into the rustle of the trees and chirping of birds. "But I'm not going to complain if you accomplish it."

"I bet you that by the end of the trip—"

"*Slade*," Blakely warns again for me to lower my voice.

I slide to the edge of my chair and lean into her so my lips are at her ear. I love the little hitch of her breath she makes when my hand rests on her thigh. "Don't worry. I know why we're here. And I bet you that by the end of the trip, Heather will be your new bestie."

"I wouldn't go that far," she says as she leans back and meets my eyes.

Her lips are right there. So fucking close it's painful not to take another taste of them.

"Do you doubt my skills?"

Our stares hold, and her eyes darken as her mind goes to the same place mine does with my double entendre. But her perfume is filling my nose, and the subtle scent of sunshine and flowers taunts me to kiss her. I'd blame it on the show, but it'd be solely for me.

"Oh, so now you like lists *and* bets?"

She's teasing me, and I flash a grin. "I like anything that has a prize dangling at the end of it."

"Do you now?"

Nodding, I glance down to her tongue, which just darted out to wet her bottom lip, and say, "I do." I shift so I'm sitting on the seat of her chair facing her, my hips bumping against hers, and place a hand on the other side of her legs.

"And what prize will we be dangling here?" Her voice is low, husky, sexy. It's a seduction in and of itself.

"How about whoever wins"—I let a slow smile crawl onto my lips—"gets a night of their choice when this is all done?"

"A night of their choice?"

"Yep." I reach out and tuck a piece of hair behind her ear, letting my fingers linger. "Whoever loses has to give the winner a night out of their choice."

"That's fair." She looks over to where another of her coworkers has ventured out onto the patio to take in this incredible view. "How exactly would we measure this though?"

"In satisfaction."

I love the flash up of her eyes to meet mine and the quick startle of her head. The way I can affect her is a heady feeling.

"That's a rather hard thing to measure, don't you think?" she murmurs

"Sometimes, but other times, satisfaction is clear as day." I chuckle. "I'll leave that up to you. How would you measure satisfaction?"

"I get the promotion."

"The promotion? And how is getting the promotion a measure of satisfaction?" I chuckle and squeeze her thigh. "I'm beginning to think you're trying to throw this bet here by giving me something to achieve that can't be quantified or measured."

"Getting the promotion would give me the satisfaction of attaining the one goal I've worked toward for years—the vice president of marketing position. If I get the job, then ultimate satisfaction is achieved."

"Essentially, you're twisting the parameter I set of satisfaction to suit your needs."

"I'm a girl who'll do what it takes to get what she wants," she says, and the playful little shrug and smile she flashes me are a deadly combination for my restraint. She's fucking irresistible. "And I want the VP of marketing job. All I need is for Heather—"

"You mean Horrible Heather—"

"*Shh.*" She reaches up and puts her hand over my mouth while I laugh, drawing attention over to us.

"Sorry. Best behavior here," I say in my nerdiest voice as I grab her hand, all thoughts of Heather gone now that our fingers are linked.

"So, it's a bet?" There's a flirtatious amusement in her eyes that's impossible to ignore.

"I still think you're putting me at a disadvantage from the start with this immeasurable parameter you've set."

"You afraid you can't satisfy me?" She trails a finger down the top of my thigh. "I thought you never backed down from a bet, Slade."

She needs to quit smiling because it just makes me want to kiss her again.

And again.

And then some.

"I don't." I lean in closer and lower my voice. "There are a whole lot of things I can't control, and you getting that position is one of them."

She twists her finger around a lock of hair while batting her eyelashes. "Don't you have faith in me, Slade?"

My name. Her lips. *Jesus.*

"Complete faith."

"Then what seems to be the problem?"

"There isn't one." I angle my head as I stare at her. "Bet taken. You'll get that promotion. I'll make sure you're satisfied."

And I don't care how subjective her satisfaction is. Scratch that. I do care. Especially when my ability to give it is being judged. The most important part is that I just extended this weekend to at least one more night with her.

Not sure why that feels so important to do before we've even started . . . but this woman.

There's just something about her.

FOURTEEN

Blakely

Satisfaction.

What man measures things in satisfaction?

Ones who obviously knows how to give it.

Why this owns my thoughts as Slade and I stroll down the pathway toward our cabin is beyond me.

That's a lie. I know why it runs on repeat in my head. I know why my body reacted viscerally to the thought of it.

Because all I could think about when he was sitting on the chaise lounge with me was our kiss last night.

Last night? It feels like forever ago and minutes ago at the same time.

And we're headed to a cabin. Yes, I said it. *A cabin*. Where we will be alone.

At night.

The man I'm lusting after. The man I want to kiss me. The man who just linked his fingers through mine as if it were the most natural thing in the world to do.

This all ties together in my overthinking brain.

There was comfort in the idea of a communal cabin with bunk beds. Sure, it would have been a pain in the ass to be with everyone nonstop, but it also would have allowed me to draw a line of propriety between Slade and me.

And now there is no safety. There is just Slade and me and nothing but a whole lot of thrumming desire in a very small space.

"You're awfully quiet," Slade says.

"Just enjoying the scenery."

He laughs, and it rumbles through the silence. "You mean the scenery in the mountains of which you despise?"

I laugh. Cover blown. "I'm not too thrilled with this agenda," I say, holding out the paper and shaking my head. "An obstacle course. Paddleboard yoga . . . I mean, I'm not really seeing anywhere how this is teambuilding."

"A fishing contest. Capture the flag. Canoe races. Relay races. Hide-and-seek." He raises his eyebrows at the grade-school games. "It sounds like your boss missed out on her childhood sleepaway camp and is trying to make up for lost time."

"I was expecting a trust course and zip line or something like that. You know, things that force us to learn to trust each other. This definitely is not what I expected."

"Says the city girl."

I shrug and give him a coy smile as we take the steps up to the small covered porch of the cabin. Within seconds, his key is in the door and he's pushing it open.

"Well, this is going to be interesting," he murmurs as he steps out of the way for me to enter before him.

I step a foot into the cabin and have to stop the panic that begins to riot within me. Everything is new and nice and clean, but the interior is, at best, twelve foot by twelve foot. There is a full-size or maybe a queen-size bed in the center of the room, and our bags are on the floor next to it. There are about three feet on each side of the bed, and there is what looks kind of like a baby changing table beneath the windows for us to put our luggage on. On the other side of the bed is a doorway, which I assume leads to a bathroom.

I'm almost afraid to look.

"It isn't much space," Slade says as he hops onto the bed and puts his hands behind his head. "But at least the bed is comfortable."

And it looks mighty comfortable. It also looks extremely small with his body occupying the space. Space that he and I will have to share while sleeping.

Memories of his kiss mix with the knowledge that we will be side by side . . . touching, and I know I won't be getting any sleep.

The cocky smirk curling the corner of his lips gives me the feeling he's thinking the same thing.

I step over our bags to get a foot of space between us and to investigate the bathroom. There's a sink, a counter, and a mirror and . . . that's it.

"You okay?" Slade asks from his spot on the bed.

"Umm . . ." This is not funny. "There's no toilet or shower." Not even remotely funny.

"Okay."

"How can you sound so blasé about there not being a toilet or a shower?" I start to freak. I mean, I'm handling this nature shit pretty well so far—outwardly, at least—but this? This isn't good.

He chuckles. "I guess I expected it," he says as if he's testing the waters. "Most camping places have a communal shower and bathroom. The one plus is Sue said there's no one else near our facilities, so we'll most likely get ours to ourselves."

"Great. A lot of good that's going to do me when I have to go pee at three in the morning and a bear comes meandering around."

"There are no bears here."

"Then why are there signs everywhere telling us to put our trash in those metal bins so as not to attract bears? *Bears*, Slade. Bears."

"They won't come around here. It's just a precaution." He angles his head up and studies me. "You're really freaked out about this, aren't you?"

"No. Yes. It's stupid."

"I'll protect you."

"Against a bazillion pound bear?"

"Don't you have faith in me?" he asks, that playful smile on his lips when he pats the bed beside him. "The plus side is, you know I'll be able to patch you up after the bear gets done with you."

"And now you're a comedian."

"At least you know I have humor to help get you through the pain," he says as I glare at him. "Come on. Forget about bears and come plot our history with me."

Freaking out about bears or talking to Slade about us, albeit a fake us?

I know which one I'll take any day of the week.

I take a single step and the fronts of my thighs hit the side of the bed as I look down at him. The black shirt against his tan skin and the biceps on full display with his arms folded beneath his head. His muscular thighs flexing beneath the denim as he uncrosses and recrosses his ankles. Those eyes, inquisitive and seductive at the same time.

He reaches out and links his pinkie with mine. "You good?"

"*Mm-hmm.*" I smile. "Sorry for the little panic attack." Then I sigh. "So, what will the best course of action be? I mean how will we explain—"

I cut off my own words with a loud whoop as he yanks me down onto the bed beside him and starts tickling me.

"Stop! Stop!" I playfully struggle until I'm on my back and he's tickling me from above. After a few moments, he lets me pin his hands against my body.

Our breathing is labored, but there is a stillness that screams if either one of us makes the next move, the other will be all in.

I wait for that next second to pass, wait for him to lean in and kiss me. There are a few seconds where I swear time stands still before his breathing slows some and his lips turn up in a smile. "You need to stop worrying, Blakely. It's simple. We'll keep it simple." I release his hands, but he keeps them where they are with one hand on my abdomen and the other on my hand. "We met in a bar. There was instant chemistry, but you walked out, afraid of how strong you felt about me."

"Is that so?"

His grin widens. "That's so. And because fate is the funny bitch she is and was determined that we end up together, we just so happened to run into each other on the street a week later."

"Very creative."

"And the rest is history."

"But it isn't." I chuckle and rest my head back and look at the ceiling. The mundane white of it makes me so much less nervous than Slade's face right in front of me while his hand heats my skin beneath its touch. "How long have we been together?"

"We told your ex five months, so let's stick with that." He props his head on his hand and settles in beside me without removing his other hand from my stomach. "You don't owe them any explanations or details. And technically, we aren't lying. The more lies you tell, the more tripped up you'll get, and then we'll be outed, so . . . the fewer details, the better."

"Why do you have to be so logical?"

I'm still looking at the ceiling, but I can feel the weight of his stare on me, and it's making me self-conscious.

"I'm sorry it doesn't have a porch swing?"

"What?" I ask and turn to look at him.

"The cabin. It doesn't have a porch swing. You said you only did the mountains with a porch swing and wine." He pats my hip. "I'm sure I can fix the wine problem, but the swing part might be a bit tough."

"You're too good to be true."

And there it is. The thought I've been thinking is suddenly out in the open, and I feel like an idiot for saying it because I can't take it back.

In perfect Slade fashion, he gives me a boyish grin before flopping onto his back. "Don't hate me when I say this, but she wasn't as bad as I thought she was going to be."

"Who? Horrible Heather?"

"*Mm-hmm.* I think I expected a fire-breathing dragon who talks like a valley girl and spits out chewed nails, but she was seemingly nice," he says.

"Of course, she was nice to the hot, young heart surgeon who sauntered into the room with a panache most would kill to have an ounce of."

"Panache?" He starts laughing.

"If I had been in your shoes—interrupt her opening speech and walk in like you did—she would have treated me as if I were a threat."

"It's the good looks," he says with a wink. My sarcastic groan has him laughing. "I'm confused. Why are you a threat if you want a different position?"

"It's a long and uneventful explanation."

"Isn't that why we're here though? I need more of an understanding of what I'm trying to tackle." He nudges me with his elbow. "So, start talking, babe."

"At Glam they have both a VP of sales and a VP of marketing position. They are supposed to have equally weighted responsibilities to drive the success of the products. We share the success, the failures, *the bonuses*."

"As opposed to having an outside marketing company?"

"Exactly. It's great in the sense that we have that whole side of our business working together, but it's bad when the two leading positions are at odds."

"And she's the VP of sales? Who is the current VP of marketing and shouldn't they be here at the retreat?"

"Debbie—the current VP—is retiring for health reasons. She's a great lady, but she hasn't been present much. We all knew she was hinting toward retirement before she got sick, but she just made the announcement that she'll officially step down once the board has a candidate to take her position."

"You, naturally."

"We can hope."

"Why does she have a hard-on for you?"

"Because she's not as qualified to have the VP of sales position as she purported to be."

"Then wouldn't that make having someone like you with so much history and experience at Glam be the best choice to be her cohort?"

"You'd think that, but this is where the let's-guess-what-Heather-is-thinking game comes in." I sigh. "It could be she found out somehow I was offered her position and turned it down."

"You were offered her position?" he asks with a lift of his brows. "Why would you turn it down?"

"Because face-to-face sales aren't my thing. I like the process of studying a demographic, of packaging a product to appeal to them, and of making them see or hear our advertising and feel like I'm talking to them specifically. Sales feels too pushy to me."

"I can understand that."

"When you don't know what you're doing, the last thing you want is someone who does know seeing when you screw up. I've noticed her make mistakes and have called her out on a few of them. Right now, I'm 'less than' her in the company's eyes—in clout, in influence—and that's just how she wants it because then it's her word against mine when she screws up."

"Hence why you're a threat." He pauses for a beat. "Is she competent? I mean, when you get the job, how are you going to handle being her equal?"

"She could be competent if she put the work in, but I think she likes the shiny title and hefty paycheck more than the job itself. She won't last long, and if she does, then she'll have to make that learning curve of hers real steep." I adjust the pillow beneath my head. "From what I hear, she's trying to smooth talk Glam's board of trustees into hiring the VP of marketing—*ahem*, her best friend—at the company she came from for the position. So, her constant cattiness is an attempt to make me look bad."

"It makes sense. Bring over the best friend so she has one surefire person to have her back and cover her ass when she messes up."

"Yeah, but she is forgetting that the board knows me and my track record, which means I'll have a bit of an upper hand there in reputation. I won't have to prove myself since I've already spent years doing so."

"And she fears you'll expose her inadequacies."

I lift my hands. "It's all a guess, but from the way she's trying to push me out, I think it's a pretty educated one."

"So, we kill everyone with kindness and then you win, which means I also win. Easy."

It's my turn to prop myself up on my elbow and stare at him. "Why do you have to be so rational? Ugh."

"Ah, but rational gets you a lot of places. I mean, all we have to do is convince the rest of your coworkers you're valuable. That will turn the tide and get people talking positively about you. Then all we have to do is somehow make Heather see that you aren't a threat to her in any way."

"You make it sound so easy."

"Don't get me wrong, I know women are vicious. I've seen it in med school and in my residency. Women don't care if you aren't trying to take their position. They care if you're a threat in general. The whole philosophy that chicks post on social media about fixing each other's crowns is a ruse. They'll fix it in public so long as they can talk shit about you in private."

I laugh, but it's halfhearted as I shake my head. "Agreed. One hundred percent."

"Okay, we need to make her not feel threatened. You help her save face with the group out there, and you'll be golden."

"Easier said than done considering she breathes that fire at me every time I talk."

"Well, it's on the Blade To-Do list, so it'll get done." He looks over at me, and I have to fight not to reach out and brush his hair off his forehead.

"Yes, it will."

"We just need to figure out who will be your in. Will it be Materialistic Maddie, who already let me know how much she spent at Nordstrom's to complete her mountain wardrobe, or Oversharing Olivia, who has already told me how she plans to make reckless love to Harley Hal in the woods."

I scoff. That sounds exactly like what those two would say to him.

"I'm not done yet," he says and lifts his hand to stop me from talking. "Then there is Buff Becky, who is upset she's missing her CrossFit challenge to be here. The irony is that she's super into her health but is shacking up with Stoned Steven."

"How in the hell did you get all of that out of one little meet and greet?"

"I'm a quick learner. Besides, I typically don't have any more than a few seconds to size people up before I treat them, especially if I'm on call in the ER. I've learned to be a good judge of character. If I didn't trust my instincts, I wouldn't have exactly offered to spend a week with you here, now, would I?"

"Thank you. Again. I . . ."

His expression softens, and in the fading daylight, this room, this bed, suddenly it feels more intimate than I expected. The playfulness is still there, but the shadows and the silence make me think about later tonight when I'll be in here alone with him.

"We should get ready for whatever's next on the agenda," I say before rolling off the bed to find the envelope that was handed to me when I arrived. "I'm afraid to look at what's on here. Do you remember?"

I glance over my shoulder and catch him checking out my ass.

That's never a bad thing.

I wait for his eyes to find mine, and there is absolutely no shame of getting caught looking when he does.

"Barbecue and bonfire, right?" he asks as he pushes himself up.

"Per the agenda, you are correct, Camp Counselor Henderson."

"Very cute," he says as he pulls his T-shirt over his head in that one-handed way guys do by grabbing it from the back of the neck.

My first thought is Paul never did that.

My second? Paul never looked like that either.

I try not to stare, but how can I not when he's all tanned skin, toned biceps, corded muscle everywhere, and he even has those glorious hip dents right above the waistline of his pants. It makes me wonder how many hours a day he has to work out to get those. To get that.

"You good?" Slade asks.

"What? Huh?" I snap my head up to catch the amusement in his eyes.

"With tonight? Are you good?" he asks, his grin widening as I try to look anywhere but at his body.

Lacy boy shorts, Blakely. You are not granny panties. You are lacy boy shorts.

With a deep breath, I find my courage and take my time looking Slade up and down.

"Yeah. I'm good."

FIFTEEN

Blakely

Two bonfires in two nights where I get to watch the flames reflect off Slade's face and dance against the highlights in his hair. Last night he was chill and relaxed—soft smiles and ocean breezes with his friends from the hospital at the beach. Tonight, however, he's playing the role of the perfect boyfriend with movements that are much more calculated.

Two bonfires in two nights with this unexpected man. I'd say life isn't too bad right now.

Slade throws his head back and laughs, drawing everyone's eyes toward where he's talking to Harley Hal about who knows what. He has a beer bottle in one hand, he's gesticulating with the other, and he has a genuine smile on his lips.

"Well, don't you two make an interesting couple," Heather says and startles me.

"How so?" *Where are you going with this?*

"It was just an observation." She gives me a tight-lipped smile instead of expounding.

"Daniel seems . . . *nice*," I say and look back toward the fire. "Just an observation, though."

In my periphery, I catch Gemma freeze over my subtle dig at Heather's boyfriend and his complete lack of interest in being here. Poor guy seems as if she's leading him around on a leash.

Maybe Gemma sees it too.

"I'm quite surprised you decided to show up," Heather tries again to land a punch, but I just smile and wave when Slade catches my eye from across the distance where of course, he's charming the pants off everyone.

And there's something about the ease he has, the ability to make me feel like we've done this before, that has me thinking we might actually be able to pull this off.

Heather clears her throat, surely miffed I'm enamored with my man more than I am with her.

"I'm sorry. You were saying?" I ask and turn my full attention toward her.

"How did the two of you meet?"

"We met at The Bitter End." Her eyes widen.

Yes, I'm cool like you and go there.

"He really picked you up in a bar?"

My smile turns sarcastic and just as biting as the judgment in her tone.

"We talked. We hit it off. I left without giving him my number. Out of the blue, we happened to bump into each other the following week and ended up going out for dinner."

"Dinner? That's all it took?"

"Slade has a way about him," I murmur like the words are a hum of appreciation as I rise from my seat. "He's not an easy one to say no to."

And without another word, I offer her a placating smile and a wink before moving across the outdoor area toward Slade.

I've let the other women play with him long enough.

He's mine, and any woman rightfully in that role would go and make her presence known.

"Hey, you," he says and reaches his arm out to pull me against him and presses a kiss to my temple. "Gemma here"—he motions with his beer toward my coworker—"was just telling me how she met her boyfriend, Ted." He points across the fire to where Ted stands. He's well over six feet tall with broad shoulders and huge hands, but there hasn't been a single instance where he's been off his phone the entire time.

"I can't wait to get to know him," I say with sincerity.

"Well," she says and puffs out a sigh, "maybe if I throw his phone into the lake, he'll actually interact." She gives a smile laced with embarrassment. "This is not his idea of a great time."

"We'll get him to put it down," Slade says. "We may have to take a guy adventure when you ladies are in a meeting. A little bonding will have him enjoying it in no time."

"Thank you. Truly." Relief floods her expression as she glances over to Heather and then back. "I just idolize Heather and want her to like him."

"Everything will be fine," Slade says, squeezing my side in lieu of rolling his eyes.

"She sure was surprised to see you," she says and bats at his arm as if I'm not standing there.

"Blakely likes to keep me all to herself, and I'm totally okay with that."

He presses a quick kiss to my lips before their conversation drifts to data infrastructure or something that makes my eyes glaze over, and Gemma slowly begins crushing on him. Her laugh becomes a little lighter, and Ted's head lifts to look our way a time or two when he hears it.

It's a beautiful night with a chill to the air and stars dotting the sky above the pine trees all around us. I refuse to think about the mosquitos waiting to bite me, or even scarier, whatever else might be lurking in the darkness beyond. Instead, I think of Slade.

Of how I'm slowly and knowingly being seduced by everything about him and how there's a strange empowerment in it. In having his arm around me and in having other women be jealous of it. Of being at his side and loving the light in his eyes when he glances at me every few seconds.

Slow down there, Tiger.

As if the powers that be knew I needed to stop overthinking in this moment, the activity director on duty—I forget what his name is—cranks up the music.

"Sweet Caroline" by Neil Diamond blasts through the speakers. Slade throws his hands up and shouts, "Sing it with me," right before the chorus hits and he belts out, "Bom, bom, bom," with his fist in the air to accentuate each word.

We all join in singing the song with him, and he grabs my hand and spins me out and then back into him. Then he puts his arms around me for a short, quick slow dance.

But it was definitely long enough to become hyper-aware of the full, long length of him against my body.

Just as I feel it, just as I want to sink into him, he spins me out so that it's me who is throwing my head back and laughing. It is me who is garnering attention and people are smiling at.

Before the laughter stops echoing around the concrete platform, Slade pulls me back in and kisses me soundly on the lips.

I freeze.

I mean, of course, it's what I want, but at the same time, there is an audience of my coworkers watching, and the attention makes me uncomfortable.

Luckily for me, the song ends and the party moves on. I take a breather to go and refill my wine and then stand on the outskirts of the fire-pit area and take it all in.

"It would behoove you to act a little more professional if you have any hope of getting the promotion."

Ah, Horrible Heather strikes again.

I know I've done nothing wrong. I know she's just lashing out because she's supposed to be the life of the party and my boyfriend just stole that away from her.

I also know I don't trust her or what she might pull to have ammo to use against me with the board.

"I won't apologize for having a good time and letting loose a little with my coworkers. Isn't that what this whole retreat is supposed to be about? Becoming a family? That whole spiel from earlier?"

She just purses her lips and sneers as Slade laughs with Oversharing Olivia.

"Oh, that's it," I murmur. "You're afraid someone else is going to steal your limelight. No worries there. But maybe if you quit trying so hard, everyone would relax like that around you, too."

SIXTEEN

Blakely

"She's mad at you, you know." There's a chill to the air that would normally make me want to go inside, but that cabin is way too small for the two of us and the desire in me that's been building all night long. I'm also buzzed enough from the liquid courage I've been drinking steadily all night to prepare myself for this moment.

For having to walk inside and sleep beside him while trying not to let my feelings grow for him.

"Do you think I care?" Slade leans his shoulder against the doorframe of the cabin as I drink the rest of my wine. "What sin should I not atone for?"

"You were stealing attention away from her."

"Then she shouldn't be so boring." He's completely unapologetic.

"You kissed me." And there I am, completely accusatory.

"And?"

"According to her, I still have to act professionally."

"I wasn't aware that you weren't." He hooks his thumbs into the belt loops of his jeans and shifts to lean his entire back against the doorframe. Shadows from the moonlight above obscure his face as the trees overhead rustle.

"I am. I was. It's just that you kissed me and acted like—"

"Like a man who's very enamored with his woman and wanted to show it." His tone is stoic, but there's a look in his eye that owns parts of me I don't want to admit to yet.

A look that tells me I'm being ridiculous for feeling like he meant it when I know better.

A look that tells me I'm off my rocker if my heart is going pitter-patter over a guy I barely know.

"Well, don't be." The words are out before I can stop them.

Slade takes a step toward me. "Did something happen tonight I'm not aware of?"

You.

You happened.

You with your dreamy smile and kind eyes and irresistibility.

You with the stupid way you make me feel—pretty, funny, wanted, heard.

"Because it's going to be a long night if you aren't going to tell me what's going on."

I'm itching for a fight because I'm nervous and because I want him. I spent the last twenty years with the same man, and what if I forgot how to do this? How to do *it*.

"It's fine. Everything is fine. We should just go to sleep because I've had enough to drink and the bed is calling my name."

"Okay," he says as I step past him, trying to keep as much distance between us as I can while I squeeze through the doorway. And, of course, I stop in my tracks now that I'm reminded how very small this space we're sharing is. "I can sleep . . . um, on the porch if you're uncomfortable with this."

I look at him over my shoulder. "Don't be ridiculous."

Torture. Absolute torture.

"Okay then," he murmurs, holding my gaze, his own asking me what's going on.

Before he can look too closely, before he can see the nerves I suddenly have despite the wine, I look away.

"Do you mind if I take a quick shower?" he asks.

"Sure. Fine. I'll change while you're out there." I motion in the direction of the communal shower.

He flicks the lights on and moves behind me toward his bag. The sound of its zipper, the pad of his feet, the distinct sounds of flip-flops as he walks out the door again with a towel hanging from his neck and his clothes under his arm.

I change into my tank top and pajama bottoms and take the time alone to wash my face, all the while refusing to admit that I'm purposely trying to pick a fight with him.

But I am because it would make falling asleep in this tiny bed a little easier. I'll be able to focus on my anger rather than making a fool out of myself for wanting him to kiss me.

Who am I kidding? I want him to do so much more than just kiss me.

I'm pulling my clothes out for tomorrow when the door opens and he walks across the room behind me. The scent of his soap hits my nose, and I know I need to apologize.

It isn't his fault I want him.

"Look. I'm sorry." I turn to find him standing a few feet from me, his hips leaning against the dresser, and completely shirtless.

Lord have mercy.

"For what?"

I chuckle because he's just being nice by saying that. "For trying to pick a fight with you."

"Want to tell me why?"

I open my mouth to give some bullshit excuse, but nothing comes out. "Because I'm trying to figure out how to howl at the moon, but I'm petrified to take the next step that allows me to do that."

Silence blankets the close quarters as he takes a step toward me. "Sometimes, you just have to jump off the diving board without testing how the water is first."

"Prisha told me you're this nice to everyone and I shouldn't read into anything."

"Did she now?" He takes another step toward me, the water from his still wet hair running down his bare chest in a rivulet that I can't seem to look away from. "I knew there was more than what you let on the other night. Remind me to tell her she should mind her own business. She can be a little overprotective and a lot like a big sister."

I take in a shaky breath when he reaches out and brushes a lock of hair off my shoulder. "So, you aren't this nice to everyone?" My voice is barely audible, and thank god for that since I'm sure my nerves are vibrating in it.

"No, I am . . . but I don't want to kiss everyone like I want to kiss you right now."

"You do?"

"*Mm-hmm.*" That rumble of sound helps to build the ache suddenly burning between my thighs. "I've been thinking about your lips for days."

"We've barely known each other for days." I laugh, but it is swallowed by the sexual tension eating up the room.

"Then I've been thinking about it for hours." He sweeps his thumb over the hollow of my throat.

"Hours?"

"*Mm-hmm.* Ever since I pretended like we needed to kiss for the sake of our cover." He brings his other hand up to cup the side of my face.

"It wasn't just for our cover?"

"No." He darts his tongue out to wet his lips as his eyes darken in the dim light of the room. "Definitely not for that."

"Oh."

"Oh?" he murmurs as his lips turn up on one side.

"Yeah. Oh." Deep breath. Don't think, just ask. "Why haven't you kissed me again then?"

With a courage I've never had before and a will bolstered by way too many glasses of wine, I step up to Slade Henderson and kiss him.

I'm hesitant at first, scared that I just overstepped, but when my mouth meets his, when his lips move in tune with mine, all of my worries fade into desire. All of my anxiety morphs into want. Need. Into anything and everything with the taste of his kiss and the smooth hardness of his chest beneath the palms of my hands.

He lets me take the lead despite the control I can feel humming just beneath the surface of his taut muscles. The minute his hands skim down the sides of my torso and his thumbs brush ever so lightly over the peaks of my breasts, I know he's just as willing of a participant as I am in this delicate dance.

His tongue delves between my lips as his hands splay over my ass and pull me against him. Through my thin pajama bottoms and his gym shorts, there is no mistaking how hard he is, and if I said the feel of him didn't stoke my fires even more, I'd be lying.

There is an electricity humming in my veins that's equal parts thrill and lust and desire and I want all three to win.

His kisses are an assault in and of themselves. Soft and tender intertwined with desperate and hungry. Need and finesse edged with want and greed. Pleasurable contradictions that I am eager to explore.

One after another.

Our soft moans fill the small space as the floorboards creak beneath our feet.

"Blake." He groans as I reach down and cup his hardness, his dick pulsing beneath my touch. The sweet, burning ache it creates between my thighs borders on painful.

He kisses his way down my neck as his fingers slip beneath my waistband and grab my hips. His caress begs for me to stay still and let him touch more of me, but when his lips close over my nipple through the fabric of my tank top, thinking coherently becomes nonexistent.

Anything but focusing on the sensations he's evoking in me become irrelevant.

"Slade," I murmur.

"*Mmm?*"

"Touch me," I say between gasps as his lips close over my other breast and suck through the fabric.

"Oh, I'm getting there," he says with a chuckle as he pushes me to sit on the edge of the bed, helping me pull my tank off. When the fabric breaks over my head, his cock is right in front of my face, pressing against the seam of his shorts.

Unable to resist, I tug his shorts down. When his dick springs free above the elastic band, I let out a gasp. It's impressive by any measure, long and thick with a perfectly shaped tip, and so gloriously hard that I don't even think twice before leaning forward and taking it between my lips.

"Oh fucking God." The three words he half growls, half moans are just as sexy as the weight of him against my tongue.

Nothing else matters but the salty taste of Slade on my tongue and how his fingers tighten in my hair as I suction around him before I slowly slide him back out.

There's just here. There's just now. There's just me saying screw the lacy boy panties, I want to be the G-string that owns every single sensation.

"Blakely." A guttural growl as his dick swells in my mouth. "Blake." A tightening of his fist so my hair pulls tight. "Blak—"

And before he can even get my name out, he yanks himself from my mouth and has his lips on mine. There's a newfound hunger in his kiss. A desperation in his touch. A sense of control snapping as he pushes my pants down, moves me up the bed, and crawls over my body, his dick heavy on my lower belly as he leans over and captures my lips again.

SEVENTEEN

Slade

Jesus Christ.

Seriously?

This woman is everything . . . every-fucking-thing. The way she looks at me. The way she responds to me. The way she asks how to howl at the moon one moment and then takes me by the balls the next without asking permission. The way she's laying there with her pussy laid bare for me to do what I want with it.

"What, Slade? Don't you want me?"

A groan slides from between my lips at the innocent tone coming from that body of hers that was made for sin.

"Oh, I want you, all right," I murmur as I let my fingertips trail over the tips of her breasts, her nipples tightening in reaction. "But I need to know this is what you want. I know you've been drinking, and I want to make sure this isn't the alcohol talking and you'll regret this in the morning."

"I'd be too self-conscious to do this with you sober." She chuckles as she slides her hands over her chest and plays with her nipples between her fingers and thumbs.

"Why?" I lean down and gently tug on her bottom lip with my teeth. "You're gorgeous and stunning and put all the other women out there tonight to shame."

"Kiss me, Slade."

I lean forward and slip my tongue between her lips, a trace of the wine still there, but everything else is pure Blakely. She's sweet and warm and everything that makes me harder than I thought possible.

"When I fuck you, Blakely, I want you to remember every damn second of it. Each touch." My fingertips skim over the top of her slit. "Each kiss." I capture her gasp with my lips. "Every goddamn sensation." I let my teeth scrape over the nipples her hands are holding in place for me. "And yes, I want to fuck you. Desperately. But I need to know your yes is because you want to and not because of liquid courage."

It was a valiant effort on my part to try to be the good guy. I was trying to give her the opportunity to blame it on the alcohol or claim she was caught up in the moment and isn't sure she wants this.

Because I sure as hell do.

She bites her bottom lip and slowly walks her fingers down her lower abdomen to the V of her thighs, which are spread with my knees pressing against them.

I glance up to her eyes and then back down to where her fingers slip between the seam of her pussy.

It pains me to watch her and not participate as I slip a condom on. But fuck if seeing the red of her fingernail polish disappear between the pink of her folds before reappearing seconds later, glistening with her arousal, isn't the sexiest fucking thing I've ever seen. Her gasped moan is the second sexiest. When I can break my eyes from watching her pleasure herself, the look on her face—the seductive eyes, her parted lips, the flush to her cheeks—is something I won't soon forget.

If I thought she had me that night in the street outside of Metta's, I was so damn wrong. This woman and her constant contradiction of insecurity and sudden confidence is sexier than I ever could've imagined. I love that about her. I want to claim both things from her in a way I can't put words to.

So yes, I was trying to be valiant, but I'm a guy. I can be noble all I want, but at some point, desire takes control.

Her answer is to slide her hand back down her body so her fingers can, once again, disappear into her wetness. It's one more soft mewl of a sigh breaking the silence.

I reach down and slide my finger over the tip of hers and take over. It's my turn to become slick with her arousal. It's my turn to slide into her warm, wet heat until she grips around me. It's my turn to be pulled into her oblivion.

If she only knew how little it would take.

It's the moan when I slip into her. It's the tightening of her muscles around me when I hit that bundle of nerves inside. It's the tensing of her legs when I add my thumb into the mix.

When I look up to her and find her eyes glazed with desire, the restraint I was testing is gone.

Obliterated.

Within seconds, I'm jacketed up and using my knees to push her thighs farther apart as I raise her hips off the bed. I resist the urgency that's trying to own me and slowly push into her. Inch by inch. Her hands grip the sheets at her sides. My fingers dig into the tops of her thighs.

"Christ." It's part hiss, part moan, and it's all fucking bliss as I bottom out within her and give her a moment to adjust to me. My vision goes hazy as every goddamn nerve within me bears the burden of restraint.

And then I begin to move.

A slow slide out that has her pussy clinging to my cock. There's something about the sight that can bring any man to his knees. Her gasped moan as my thumb circles over her clit before I delve back into her warm, wet heat again.

The slow seduction of our hips becomes a little more urgent with each and every drive in.

The jiggle of her tits when our hips slap.

The ache in my balls as the pressure builds.

The bow of her back every time I grind against her.

"Slade." Pull out. "God, yes." A mewl. A slide of her hands between her thighs to help push her over the edge. "I'm almost there." Her wetness coats my balls.

As her cry fills the room, it's loud and laced with abandon. She arches her neck, her lips falling lax with each wave of bliss that hits her.

If the feel of her isn't enough to pull me over the edge, the sight of her—hair wild across the sheets, fingers tightened, body taut with pleasure—sure as hell does.

And I do. I crash over the cusp with my hips pumping and my thoughts on her and this and how fucking incredible she feels.

How fucking amazing she is.

My lips meet hers one more time before I rest my forehead on hers as a million thoughts fight for attention, but the biggest of all of them is *wow*.

Just wow.

EIGHTEEN

Blakely

Oh. My. God.

I slept with Slade.

Well, more than slept with him, but yeah. I did. And now, in the early morning hours as it sounds like a damn Snow White sing-along of forest animals outside the cabin, I'm laying here with his leg slung over me while *not* freaking out.

Maybe I'm freaking out a little, but it's because it really happened—every slow slide in and out of his glorious cock—and not because I don't know what to do or say when he wakes up.

Should I be freaking out? Should I be worried that he's going to go into that I've-had-her-now-I-don't-want-her mode Paul went into after the first time we had sex.

But I'm not.

Instead, I keep my eyes closed and relive every moment from last night in my head. Of course, there is a smile on my face, because how can there not be?

Kelsie would be proud.

It's stupid to think, but that doesn't make it untrue.

I stretch some and feel the glorious ache of a night well spent in all the right places.

So, this is what a rebound feels like. Carefree. Hassle-free. Fun. Satisfying.

Slade shifts behind me, and when I feel his obvious erection against my back, I jerk away out of reflex.

Slade chuckles. "Why are you so scared of it now when last night you were singing its praises," he murmurs in that half-asleep, husky tone that does funny things to my insides. He slips an arm around my waist and pulls me flush against him before he props his head on a hand and rests his chin on my shoulder. "Uh-uh. You don't get to blush. Not after last night. Not after what you did to me."

What I did to him?

Is he telling me that he thought last night was as good as I thought it was?

He tightens his arms around me as his breathing evens, but there is no way in hell I'm falling asleep again. My mind is as awake as my body is, and it's all because of him.

It all feels a little too easy, though. My first time with Paul left me wondering if it had been a mistake, while this? This is just comfortable when it should be awkward.

He shifts again, and I tense when his dick hits me again.

"It's perfectly normal, you know? *Morning wood.* I could get all doctor-ly on you and give you a really long list of complicated medical terms to explain why it does what it does, but I'll just say it's indicative of a healthy male. You know, in case last night wasn't proof enough for you." His playful tone is all I need to hear to know he really is too good to be true.

"No explanation is necessary."

"So, it was proof enough for you?"

I look up to find a grin wide on his lips and his eyes half-open.

"I thought we were supposed to measure things in satisfaction?" I quirk an eyebrow.

"True. Very true. I guess I need to up my game then."

I freeze when he stretches, partially rolling on top of me, my body awakening fully to the feel of every long, hard inch of his weight on me.

"What?" I laugh.

"Getting my satisfaction ruler out."

Slade grabs something off my nightstand and then retreats to his side of the bed. To my surprise, he's holding the napkin from our dinner at Metta's up in the air so we can both look at it.

"What? You kept it?"

"Of course, I did," he says. "You didn't think I was going to leave Blade's To-Do list for just anyone to accomplish, now did you?"

Blade's To-Do List:
~~Make Paul regret he ever let you go.~~
Figure out our history: when we met, how long your legs really are, pet peeves, etc.
Make Horrible Heather see you differently.
Win your co-workers over by being fucking awesome.
Convince everyone we are madly in love and meant to be.
Get the promotion.
Find the real Blakely again.
Fall hopelessly in love.

"Why is the first one crossed out?" I ask.

"Because he definitely knows you were the better choice."

"Whatever." I laugh and swat at him.

"No, I'm serious. He couldn't keep his eyes off you that night."

"He can look all he wants. There is no going back there with him."

"Really?" he asks.

"Definitely."

Silence falls over the small cabin. "We're halfway to crossing off the second one," he murmurs.

"We are?"

"We know our history." He shifts onto his elbow, a gleam in his eyes. "We just need to see how long those legs of yours are."

"I figured you had plenty of time to study them last night."

"I was a little busy enjoying other things." His dimple deepens with his smile, and between that and the look in his eye, that delicious twist in my lower belly tightens.

He runs his hand down the length of my hip to my knee, his hand resting there like an electric shock to my system.

"And how exactly do you plan to measure their length."

His lips twist as he fights a smile. "In hands."

"Like a horse?" I laugh.

"I'm surprised a city girl like you knows that." His hand runs back up to my hip, and when it moves down again, it takes the sheet with it. "There are other means of measurement, you know."

"Like?" I ask, not trusting my own voice to speak.

"Like with my tongue."

"Oh." It's little more than a squeak.

"You seem to make that sound a lot," he teases as my pulse starts racing and the delicious soreness from last night begs to be tested again.

I'm not sure what it is that makes me turn to look at him at the exact angle that I do, but it gives me a clean line of sight to the nightstand.

And the digital clock that tells me I have ten minutes to get to my first meeting.

"I'm late!" I shriek as I bolt out of bed like a woman on a mission.

His chuckle rumbles through the room as he props his pillow against the headboard and leans back against it to watch me scramble.

I run to the bathroom, too preoccupied with being late to worry about being attacked by a bear. Five minutes later, I'm back in the room, hopping from foot to foot, trying to put my shoes on.

"What's this morning's meeting?" he asks.

"Who knows? How to berate your employees so they hate your guts?" I mutter.

"Sounds like a fun one."

I glance over to him as I grab my notebook. His hand is behind his head, his hair is sticking up from the fingers he just ran through it, and one of his tanned legs is wrapped around the white sheet.

He's breathtaking. Even in my flustered state, it's hard not to notice.

"I'll be back at God knows when to get ready for our first group activity," I say with a fake pump of my fist in excitement.

"Can't wait." He smiles.

"What are you going to do while I'm gone?"

"Cause some trouble." He shrugs. "Wreak some havoc."

He already has.

On me.

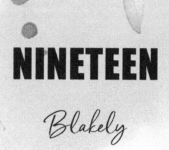

NINETEEN

Blakely

"Let's start with you, Blakely, since it seems you couldn't be bothered to make it here on time this morning." Heather's smile is anything but warm as she tries to pass off her comment as benign.

"Gladly." I sit up straighter in my chair, refusing to take the bait. "What would you like to start with?"

Heather takes a sip of her coffee as the rest of the ladies sitting at the circular table pull out their pens to take notes.

"And what's the point of this?" Minka asks. Clearly, she isn't a morning person and is probably pissed that she was here on time when I wasn't.

"Our goal is to better understand how to be constructive with criticism in order to keep the team moving forward." She glances down at her pad of paper. "I'm going to give you a scenario, Blakely, and then you explain to the group how you'd handle telling your coworker that the idea doesn't fit with the direction the company is taking on a campaign."

"Okay." But I don't trust her as far as I can throw her.

"Let's all look at the first slide, shall we?"

I glance to the screen, and my brow slightly pinches with confusion. Even though my name is blacked out, I know it's my proposal and graphics from a campaign I spearheaded a few years back.

"As you can see here, we have a well put together proposal, but it completely misses the mark. The person has no vision. She clearly doesn't understand the demographic or how to target them. This proposal would be dead on arrival once it hit my inbox, and I'd wonder if the employee who handed in something like this rubbish was qualified to work here."

When Heather completes her spiel, she turns her attention from the slide and levels it directly at me.

I have a very short time to figure out if I want to challenge her, and if so, how exactly I go about doing so without pissing her off and rallying her minions to her defense.

She's such a bitch, and the smarmy smirk on her face and her shady example emphasizes it.

"Blakely?" she prompts.

Heather vs. Blakely: Round One.

I take a deep breath and speak. "As her boss, I'd sit with her and ask for more specifics. Why she chose to market this demographic. What factors she considered while making her plan. What her secondary goal was with this proposal."

"Secondary goal?" Heather asks.

"Yes. Obviously, the main priority is to produce sales, but what else is Glam trying to achieve? Brand awareness? Repeat customer purchases? A new customer introduction into our line of products? There always has to be a secondary goal to a campaign. So, that's what I'd ask my employee because every idea deserves to be heard regardless of what you think on the onset. You never know what other ideas it might spark."

Heather continues to stare at me while my coworkers nod. I wait until she goes to speak, and I continue, purposely cutting her off.

"The question is, how did this campaign do?"

"How would I know?" she scoffs.

"Well, there is a date on this campaign, so we know it was run. If you click on the second tab of that spreadsheet right there, it will tell you just how well it did."

"That isn't needed," Heather says and switches the screen.

"If you're going to criticize my work in front of my coworkers, then at least show the whole picture."

There's a sharp intake from my right by Cliché Karen as others shift uncomfortably in their seats.

"Criticism is how we learn," Heather says, a sharp rebuke in her tone.

"If that were the case then you'd be fair and look at the whole picture. You'd click on that second tab and show that despite your comments about the campaign, our launch was successful. The new line we were pushing had one of the best releases to date on top of a forty percent spike in overall sales. That spike sustained for four months, which is longer on average than others. So, while the campaign may seem dated to you, it was actually quite successful."

Funny how when I finish, it seems all of the air has suddenly been sucked from the room.

"Moving on," Heather dismisses with a quick shake of her head. And on she drones from one slide to the next. None of them mine like the first one was, but they are someone's nonetheless.

By the time we've worked through her slides, nature is calling me. And I don't mean going to the bathroom. I mean the outdoors that I've never liked before now seems a hundred times better than being in this stuffy room with Horrible Heather.

That, and I get to see Slade again. The thought makes me giddy like a high school crush. I should be ashamed of it, but I'm not.

"So, we'll see you in forty minutes down at the dock for paddleboard yoga, everyone!"

I catch Gemma's wince and am glad that I'm not the only one who isn't fond of the combination of two activities. On their own, I can manage, but putting them together is going to be a disaster.

"Blakely, can I have a word?"

The air deflates in my chest, but my voice remains chipper. "Sure. Yeah." I keep my back to her with my hand on the door.

"I wasn't trying to offend you with the critique today."

I plaster my *fuck-you* smile on my lips when I turn to look at her. "Of course you weren't. You were too busy pointing out to everyone how inadequate I was in an effort to undermine any support I might have for the VP position."

"I'd never do such a thing." She crosses her arms over her chest. "You have more experience than anyone for the job."

Exactly. I have more experience than even you.

"Barbie was telling me all about her run-in with you and Slade last week."

"Oh?" I've been waiting for this to come up.

"She was just saying how Paul thought it was interesting how you'd been hanging on to hope that the two of you would get back together and then, there you were, with Slade. Pretty convenient if you ask me."

I laugh and hope I pull it off. "*Convenient?* Just because your bestie is marrying my ex, it doesn't give you the right to have any commentary on my personal life. Paul lost the right to have any thoughts or opinions about me a long time ago, so I wouldn't put much stock in his opinions considering he knows nothing about me. Now, if you'll excuse me, I need to go and get my suit on for paddleboarding."

Right when I reach for the doorknob, her words hit me from behind. "Good luck trying to keep a man like that."

I freeze as I try to figure out how to respond. I think of the girl in the bar and how I let her scare me away without my saying a word. I think of how I vowed to never cower from a comment again, and then I rationalize that I don't have a choice but to walk away without a word this time.

Why give her more fuel for her fire? Why bark back when I know she's looking for a fight?

I grit my teeth, swallow my urge to lay into her, and then turn and look at her with the professionalism I don't really feel. "For someone who's spent the last twenty-four hours preaching about us coming together as a team, comments like that from our team leader seem counterproductive. But what do I know, I'm just the person who turned down your job before they offered it to you."

TWENTY

Blakely

I yelp when arms wrap around me and pull me off the path toward the cabin. Like full on freak out. In those few seconds, I lived my own horror story in my overactive imagination. One where I'd been abducted off the trail at Red Mountain Lodge, never to be seen again. Slade would search endlessly for me to no avail before vowing never to be with another woman because I was his everything.

My ridiculousness lasts only seconds before my *abductor* spins me around and slants his lips over mine.

"Slade." His name is a breathless pant of relief before I get lost again in the carnality of Slade's kiss. In the desperation I can taste on his tongue and the need I manifest by fisting my hands in his shirt. I allow myself to forget what Heather said and how much it has owned my thoughts since leaving the meeting room a few minutes ago.

Slade and his lips are exactly what I need.

"What was that all about?" I murmur when the kiss ends and he leans back.

"I needed a little something to motivate me before I have to go do this next activity."

I reach up to pull a piece of leaf from his hair. "Paddleboard yoga not your thing?

"Is it anyone's thing?" He laughs, pointing to the cabin. "Go get our swimsuits on?"

I nod and playfully stomp my feet like a kid. "Do we have to?"

"Unfortunately, yes, or it defeats the whole purpose of coming here." He lifts a chin back to the direction where I came from. "How was your meeting?"

"Oh so fun." I shake my head. "Not."

"What happened?"

I avert my eyes and shove Heather's comment from my mind and pretend that the inadequacies it evoked aren't still there.

It's funny how I can handle her bashing my work without a second thought, but when she implies I'm not *enough* for Slade, I have a little mental health lapse.

I force a smile onto my lips. "She was just being her charming self as per usual."

"Dare I ask?"

"Nope." I shrug it off. "Not worth both of us having our mood ruined."

"Hey?" he says and gently pinches my chin between his thumb and forefinger to direct me to look at him. "Screw her. She isn't going to stand a chance once we put our plan to win her over in motion."

"We have a plan?" I ask and raise my eyebrows.

"Do you think I ever don't have a plan?" he asks with a flash of a smile before linking his fingers with mine and directing us back to the trail.

"What is it?"

"Hell if I know." He laughs. "Right now, it's to go and have a blast making idiots of ourselves as we try not to fall into the water."

"That's a plan?" I glance his way and love the sheepish smile he gives me.

"It seems like you being happy pisses H-squared off, so while it won't exactly win her over, it'll still feel good to just be happy." He shrugs. "And who knows, it might be contagious and others might end up admiring you for just being you. If you win over the masses, she'll have no choice but to follow."

"That's a very sound plan."

"Did you doubt me?"

We swing our arms back and forth as we walk toward the cabin. I try to clear my mind of all of the negativity from earlier and just enjoy this simple moment with Slade as much as I can.

"The way I see it, it's officially day one, so we need to turn it up some."

"Is this you figuring out your plan?" I tease and get a boyish shrug in response.

"What do you know about me so far?"

"You like bets. You're pushy." *You're adorable.*

"And I'm competitive as hell."

"So?" I ask as the cabin comes into sight.

"So, we're going to win every damn challenge."

I laugh. "You don't exactly win at yoga, Slade. It isn't a team sport."

"No, but you can win by captivating others. Making them want to be more like you, who is charming and welcoming, instead of being like her, who is controlling, demanding, and off-putting."

"Easier said than done since they're all friends with her," I say as we walk up the steps to the door.

"That's where I think you're wrong. Give them a lifeline, and they'll take it," he says, and before I have too much time to think about his comment, he pushes open the door. "I'll wait out here while you change into your suit."

"I thought we were coming here for you to get changed?" I set down my notebook and pull my hair up into a messy bun.

"I already have my board shorts on. Get your suit on."

It's my turn to laugh. "You actually think I'm going to open myself up to criticism around those perfect bodied women I work with? No freaking way. I'll take my carbs and my rounded curves and wear my tank top and shorts"—I hold them up as if he doesn't know what a tank top and shorts look like—"thank you very much."

Slade chuckles, but when I don't move to get a suit out, his amusement fades. "You're serious, aren't you?"

"What part of you thought I wasn't?" I laugh and play it off. "All I hear about at work is how perfect they are compared to everyone else.

The last thing I want to do is put myself in the position for them to judge me even more."

"And what exactly would they be judging you on, Blakely?" he asks as he walks up to me, brows furrowed. "Because I certainly don't see anything they can pick apart."

A hundred things zoom through my mind. How the skin on my legs isn't as firm as it used to be. How my tummy isn't perfectly flat like theirs are. How my boobs definitely aren't as perky as they were ten years ago. All the imperfections I see when I look in the mirror blare in my head like a tornado siren.

Most of all, I don't really want Slade seeing them in broad daylight either. I mean, sure we had sex last night, but it was in the dark. Moonlight glow never makes anything look bad.

"Blakely?"

"It's nothing. I'm just—"

"You're just refusing to own how gorgeous you are."

Thump. There goes my heart when my heart isn't supposed to have any skin in this game.

"Whatever." I roll my eyes.

"Oh. I know what it is. You don't want to show them up with that incredible body of yours."

"I'm beginning to think that trouble you said you were going to get yourself into was in a liquor cabinet somewhere," I say, and a coy smile plays at the corner of his mouth. The sight of it says he's up to something. "What?"

"I dare you to wear it, Blakely."

"Nice, try, but I'm not like you. I don't accept dares." I move toward the small bathroom.

"C'mon, everyone loves a good dare," he says to my back.

"Not this girl." I lift my hand and wiggle my fingers.

"I'm so disappointed in you," he says dramatically, and I hate that I feel like I'm letting him down.

No, not letting him down.

Letting myself down.

The man's been inside me. Did I really think he was going to balk at seeing that the backs of my thighs might have a dimple here or there?

"Okay then . . ." He sighs and sits on the bed.

Mad at myself and pissed that I'm so in my own head about this that I can't see the forest through the trees, I blurt out. "Wearing a bathing suit isn't even a good dare in the first place."

"No? What exactly is a good one then?" he asks as he leans back on his elbows.

"I don't know, but that isn't it." I laugh because this conversation is ridiculous.

"A dare is something like, I dare you to somehow knock Heather and her perfect yoga poses into the water so she doesn't look so perfect anymore."

"Deal."

Slade replies so quickly that I think I get whiplash from snapping my head up swiftly. "No. That is just an example because I'm pissed at her for now. For earlier." I force a smile onto my face. "Do *not* push her into the water."

He bites back a smile and shifts so he can hold his hands up. "Accidents happen."

"I was joking."

"Partially," he says through a laugh. "How about this? You put your suit on and Horrible Heather is saved from her mascara streak demise."

"What's in it for you?" I ask.

"For one, I'll have something to concentrate on while trying not to lose my balance and fall off the paddleboard." He lifts his eyebrows and lets his eyes roam down my body.

"And two?"

"And two, we're trying to find Blakely again." He points to the napkin on the nightstand and continues, "Not caring what people think is part of that."

"You're incorrigible."

"You act like you're surprised."

TWENTY-ONE

Blakely

I put the damn suit on.

Not because he told me to but because he was right. If I'm going to be wearing lacy boy panties, then I sure as hell should be able to wear my bathing suit.

It isn't anything revealing, by any means, and I have to admit that I don't feel as insecure as I thought I would.

My coworkers have imperfections just as I do. Now I need to work at seeing myself as just as beautiful as I see them.

"It's all about balance and finding your chi," Heather reiterates, continuing what sounds like lines she found in *Namaste Magazine* or whatever yogis read. "Inner peace exists if you look for it."

If I thought Horrible Heather was self-righteous before, I was wrong. She's reaching for new levels right now. Though, I shouldn't have been shocked when she anointed herself as the instructor.

Don't get me wrong, I'm all for yoga. I've taken classes before, I've become mindful, and I've released the negativity. But relaxing is not exactly something I want to do with my boss who was a catty bitch an hour ago.

Also? She's suggesting we do poses that are far from beginner. She's either setting us all up to fail so she looks awesome or is so wrapped up in herself she hasn't thought otherwise.

As it is, four of the significant others skipped out on this bonding experience. I'm sure Slade was wishing he was one of them.

"Hold these poses as if they are prayers. Worship your body as if it's a temple."

Don't look at Slade.

Don't look at him.

I bite the inside of my cheek as I struggle not to laugh. Heather calls for another pose, and of course, I have no idea what she's talking about, so when I look up to see what I'm supposed to do, her eyes are laser focused on me.

I bite down so hard it hurts.

"We should be focusing on our inner light and not laughing at our inner-selves in this moment."

Jesus. Really?

"It's obvious that some of us are struggling with finding the maturity it takes to do this activity."

"Sorry," Slade says as he almost loses his balance. "This isn't the easiest thing to do for a guy who's never done it before."

"Would you like me to paddle over and try to help you pose?" she asks, turning on the charm. I get the glare, and he gets the offer. Figures.

"I'm good," he says. "Carry on."

And she does. She moves us through the mountain pose, forward bend, cobra pose, and downward dog, all of which I know by name now because she repeats them so many times. It's as if she's trying to convince us that she really knows her stuff. And with each repeat of the pose, I can see Slade not only struggling with his balance like I am but also fighting back his amusement over how damn serious she's taking this.

Or maybe I'm just distracted by him.

I know I'm supposed to have my head down for the current pose, but I look up to take in everyone around me. They all look so serious and are trying so hard that it makes me think I'm the one being a judgmental bitch.

Or maybe they are all just better at faking it.

I hear a snickering to my left and look beneath my raised arms to

Slade, who is failing horribly to succeed at the pose. Our eyes meet, and the snicker he has turns into a laugh.

"Can we please try to focus?" she asks, becoming irritated.

But Slade's laugh is contagious.

So much so, that I start giggling.

Then, of course, he laughs harder and loses his balance, which wasn't that great to begin with. I break my pose, unable to hold my laughter in anymore, and just as I do, Slade loses his struggle to stay on his board. Rather than falling innocently into the water, he shifts his weight to the side I'm near so that when he hits the water, his body hits the edge of my board, taking me down with him.

When I resurface, I'm giggling so hard I can barely breathe. Slade's beside me, helping to push me toward my upside-down board, coughing through his own laughter.

Conveniently, his hand finds my ass and squeezes. I yelp and splash water in his face, both of us going under water again before surfacing in another fit of laughter.

For a minute, I forget that everyone is around us. I'm lost in the moment of our laughter and the water and not caring, which is the best feeling ever.

I float on my back until my giggles subside and my feet hit another paddleboard. I look up to see Buff Becky biting back her own smile as she flicks her eyes over my shoulder to where Heather no doubt is shooting daggers at me.

"Can we get going? We are on a schedule as you know," Heather says, her irritation clear.

"Sorry," I say like a scolded child who doesn't care as I swim over to my paddleboard, which Slade has flipped back over for me.

Of course, I have to figure out how to get onto it without making more of a scene, but Slade beats me to it. He hoists himself onto my board and locks his hand around my wrist to help pull me up.

On the third try, he finally has me out of the water, and as I finally get my knee up on the board, Slade loses his balance again.

His yelp is loud and loaded with amusement as he falls in what feels like slow motion. He flops on his back right next to Heather's board, and in her overreactive attempt not to get hit by the huge splash that is about to hit her, she jerks her body to the right and promptly loses her own balance.

I stare in shock as she falls face-first into the water.

TWENTY-TWO

Blakely

"**D**id you really have to say that?" I ask, my cheeks and my sides aching from smiling and laughing so hard despite his comment to Heather when she resurfaced, sputtering mad.

He pulls on both ends of the towel wrapped around his neck. "It was all I could think of in the moment."

"Tag, you're it?" I shake my head, reliving how I choked on my next breath after he tossed those words at Heather when she resurfaced.

"Everyone else thought it was funny. They laughed," he says unapologetically.

"Funny or not, you just put the biggest target on my back."

"Hate to break it to you, but based on the look she was leveling your way, she already has one there. Now she's just readjusting her aim."

"And that's supposed to make me feel better?"

"No, but something has to push this to a head between the two of you sooner rather than later so"—he bends into a deep bow and flourishes a hand—"glad to be of service."

"So, it was on purpose, then?" I ask again because he hasn't given me an answer one way or another. Instead, he gives me that adorable shrug and casual lift of his hands. "You're maddening."

"I know." He grins. "And you love it."

I stand in the tiny cabin with my hands on my hips and know he's right—I do. He's the reason this stupid retreat has pulled so much laughter from me. He's the reason I've forgotten about bears and mosquitos and whatever else lurks beyond those trees and have actually enjoyed myself some.

"I'll get you back somehow."

"I count on it."

"Go take your shower." I wave my hand at him.

"Hey, Blakely?"

I look over my shoulder at him. "Yeah?"

"Thanks for wearing that suit." He gives me a wink and doesn't say another word before jogging down the steps of the cabin with his towel over his shoulder and his clean clothes tucked under his arm.

I don't know how long I stare after him, but I'm sure I have a goofy smile on my face that needs to be reined in somehow. But how? Why? Isn't this what letting go of my past is supposed to feel like? Isn't this what enjoying the now is supposed to be like?

Why does him thanking me for wearing a suit make me feel so good when I should have worn it to begin with?

Before I can think too much about this onslaught of feelings . . . this lust that seems so very real when there is no possible way it can be in this short amount of time, my phone alerts a text.

I laugh when I look at it, surprised at her restraint in texting instead of calling.

Kelsie: Dare I ask if you're regretting that decision to shave yet?

Me: I shaved before I left.

Kelsie: I guess the only other question left is, has anyone seen your handiwork?

I stare at the text, and a part of me wants to toy with her while the other part of me is dying for her to know how everything is going.

Me: The outdoors doesn't seem so bad after all.

Laughing, I toss my phone onto the bed just as the perfect way to get Slade back hits me.

I need to act fast to make it work.

The next few minutes are spent with adrenaline coursing through my veins while I bite back the laughter that seems to be flowing freely today.

Then I wait.

It's probably another five minutes before I hear my name being hollered from the communal shower.

"Are you sure that's how you want to play, Blakely?" he warns playfully. "No skin off my back."

I'm sitting on the steps of the porch with his clothes and towel dangling from my fingertips and the grin to beat all grins on my lips.

"Did you forget something?" I call out to him as he exits the shower with nothing but his birthday suit on.

This was supposed to be a trick on him, but I didn't realize it was going to be one on me too. How am I supposed to watch him close this distance in all his gorgeous splendor? His hair is wet, water drips off his chest, his cock bounces off his thigh with each stride, and a devious desire sparks in his eyes.

"Didn't forget a thing," he says and then whistles as if he walks naked every day across a camp. "Good thing I still had my shower shoes on though."

"Good thing."

"Or it might have been a *prick*-ly walk back."

"*Prick*-ly, indeed," I murmur, not bothering to hide my long, appreciative look at him when he steps into the shade of the cabin. I hold the green beach towel a bit higher. "You seem to be a little wet? Did you need this?"

"I need a whole hell of a lot of things." He returns the languorous appraisal before meeting my eyes again. "Turning the tables on you, making you a little wet, might just be one of them."

His words burrow under my skin until my body reacts viscerally to them. My nipples pebble. Chills blanket my arms. That slow, sweet ache begins to simmer because the memory of him makes the promise in his words burn that much brighter.

"Is that so?" I ask.

He takes a step toward me, his cock growing harder with each passing second. "You know this means war," he says, grinning wickedly.

From one beat to another, he's charging up the stairs. I yelp and run into the cabin. It's not lost on me that I'm running into a small room with only a bed with a naked, sexy man in hot pursuit. Within seconds, he has his arms around my stomach, his hard length pressing against my ass as he pulls me against him.

"Someone's feeling a little feisty today, is she?" he murmurs against the curve of my neck, the scrape of his jaw lighting little fires everywhere across my skin.

He slides his hands up to cup my breasts and play with my nipples through the thin fabric of my bathing suit, and his mouth sets a course toward devastation just below my ear.

"If you can't handle the heat . . ."

His chuckle rumbles from his chest into my back.

How can I want him this much already? It isn't just the incredible sex we had last night—well, *it is*, but it's also the way Slade makes me feel. Youthful. Vibrant. Carefree. Nothing like the proper debutant Paul needed for his stuffed-shirt meetings and his I-should-be-serviced-with-a-blow-job-for-closing-this-merger attitude.

"If you don't stop, we might be late to the next activity," I murmur and then moan as his fingers cup my sex.

"That's the point."

My neck arches, and my head falls back against his shoulder as he slips his fingers beneath the fabric and finds that soft bundle of nerves there. I lift my foot onto the bed to give him more access, to beg him to take what he wants because hell if it isn't up for the taking.

Between his kisses, the gentle scrape of his teeth against the slope of my shoulder, his fingers moving masterfully, thoughts of being late for a second time today flicker and fade.

There's no way I can concentrate on them when he's doing this.

"Slade." His name falls from my lips as a moan just as he turns me around and slants his mouth over mine. Where last night was us easing into whatever this is, today is him taking what he wants, and a small thrill shoots through me at the same time his teeth tug on my bottom lip.

The knock on the door startles the shit out of us.

My first thought is how loud was that moan I just emitted?

My second is that I want whoever is there to go away.

Our lips meet again, this time a giggle escaping my lips as my body tremors with the desire coursing through it.

"I should get it," I murmur between another kiss.

"Unless it's Horrible Heath—"

"*Shhh!*" I say as I cover Slade's mouth before he can finish the nickname. With my luck, it's her on the other side of the door.

His tongue licks over the palm of my hand covering his mouth, and I throw my head back and laugh.

"I'll be right there!" I yell to the door.

Another kiss.

"You should get that," he says.

Then another.

"I should." I take a very painful step back and laugh at him standing there buck naked. "You should cover that thing up," I tease and throw the towel at him.

"To be continued," he mutters, and I laugh again right before I open the door.

TWENTY-THREE

Slade

"**G**emma!" Blakely says as she slips outside and shuts the door behind her.

I picture the woman. Shorter with curly hair, a great smile, a little timid, and definitely a tad germophobic. The woman pulls out hand sanitizer every five minutes.

She also has shit timing.

They make small talk as my hard-on fades and my thoughts scatter all over the fucking place.

They are mostly of Blakely.

Of the color that lives on her cheeks and the smile that has owned her face nonstop since I met her on the trail this morning. Whatever the hell happened at her meeting this morning got to her enough that there were storm clouds in her eyes when she deserves only rainbows.

Plus, she wore the bathing suit.

She thought it was about me getting her into it when I'd much rather have her out of it, but it was so much more than that. It was about how when she doubts herself, she becomes flustered and then defensive. Her not wanting to wear it had nothing to do with her damn coworkers and what she deemed were their perfect yoga bodies. It had everything to do with her and how she sees herself.

Not sure what that douchebag of an ex did to her self-esteem, but fuck him.

I'm making it my mission to rid her of her insecurities one by one.

It's the least she deserves.

Her laugh sounds off again, and my balls tighten. This woman. She has gotten a hold of me somehow.

"The reason I really stopped by is kind of embarrassing," Gemma says and catches my attention.

"What's wrong?" Blakely asks.

"Oh. No. Nothing is wrong," she says, and when I peek through the blinds, I can see her blushing and shifting her feet. "It's more . . . I just wanted to say how envious I was of you today. We all thought the whole paddleboard yoga thing was more for Heather to show off how good she is at it instead of bringing us together as a team."

"She is good at it," Blakely says softly as I step into my shorts and pull them up. "But why were you envious of me? I fell off the paddleboard and couldn't stop laughing."

"Exactly," she says, her smile growing more certain. "You and Slade were laughing and having so much fun while the rest of us were afraid to breathe wrong for fear of getting reprimanded. You just didn't care."

Blakely sighs in that way that says she is treading lightly so as not to offend, but at the same time, says she hears her coworker. Such a perfect boss sound. "Of course, I care, but—"

"We can all see that she's out to get you, and yet, you aren't afraid." She giggles nervously, as if she can't believe she just said that. "It's about damn time."

"Oh. I—I wasn't aware it was so obvious."

"We see more than you think we do—or, at least, I do," she says. "Do you want to walk to our next session together?"

"Um, yes. Sure. Let me change out of my suit first. I'll be just a second," Blakely says.

A second later, the door opens and shuts and Blakely stares at me as if she's shocked.

"Don't look now, but I do believe another thing is getting crossed off our Blade To-Do list," I whisper so Gemma won't overhear.

"You heard us?" she whispers back as she walks over to her suitcase.

"I did."

Her back is to me as she slides her arms out of the bathing suit straps and begins whatever voodoo it is that women do to get their bras on. "She's one of the ones I thought was a die-hard Heather cheerleader."

"Not anymore, it seems," I murmur, rather enjoying watching her get dressed. There is an efficiency to it that is equal parts admirable and sexy.

"All because we were laughing." She pulls a shirt over her head and it hangs just below her butt. "All because we were having a good time."

"You proved you weren't scared of Heather's wrath." She steps out of her suit and slides a rather sexy pair of lacy panties up that mile-long stretch of legs until I can't see them anymore. "Hope can be contagious."

She glances over at me again and laughs. "Hope?"

"Hope." I take a step toward her. "When people give it to them, even in such a simple form as laughter, it's contagious." She steps into a pair of jeans. "I see it all the time in the hospital."

"I think you're giving me too much credit here." She turns as she tucks in her shirt and fastens the waist. "For all I know, I'll go to this next session and this whole conversation will be moot."

"I doubt it." I take another step toward her. I brush back a lock of her hair that's fallen loose from her ponytail and tuck it behind her ear. "But if I'm wrong, I'm going to be pissed we were interrupted." I lean forward and kiss her smile.

"I'll make it up to you."

"Famous last words," I say and walk toward the door and open it. "Hey, Gemma. You doing okay? Not too sore after too many Downward Dobermans?" I joke. "What's Ted up to?"

Her laugh says it all. "Frustrated that he has to be here. He isn't exactly a yoga man."

"I think it's apparent that I'm not either." I grin. "It hasn't exactly been a blast for the men."

"Should I worry that you're formulating another plan?" Blakely asks as she closes the door behind her.

"I am." I wink at Gemma. "I plan on changing the male perspective a little while you ladies do whatever it is you're doing next. You okay with that?"

"Do I want to know?" Gemma asks.

"Nope." I press a chaste kiss to Blakely's lips. "But you'll thank me for it."

TWENTY-FOUR

Blakely

"Hey man, I hate to ask, but can you check on her for me?" Slade walks from one side of the dock to the other and chuckles softly. "Nah. Same old bullshit. They have to wait for her to wake up. No decision until then." His shoulders are tense, and he pinches the bridge of his nose in what seems like frustration. "I appreciate it. Yeah, I can hold."

Slade doesn't speak for a few moments as he waits.

"Christ," he finally mutters, his shoulders sagging. "Thanks for checking. I know the position I put you in by asking." He nods. "Sounds good. Later, man."

"Shit." He hisses the word to himself as he takes a seat on the end of the dock.

Watching him for a few seconds, I debate whether to leave him be or approach him. He seems so lonely that I know I can't just walk away. Not after he's been my biggest cheerleader.

I know he knows I'm there as my footsteps vibrate the dock, but he just keeps his eyes on the water ahead.

"Hey," I murmur.

"Hi." He doesn't look my way.

"Can I sit, or do you want to be alone?"

"Sit. Please." He looks up at me and offers a smile that doesn't reach his eyes. "Of course, sit."

I take my flip-flops off beside where his are and take a seat next to him, letting my legs dangle over the side so that my toes skim the water. We sit in a comfortable silence for a few minutes as I enjoy the feel of the sun's warmth on my cheeks and the sparkle of its rays on the water around us.

Even though our hands are behind us, he manages to slide his closer to mine and hook our pinkies together.

I'm not sure why the motion makes me swoon, but it does.

"Everything okay?" I finally venture to ask.

"Just work."

"Want to talk about it?"

"Not really."

"You said you needed some outdoor therapy. Does it have to do with whatever that call was about?"

"*Mm-hmm.*"

"Okay," I say and rest my head on his shoulder. I smell the slight scent of beer on his breath and laugh. "Should I ask what you and the husbands, boyfriends, playthings did while we were in yet another mind-numbing session, or is it better if I don't?"

"We may have partaken in some libations, and I may have been the bartender." He gives a short chuckle. "Needless to say, Testosterone Tom, Stoned Steven, and Baseball Bobbie might just be in good moods for to-night's festivities."

"How drunk are they?"

"They're just very happy." Yeah, I don't want to know. Whatever bonds those guys made are theirs, so I don't dig.

"Thank you for that," I say and press a kiss to his shoulder in appreciation.

More silence passes between us as the sun slowly begins to fall to-ward the horizon and the sky begins to dance with color.

I can't say that I mind sharing this with him.

"Tell me something about you that I don't know," I say, suddenly curious about who this man is.

"Like what? You know the basics."

"Your mom. That first night we met, you said you had a meddling mom. Tell me about her. My mom is so distant and busy with her life in Michigan, that I miss the love that's equal parts annoying and welcoming."

"True." He nods before falling into a contemplative silence for a beat. "She's crazy, but she means well."

"You said she was out here visiting?"

"Yeah, and as much as I love her, I'm glad that she's gone." He chuckles. "She has a way of taking over everything and knowing things before I do."

I laugh, loving how the mere mention of her has the smile finally reaching his eyes.

"And your dad?" I ask.

"He's incredible in his own right. He's a plastic surgeon who only deals in reconstruction after mastectomies."

"Is that why you got into the field?"

"I like to say I went into medicine because I want to save people, but yeah, I'm sure a part of it is that I wanted to make him proud of me."

His candor is refreshing. I'm used to having to pull teeth to get any kind of reaction from a man.

"Why the heart?"

"Because isn't that where everything begins and ends?" he asks, his eyes locking onto mine. "*With the heart?*"

I'm speechless. I'm sure he doesn't mean his words how I take them, but they still hit me in such a profound way.

"Yes." My tongue feels heavy in my mouth. "It's true."

"My mom used to be a therapist. She helped women cope with the loss that comes with that kind of surgery. Many women try to convince themselves they're only breasts and they can live without them, but it's a huge hit to the psyche, and she'd help them get through that."

"I can't imagine. It must feel good doing a job that makes people better."

"It does, but you do the same."

I laugh at his attempt. "I appreciate you putting it on the same playing field, but it isn't. Saving lives and selling makeup isn't really comparable."

"It's all about perspective. How do you know the makeup you've sold hasn't helped someone to feel good about themselves when they've looked in the mirror? How can you discard the fact that for some people out there, a small boost to their self-esteem can mean the difference between falling into the depths of depression or a having a great day."

I shift my head to just stare at him.

"What?" he asks.

"Do you always have this outlook on things? I mean, where did you knowing how to look at things through a different lens come from?"

He gives a sheepish shrug. "I don't know. Reading. Listening to others. Watching way too many people's lives end too soon in the ER forced me to look at the positive in everything. If I don't, I'll get pulled under the weight of it too."

"It's pretty amazing if you ask me." His fingers on top of mine squeeze, and I go back to resting my head on his shoulder.

"Is that how they met?" I ask, thinking of his parents again. "Your mom and dad, I mean. Through their work?"

"The story they tell is that she saw him across the room at the hospital Christmas party. He was talking to two other women, but she said he locked eyes with her, and she knew he was the one."

"Love at first sight?" I ask in disbelief.

"According to her, it was. It took him a few days to chase down who she was and find her. She says he took too long, but they've been together ever since." There is so much affection in his voice, I can't help but smile. "But that was thirty-something years ago."

"I guess it's good to know it's really a thing that's out there," I murmur under my breath.

"I guess. Either that or it's fate having you be at the right place at the right time." He chuckles. "Who knows? It isn't something I put much thought into. What about you? You said your mom lives in Michigan?"

"There isn't much to tell. My father was never in the picture, so it was just us, and that woman is a whirlwind. I think she spent so much time living for me as a single mother that now she's busy living for her. We aren't as close as we used to be, but she fits me in when she has time." I'm not bitter about it and love that she's finally enjoying the life she deserves.

"Was she a fun mom?"

"I think unconventional is more like it. School wasn't always mandatory but traveling was. Dress codes were the devil and wearing the loudest thing possible was more acceptable. Why take civics class when you can go out and protest? The type-A part of me bucked that type of upbringing, but I can appreciate it now."

"Was it hard growing up without a dad?"

"It's all I ever knew, so to me, it just was. Of course, I was desperate to have one so I could be like other kids, but my grandpa was always there, being my dad when my mom couldn't be. I've recently wondered if that's why I clung so tightly to my marriage for as long as I did. It died years before either one of us realized it. Now that I've gotten some distance, I realize it was more my fear of failing that kept us together more than anything."

He chooses not to opine, and for that, I'm grateful. The cold water on my toes, the sun on my cheeks, and the warmth of his skin beside me are too perfect to follow that line of conversation.

TWENTY-FIVE

Slade

"At least the guys are a little livelier now, huh?" I ask as Blakely and I try to figure out where we want to set our stuff for movie night under the stars.

Sounds luxurious. It is not.

A portable screen has been set up at the bottom end of an amphitheater. There are grass sections about ten feet wide that are then portioned off by a curved concrete step about a foot high before another section of grass. All in all, there are ten different levels of grass seating for us to spread out on.

There is also a concession stand, complete with cocktails, set up to the side.

We make our way up the levels, my eyes already scoping out the highest one . . . and for good reason.

Testosterone Ted lifts a beer bottle in greeting as we pass him, and Gemma waves animatedly at me. Harley Hal shouts from where he's sitting in a lawn chair while Baseball Bobbie lifts his hand in a mock salute.

We definitely bonded over the shots we took and the gripes we made about Horrible Heather. Gripes none of them would ever have voiced in front of their wives or girlfriends, but after a little alcohol, were totally fine expressing in front of me.

"I'm beginning to think us women need to break into the bar too."

She laughs. "Maybe then we'd all relax and bond some instead of always being on edge."

I tug on her hand and pull her closer so I can kiss her right in the middle of everyone getting their stuff situated. This time, it isn't for show. It's because I want to.

Hell, I wanted to on the dock but told myself not to. She's going to start thinking the only reason I asked to tag along is to have sex with her, and while I'm not going to lie and say that isn't a bonus, it isn't the real reason I came.

Sitting at home and waiting for Ivy to wake so that a decision could finally be made on whether I'd get to return to my residency was weighing too heavily on me. I needed a break.

She leans back when the kiss ends and the smile that lights up her eyes is worth everyone watching us right now. "What was that for?" she asks.

"For the dock." It's all I say before I grab her hand and lead her to the back of the makeshift movie theater.

It was for her silent comfort when I found out the latest on Ivy was more of the same. It was for her reminding me how lucky I am to have the parents I have and the upbringing I did, and for just sitting with me and watching the sunset with our fingers linked and no words spoken.

"You want all the way up here?" she asks as I lay out the blanket and then she tosses some pillows against the concrete wall for us to rest our backs against.

"*Mm-hmm.* It's optimal viewing up here."

She gives me a look that says she doesn't buy it. And she shouldn't because I don't give a shit about watching the movie *Horrible Bosses.* I mean . . . the irony there is that Horrible Heather chose it.

Maybe she has a sense of humor after all.

It doesn't really matter. I have other plans for us.

Like sneaking off to finish what we started earlier.

It takes a few minutes for everyone to get settled, and Blakely and I drape the huge Pendleton blanket over us. There's a chill to the air tonight that makes her snuggle in closer against me, and I'll take it.

Horrible Heather and her boyfriend, who I've nicknamed Dismal Dan since he refused to join us guys earlier today, stroll in right before the lights at the front of the amphitheater flicker to tell us the movie will be starting soon. Of course, it was perfectly planned for her to have center stage. Anyone who can't see that is blind.

She gives her fake little finger wave to everyone, and then like a queen, she takes a seat in the middle. Perfect. She's far away from us.

The lights dim completely, the movie begins to play, and people become settled.

"What happened today with her?" I ask quietly.

"Nothing that really matters."

But there's a discord in her tone that tells me differently. I lean over to whisper in her ear, and I love the hitch of her breath when I do. Affecting a woman is never a bad thing.

"I completed your dare this morning," I murmur. "I do believe it's my turn to pick the next one."

Her laugh draws a few pairs of eyes up to where we're seated. "You forget, I don't accept dares."

"I'll convert you yet." I run the tip of my nose around the shell of her ear and feel her body shudder in response. "You cold?" I ask when I know that shiver was so much more than that. "Come closer. I'll keep you warm."

And she does. We reposition so that she's sitting between my spread legs, her back is to my front, and my chin is on her shoulder.

Of course, with my dick pressed against her ass, all I can think about is what we were doing when we were interrupted earlier.

My hands are on her waist, so I slide them beneath her bulky sweatshirt so that my thumb can rub aimlessly over the band of her yoga pants. She settles tighter against me, and her hands move to rest atop my forearms.

I let my hand linger there for a few minutes before walking my fingertips under the band of her pants.

"What are you doing?" she murmurs in mock protest, her body tensing as her fingers tighten on my arm.

"Making sure this movie is memorable," I whisper in her ear. "And I can't seem to keep my hands off you."

Her only response is to push my hand lower in consent. And I do. I find my way between her parted thighs, hidden by the dark of the night and the thickness of the blanket.

I run my fingertips over the top of her mound in lazy circles before adding my other hand to the mix and sliding it below. Within seconds, I've parted her lips so that I can have a little better access.

I grit my teeth to hold back the groan I want to emit when I slide my fingers lower, finding her already wet and wanting.

Her contained moan is an aphrodisiac in and of itself. The sound embodies how I feel every time I look at her: want wrapped in need and desire forged with lust.

She coats my fingers so that when I slide back up to where my other hand still has her parted, I'm able to find purchase on her clit. I take my time with slow circles over the bundle of nerves. My movements are lazy, my intentions are singular.

There is a heightened awareness of what we're doing, knowing we could be caught, and it has me noticing every little thing about her. The dig of her fingernails into my skin. The lift of her hips into my hand. The grind of her ass against my cock. The stuttered laboring of her breath. The scent of her arousal that's like a pheromone egging me on.

I create a rhythm: play with her clit for a little bit, adding friction so it swells before slipping back down and into her center and fingering the rough patch of nerves there. All the while, my lips focus on the skin just below her ear, which I learned last night is one of her most sensitive erogenous zones.

So many places to get a response from. So many ways to bring her pleasure. So many means to get her to the end.

Do I want to flip her over and bury myself in her? Hell yes. But there's also something incredible about knowing I can bring her to this point with my fingers alone. There's something heady about testing her limits and seeing just how far she's willing to go. And goddamn it, there's something to be said about anticipating her coming undone.

Her breath becomes shorter pants, and I survey everyone near us to make sure no one is paying attention as I work her toward that edge, one finger at a time.

And just when she gets close, just when I can feel her body tense and my hand becomes soaked, I whisper in her ear, "I dare you not to come."

TWENTY-SIX

Blakely

"You're such a bastard," I say as I push Slade from behind.

But I don't mean it.

Not a single word of it.

Not when I'm riding that high of disbelief and desire that he left me with during the movie.

He walks in front of me, hands in his pockets, whistling a tune as if nothing happened, while I'm back here, slowly reliving every single adrenaline-filled moment of it.

Heck, I've never done something like that in a movie theater with a boyfriend before, never mind in an intimate setting where my boss and coworkers were so damn close.

How did no one notice?

How did no one mistake the laugh I barked out when Slade made that dare two seconds before I actually came for what it really was?

And oh my, did I come hard.

It had to be the thrill of being caught that edged that orgasm. That, or it's just what Slade does to me, and I'm not sure which one unnerves me more.

"You can call me a bastard all you want, but I do believe I won that dare."

"You played dirty," I say as I jog up next to him.

"Only when it's fun and games," he taunts me with his grin.

"What if we had gotten caught?"

"But we didn't," he says and takes the final steps up to the cabin.

"What would even make you think to pull that?" My straight and narrow brain has a hard time computing.

"Because, sometimes in life, Blakely, you need to do what you want, and right there in that amphitheater, watching that stupid movie, I wanted you. Simple as that. I couldn't get you out of my head, so I wanted you to feel how I felt."

"Oh."

"There's that word again." He puts the key in the lock, twists, and then pushes the door open.

He turns to face me, the light inside haloing around his silhouette. There are so many things about him in this moment that hit me like a sucker punch in the gut, and I struggle with words as I try to fathom how this all happened so quickly—the bar, the napkin to-do list, *him*, and my growing feelings for him.

But I don't have an answer.

It isn't possible.

A lopsided smile slides onto his lips. "Don't look now, Blakely," he whispers as if we're the only two people left on earth. "But you might just be figuring out how to howl at the moon."

As I watch him watch me, I try to figure out if I should be annoyed with him for pushing my limits like he did tonight or love him for it. Our eyes hold across the short distance, nature a symphony in the night around us, as his grin widens and taunts.

With a pretend howl, which likely sounds pathetic, I launch myself at him. Lips and hands and bodies collide, as I jump into his arms.

He stumbles backward, caught off guard, but his laughter rings out as he kicks the door closed behind us.

Our laughter turns into moans.

Our fantasies meld into reality.

TWENTY-SEVEN

Blakely

As I walk back from the camp showers, my hair is wet, parts of me are unabashedly sore, and I'm so not wanting to leave my laughter with Slade for my misery with Heather.

But it isn't as if I have a choice.

I clomp up the steps with my shower stuff clutched in my hand and smile when I see the napkin taped to the door.

Blade's To-Do List:
~~Make Paul regret he ever let you go.~~
~~Figure out our history: when we met, how long your legs really are, pet peeves, etc.~~
Make Horrible Heather see you differently.
~~Win your co-workers over~~ by being fucking awesome.
~~Convince everyone we are madly in love and meant to be.~~
~~Get the promotion~~
~~Find the real Blakely again.~~
~~Fall hopelessly in love.~~

I study the list and laugh at his half crossed off items. When I go to open the door, though, it's locked.

"Hey," I say and knock on it. "Open up."

"Not until you give me the secret code," he says from behind the slab.

I hang my head and bite back my grin. "Funny. C'mon, I need to get ready so I'm not late today."

"You have plenty of time."

"Open the door, Slade."

"What's the secret password then?"

"Thirty-six inches," I say, knowing that was his rough (and wrong) estimate of the length of my legs last night as he ran his tongue up my inseam. Just the thought of what that tongue did to me has me shifting on my feet.

"While I do think we need to try to measure them again just to be sure, that is not the password."

"Then why is it crossed off the list?"

"Because sometimes we need to feel accomplished, and after last night," he says, "I feel accomplished."

"Slade." My voice is a warning.

"The code is: Slade is a stud," he says.

And while I may agree, I let the smile play at the corner of my mouth before giving him what he wants. "Slade is a stud," I moan the words, playing them up for maximum effect, but nothing happens. The door doesn't unlock. Nothing. "Slade, I gave you the password, now open the door."

I can hear his chuckle from the other side. "That's not the password, I just wanted to hear you say that."

"Bastard," I mutter playfully.

"I can't hear you, what was that?"

"Slade." I sigh, but it contradicts the smile I can't stop smiling.

"Fuck you, Heather," he says.

"What?"

"That's the password. Fuck you, Heather."

"I can't say that."

"Sure you can. I'm sure you've said it a million times in your head. Now you just have to say it out loud.

"Someone might hear me."

"I won't open the door until you say it."

My shoulders sag, and I shake my head while laughing because I know from experience he won't give up until I say it. "Fuck you, Heather," I mumble.

"What was that?"

"I said it. Now will you open the door?"

"I couldn't hear it. You need to say it a little louder."

"You're maddening."

"And you love it."

And I do. I can't deny it. Who else would have me shouting passwords through a door?

"Fuck you, Heather," I say a little bit louder.

As soon as I say it, he yanks the door open, and Slade is standing there in his board shorts and a Henley with the long sleeves pulled up to the elbows. His smile is wide, and his eyes sparkle with mischief as he runs a hand through his hair.

God is he gorgeous.

"Are you happy?" I ask.

"I'm always happy. I think the question you wanted to ask was, am I *satisfied*." I glare at him. "And as you know, satisfaction is a *hard* thing to measure."

"Funny."

"Do you know what your goal is today in the plan to take Blakely back?"

"I think I'm afraid to ask."

"It's your turn to stand up to her today. If she pops off to you in the meeting this morning, or any other time, stand up for yourself. You're gaining traction with your colleagues so you'll have them silently rooting you on."

I don't give an answer because what he's asking of me isn't the easiest thing to do, and if I tell him I will and then fail, I'll hate disappointing him.

"C'mon. Find that girl of mine who was howling at the moon last night and let her loose."

"I knew you wouldn't be able to resist calling," I say in greeting as I stop just short of the amphitheater to talk to her before heading into my meeting.

"You know I'm dying to know what's going on," Kelsie says, her voice almost a squeal. "Have you gotten horizontal yet?"

"To sleep? Yes. I do believe sleeping works much better when you're horizontal."

"Oh, you're sassy. I haven't heard that in quite some time, which leads me to believe that you have, in fact, played with Slide-It-In-Slade."

My grin is automatic and so is the need to tell her I have. It isn't because I want to brag but because I'm so damn happy. "Perhaps."

"That's a definite yes. Why are you not screaming it from the rooftops? Or why are you wherever you are talking to me and not in bed with him?"

I chuckle. "I'm heading into a meeting, so he's back in the cabin getting ready to round up the men and do who knows what with them. Whatever it is, I'm sure it will be a lot more fun than what I'm about to endure."

"That bad, huh?"

I twist my lips for a beat as I think of how to answer. "Actually, it isn't bad at all if we exclude the times I have to spend with *her*," I say, glancing around to make sure no one is in earshot. "I haven't laughed this much in a long time."

"Don't give me a pause like that," she says, her voice turning serious. "I know you well enough to know a *but* always comes after your pregnant pauses, and it isn't the kind of butt that comes on some sexy young doctor." I don't reply. "Spit it out, B. Was the sex that bad?"

"No. God no." I laugh and then pinch the bridge of my nose. "He's awesome, and each time has been great—"

"Each *time?*" She coughs the word out. "There's been more than once?"

"Yes. No. *Grrr,*" I say with a part laugh, part sigh.

"You aren't supposed to sound unsure of yourself after having incredible, mind-blowing sex, which I'm more than sure it was, so why do you?"

"I don't know what to say."

"Words. Words are what you say."

But she doesn't push as the silence fills the line, and I figure how to articulate my thoughts. Maddie sees me across the way as she enters the building and lifts a hand in a wave. "How is it possible to feel on cloud nine with a man who I barely know but truly feel like I know, Kels? And even worse, I'm really happy, which is probably just from the endorphin rush from being with him the past couple of days. And I won't bother getting into why I'm already silently panicking over what happens when this ends, but I am."

"Oh Jesus. Did we take our overthinking pills this morning?" She laughs.

"It's me, isn't it? I always overthink. And, of course, I need to get inside, so I can't talk—"

"Then I'll be quick." She tsks. "You're allowed to be on any damn cloud you want without shame. Who says you don't know him? Sometimes you simply have a connection with someone, and maybe Slade's that someone. From the start, this whole thing with the two of you has been unexpected and weirdly right. So, don't question the universe. Just accept it."

"Uh-huh." She's crazy, but I nod in silent agreement.

"You aren't happy because you're with him. You're happy because of how he makes you feel about yourself. You're happy because you had some good sex with someone who I assume is treating you right. You're happy because of you. Sure, he might point things out that make you see things differently, but no one can make you *feel* happy but yourself. So, wipe that nonsense out of your head."

"I have to go," I say and start walking across the grassy area toward the meeting room.

"And lastly," she says as if she didn't hear me, "it's normal to wonder what happens next because something attracted the two of you to each other. If it truly is a rebound, then it'll run its course, and you'll rebound off him and bounce even higher. If it's something more, then only time will tell. It's been days, stop freaking."

The problem isn't that I'm freaking out, it's because I'm not. It has been days, and parts of me swoon way too much at things Slade says, and I know my feelings are involved when they have no business being involved yet.

TWENTY-EIGHT

Blakely

"**A**re you having a good time?" I look over to Oversharing Olivia. Her smile is wide, and I don't one hundred percent trust its sincerity.

"Yes, and you?" I ask.

"Between you, me, and the fencepost, we need to be doing less activities and more drinking. I feel like this is all staged. Too set-up. We get enough of this at work." I glance around to make sure no one is paying attention. "I mean, how are we supposed to bond if every activity has us paired with our men? That defeats the purpose of bonding. It tells me Heather didn't really plan this out." She glances to the doorway Heather just walked through. "Either that, or just like this late entrance, she gets off on all of us waiting for her to make her grand entrance."

I open my mouth to say something, but I hesitate, still not trusting that she's being genuine.

It's better if I just smile and nod and toe the company line that I support Heather instead of publicly questioning her.

"Hey. Hi," Gemma says, her cheeks flush.

"Hey, Gemma," I say as Olivia smiles at her.

"I was wondering if maybe you'd be my partner in the canoeing challenge we have later. I mean, that's if Slade isn't participating in this one, and—"

"Hal's sitting that one out," Olivia says.

"Sure," I tell Gemma, knowing Slade won't mind. He's more excited for the fishing challenge than the canoeing one anyway.

"You're a lot of fun to talk to and—"

"What's the point of all of us team bonding and bullshit if we're only doing challenges with our boyfriends?" Olivia interrupts Gemma again and repeats herself. "Doesn't that defeat the purpose of learning to trust each other as coworkers when we're never exactly challenged to work together?" She snorts and rolls her eyes in a way that has me actually thinking she isn't in as much love with Heather as I thought.

It's the second time Olivia's brought this up in the conversation. She's either looking for an affirmation or is waiting to see if I'll badmouth Heather so she can run and tell her.

I gauge how to respond and opt for a cautious approach.

"True," I muse as Olivia nods and lifts her eyebrows as if to see if I'm going to do something about it. "Slade and I discussed the same thing last night."

"It wouldn't take much—"

"Good morning, *friends*," Heather says as she strolls into the room, thrilled with all of the attention angled her way. "I'm so excited to spend another wonderful day cementing our bonds and intertwining our thoughts," she says and does the Namaste gesture with her hands.

Did she drink a cup of kindness this morning, because this does not sound like her.

"A few things before we start. I guess, last night there was a bear roaming through camp," she says as everyone at the table looks back and forth at one another with annoying, excited chatter as I sit still, rooted in my chair. "What's wrong, Blakely?"

I clear my throat. "Nothing."

"You seriously aren't worried about there being a bear out there are you?" Her voice is akin to microblading. It leaves tiny cuts across my skin over and over, and no matter how uncomfortable it gets, I always tell myself they are worth it when I know they aren't.

"Well, the camp staff wouldn't have asked you to mention it to us if it weren't a concern."

"Blakely Foxx scared over a bear. How cute is that?" She laughs and waves a hand my way. "You should probably be more scared of me than of a bear."

"It doesn't concern you at all?" I ask.

"No. But if it did, I'm the team leader, and I wouldn't show it because I am a firm believer in leading by example. Showing your fear isn't exactly doing that, now is it? She would buck-up and take one for the team." She stares at me, that smirk I hate toying at the corners of her mouth, taunting me to question her. "If you have any hopes of advancing, you best figure out how to put on a braver face."

Every part of me roils at her comment and public reprimand, but I bite my tongue and just smile as if I know something she doesn't.

I think it hits its mark. Her jaw clenches. Her hands fist, and I know the moment she realizes it because she shoves them behind her back. And that lone eyebrow of hers shoots to her hairline as she contemplates what exactly the ghost of a smile on my lips says.

"We're wasting time here." She turns her attention to the rest of the group. "Now on to today's topic . . ."

And so she goes in to a long diatribe about the purpose of diverse thoughts while single-handedly shutting down every person's opinion in true Heather fashion.

The entire time we're having our discussion, I'm preparing myself for what I'm going to say after. Line by line. The tone I'll use. The way I'll move my hands so she doesn't read the nerves running rampant underneath. Everything.

When the time finally comes for everyone to leave, I stay in my seat until she notices me still there.

"Is there something you needed, Blakely?" she asks with that sharp snap to my name.

"I'm just trying to figure something out."

Her hands stop stacking papers, and she very deliberately lifts her head so her eyes meet mine. "And what exactly is that?"

My heart is racing, my pulse pounding in my ear.

"Why it is you constantly feel the need to cut me down and criticize me in front of my coworkers? If you're that unhappy with my work, why haven't you just fired me?"

Her body jolts in surprise before she recovers, but she's blinking too rapidly to pull off appearing unfazed. "Excuse me?"

"You heard me."

"I did, I'm just surprised you have enough of a backbone to ask." She leans her hips on the table behind her and crosses her arms over her chest.

"I have plenty of backbone, Heather. I've been in this game long enough to know it's best to choose when to use it."

"And you choose now?"

"It doesn't seem that you discriminate when it comes to me, so why should you be offended that I chose right now, when we're alone, to ask you?" I flash a catty smile. "I mean, unless you'd rather I confront you in front of the team. I think that my doing it this way is the proper way to be a leader. Don't you?"

"You've always thought you were better than me."

You're correct on that one.

"You're the only one who has ever thought that, so that's on you," I say and rub my palms on the thighs of my jeans. "So?"

She licks her lips, and her expression turns calculating. "Just because you've been here a long time—you know what? Never mind."

"No." I stand, hearing words that affirm everything I've thought about how she looks at me. "Just because I've been here a long time, what?"

Heather pushes off the table and shifts on her feet. "You seem to be the board's darling. That's the only justification I can find as to why you've lasted this long when no one else has."

"Like I've said before, I'd think you'd look at that as a positive. I know what the board wants out of our department. I know how to approach them to get approval on out-of-the-box ideas. And my experience and tenure at Glam allows me to see how a different age group might look at a campaign geared for a younger subset."

"And your tenure just might be the only reason you still have a job," she grits out.

"Excuse me?" Finally. Something solid as to what her problem with me is.

"I can't fire you because the board would not take too kindly to it."

"So, what? You're just going to make my life miserable until I quit?"

Why did I not think to record this conversation on my phone?

Her grin widens, and she winks. "That's the plan."

And then she walks out.

TWENTY-NINE

Slade

M y legs burn and my muscles are definitely feeling last night's alcohol and possibly the killer sex I had as I jog the last quarter mile back to the cabin.

Mission accomplished.

Get a run in. Scope out the best fishing locations for the "competition" we're supposedly having today. Get back in time to see just how well Blakely kicked Heather's ass.

Thank god. It's all I can think as the cabin comes into view through the thick of the trees.

This is what I came here for. The outdoors, some clean air in my lungs, and a little distance from everything. A distraction to pass the time while I wait for the call to reinstate me.

And it can come any fucking time.

The one thing I didn't see coming was Blakely becoming part of that expected reprieve.

Out of breath and feeling that much better for it, I jog up the steps and am surprised when I find Blakely back already from her morning meetings.

"Hey . . ." I say, but my words fade the minute she turns her back to me and shoves away what I can only assume are tears because I can't see them. "What's going on, Blake?" I ask, my voice softening as a million fucking things that bitch Heather could have said or done run through my mind.

"I'm fine. It's nothing." Her voice is muffled as she rummages through her suitcase aimlessly to avoid me.

"You crying in our cabin isn't nothing."

"You just—you don't understand."

"Look at me," I say. It takes her a second, but when she does, it guts me. Her eyes are rimmed in red, and even worse, the spark is gone. "Why do you put up with her?" I ask without knowing an iota of what happened. All I do know is this is the second time in as many days that Heather has put tears in those emerald-green eyes, and I'm sick of it. "Because the no-nonsense woman who I first met in that bar, the one who had me laughing and then wanting? The one who had me plotting and planning on a napkin after pretending to be something we weren't? The one who was laughing so hard she couldn't stop yesterday when we were, god forbid, breaking all the yoga rules . . . that no-nonsense woman would tell her boss to go to hell."

She shakes her head. "That woman isn't me." The laugh that falls from her lips is loaded with doubt. "She's a fake who is trying to prove her worth and is doing it miserably."

"That's where you're wrong. That is you. You're refusing to see it."

"Says who?" she demands.

"Says me."

"You don't even know me." Her words are soft yet biting.

I do believe that Blakely Foxx is angling for a fight, and maybe if I give it to her . . . maybe if I piss her off enough, she'll turn around and direct that anger where it needs to be focused.

I take a step toward her, my eyes demanding more. "I don't think you know yourself, Blakely. You keep saying you want to find her, but you keep burying her beneath everything you're afraid of. Maybe it's time you stop using the old you as an excuse and let the new you just be."

Her bottom lip quivers, and I hate the sight of it. "Go to hell, Slade."

"Is this our first fight?" I ask and chuckle. "Is that what we're doing? Should we go back toward the main building and do it there so everyone in camp hears us and knows we're a legitimate couple? It would give you another excuse for why we didn't work out in the long run. For why it seems you can't stand up for yourself and just take what you fucking want."

Your promotion.

Your pride back.

Me.

"What?" she snaps at the low blow.

And it *was* low, but it was also said to get her attention.

It sure as hell got mine too.

Me?

What the hell is that shit all about?

I don't have time to figure it out. Blakely is standing in front of me with parted lips and wounded eyes, and fuck if I hate that I put it there but still want her to call me on it and own every damn thing I've said.

"You heard me," I provoke.

"I did, and all I hear is arrogance."

"Well, someone has to say it."

"You don't get to speak for me," she says and jabs a finger against my chest to emphasize her words.

"Then you better start doing it for yourself because your silence is your own worst enemy."

"Stop talking."

"Not a chance in hell. You need to hear this."

"Get out." Her body vibrates with frustration not very different from the kind I feel. Only hers is because she doesn't want to hear it, and mine is because I finally want her to see what an incredible person she is. The woman Paul never allowed a light to shine on. "Please. Just go."

A tear slides down her cheek, but she blinks back the rest before another one falls.

Christ.

"Fine," I say with my hands up. "I'll give you your space, but only after I say what I need to say."

"Save your breath," she mutters.

"I don't know what you see when you look in the mirror, Blakely, but it definitely isn't the same thing I see when I look at you. You fight me on wearing a bathing suit to go in the lake, you religiously put all those lotions on what you call your crow's feet at night, and you wonder why you don't measure up to the flighty people you work with. You make excuses why you can't, why it's better to bide your time than rock the boat, and then you wonder why they look at you differently."

"Slade—"

"My turn, Blakely. That's twice now you've come back from a meeting with tears in your eyes, so this is my turn." I hold my finger up to stop her. "Do you want to know what I see when I look at you? That bathing suit you argued over putting on yesterday because you thought you were fat or looked bad or whatever the hell reason you had? You put it on and looked in the mirror and cringed. You want to know what I saw? I saw your curves. The ones I want to map one by one with my hands. They're sexy and beautiful and—"

"Slade—"

"I don't see the lines around your eyes that you crack jokes about. I see evidence of laughing and living, and damn it, I want to know the story behind each and every one of them. You're so damn hung up on your age, Blakely, but when I look at you? *I just see you.*"

She shakes her head to reject my words, but I nod to contradict her.

"I've heard you talk to your coworkers and have seen you betray yourself almost every time. You downplay your knowledge so you don't step on toes. You know the answer to every question Heather throws out at you, but you're petrified to know too much or be too smart because you'll piss her off. Well, fuck her, Blakely. Goddamn own who you are. Be the woman you are." Rage eats at me. The kind that stems from wanting to help someone but knowing you can't do it for them. All you can do is show them the road and hope they fucking drive on it.

"It's your doubt that kills you, and I've sat here and wondered why. Why do you not think you deserve this? The respect? The promotion? The laughter? The admiration? I've told myself Paul's to blame for all of this, for wearing you down and killing your self-esteem. It's easier than thinking you are choosing to be this person . . . but he can't be your excuse all the time. You're the one who has to look in the mirror every day, and until you can like who you face, until you see the same woman I admire looking back at you, you're going to struggle at your job and you'll definitely struggle with accepting the fact that *I like you, Blakely Foxx.*" I take a deep breath and step back as her eyes flash up and meet mine. "I like you, and I'm not quite sure what to do about it because this isn't like me. I stick and then move. I don't form attachments . . . but there's something about you that begs me to figure you out. There's something in me that's telling me you're worth it even if getting you to see it is a pain in my ass."

I'm not sure if she's as shocked as I am that I just said that, but there's a hitch in her breath and her shoulders shudder as if she's holding back a sob.

I feel like the asshole.

"This is on you." My voice is low, barely audible. "You want the promotion? Then take it. You want to tell Heather off? Then tell her. You want me? Then love the new Blakely first because that's who I want to laugh with. Not the one you think all these people want you to be— whoever that is. Just the you from the beach bonfire who was willing to dig her toes into the sand and howl at the moon. Just the you who hates the outdoors and drinks whiskey at a bar after a long day at work and tells off men who try to talk to her. Just the you who is willing to go along with crazy schemes like the one I concocted because I feared I wouldn't get a second glance otherwise. That's who I'd pick every time. Hands down. *Just you.*"

There's hurt and denial and a myriad of other emotions I've drummed up swirling in those eyes of hers, but she needs to figure this shit out.

I don't give her a chance to respond because I've said too much. I've called her on the carpet when I have no fucking right to.

Without another word, I slam the tiny door behind me and jog down the steps, needing to clear my own head.

Needing to wrap my own thoughts around my own admissions.

THIRTY

Blakely

You're right.

    Holy shit. Is that how people see me?

    Wait. Come back.

All of those would have been reasonable responses to Slade to get him to stay.

But I didn't say any of them.

Not a single damn word. All I did was sit there angry at him for being so brutally honest, rejecting the things he said instead of owning them.

Just you, Blakely.

All those truths kept ringing in my ears, overshadowing some of the more major ones he said.

I like you, and I'm not quite sure what to do about it because this isn't like me.

I let him walk out when I should have called after him.

I'm supposed to be finding myself, and every time I really need to be the new me, I can't seem to summon her.

Like how in the middle of his rant, the new me just wanted to grab him and kiss him senseless. The problem was the old me was scared to death to do so because it's so out of my norm to take what I want.

And, oh, how I wanted.

So here I sit, second-guessing my actions and frustrated that I am.

There are a million ways the conversation could have gone had I spoken up instead of letting him walk away. Like I could have told him he was absolutely right and that I'm trying hard to to find the Blakely Foxx he is telling me he sees hiding.

"You okay? You seem a little preoccupied."

I look over to Gemma and smile as I run the paddle of the canoe through the water. "I'm fine. Sorry I'm so quiet. I was just rehashing a conversation in my head. I didn't mean to be rude."

"Rehashing because you're thinking of all of the things you should have said or rehashing because you gave as good as you got and you're proud of yourself for it?" She quirks a lone eyebrow above the line of her sunglasses. "I'm typically in the former camp."

"Yep. Me too." I laugh. "And yes, that's exactly what I was doing. Thinking of the million things I should have said instead of the giant nothing I did say."

"Should I assume you're talking about Heather?" she asks, lowering her voice and glancing around even though the closest canoe is over a hundred feet away.

I wasn't, but if the shoe fits.

"I think that's how I feel after every conversation with her." I chuckle and rest the paddle across my lap.

"I should have spoken up when she said that to you this morning. About the bear."

"I can fight my own battles, but thank you for the thought," I say.

"Bears scare me too." She laughs nervously. "Just like Heather does."

Now she has my undivided attention, but I tread carefully. "All bosses are a little intimidating."

"You aren't."

I startle at her comment. "But I'm not your boss."

"You will be soon enough."

"Gemma," I sputter, "what gives you that impression?"

"I was having drinks with Minka last night after the movie and talked while the guys talked sports." She rolls her eyes and takes a sip of the alcoholic cider she smuggled in her backpack.

"Okay." The word is slow and reflects the caution I feel.

"We were talking about this trip. We both brought up the notion that it's weird we're here on this retreat to become a stronger team and yet Heather's made damn sure that none of us actually do the bonding part."

I nod, not wanting to look like I'm fishing for whatever it is she wants to say.

"Did you see the look on her face when I asked if I could be paddle partners with you? Her eyes bugged out of her head."

And she's right. Heather's disdain was written all over her face when Gemma raised her hand and said she wanted to partner up with me.

"I think she was a little more miffed that the husbands—well, except for *hers*—opted to go drink with Slade again. I don't think her being flustered had anything to do with you asking to be my partner."

"Can you blame them for wanting to drink with Slade?" Gemma laughs. "I'd join them if I could. And she *was* miffed, Blakely. I know you have to take the high road here, but I don't. All I know is Minka said Heather is all about assigning partners so she can control who talks to who. She wants to make sure she has an ally with each pairing so we don't talk shit about her." She holds her hands up in front of her in dramatic fashion. "Because whoa! It's not like we're adults who aren't going to talk on our own volition anyway."

"True."

"Anyway, it's like she planned this whole retreat for us so the board gets the impression she's being a good boss, but it's all for show."

"Show for what?"

"To give her some bonus points since you steal most of them."

"Please." I laugh and play it off but am so very curious what she means. "She has more clout than I do."

"She really doesn't." She takes another sip. "Minka says that's why she's terrified of you."

"*Me?* But I don't want her job."

"But you could have had it, and isn't that just as daunting to the person who took it? To know there is someone in the wings the board thinks is more capable of doing the job than you are? To know that you were second choice?"

"Can I have some of that?" I ask of her flask. I take a swig when she offers it, needing a moment to collect my thoughts. I let the alcohol burn down my throat and warm my belly as I look out over the lake. "Thanks."

"The way we see it—"

"We?" I stutter over the simple word.

"We. There are a few of us who are Team Blakely. A few who are just there to collect a paycheck. And then the two Heather brought with her when she moved over to work here at Glam are obviously on her team." She meets my eyes like I'm crazy for not realizing there was a 'we' component here. "But yes, there is a *we*, and we've got your back."

"I wasn't aware any of you felt this way."

"We do, but we have to thread the needle just as carefully as you have been because we don't have the backing of the board. She is our boss, after all, so we can't exactly roll our eyes in front of her. We see it. We're rooting for you. Just know that."

"I don't even know what to say." This time, I take the flask without asking as the whole notion hits me that I have all this silent support I didn't even know I had.

"Anyway. The way *we* see it is that you're the only one who knows the ins and outs of Glam. The board freaking loves you, and as hard as she's pushing for her best friend for the position because she needs her—"

"What do you mean, *she needs her?*" I all but chuckle over the question as I play it off. I thought I was the only one privy to Heather's scheming.

"To cover for her and save her ass?" Gemma's eyes grow wide. "Surely, you know this and are just being professional. I mean, after that first brainstorm session we had on how to brand the new Goody-Girl eyeshadow palette when you corrected her facts like five times. You played it off like her lack of preparedness was understandable because she was new, but we all saw it."

"I didn't realize it was so obvious," I murmur.

"Girl, she's been gunning for you ever since." She waves a hand at me.

"But don't you worry. She can lobby for her best friend to get the job all she wants, but we've made sure to drop hints to management that you're the one for the marketing position."

"Thank you. Truly." Her words bolster my confidence. "But rumor is she gets final approval on their choice since the positions work side by side."

"Is that why you're being so cordial and taking her shit? Because you need her approval?" she asks, putting the exclamation mark on this whole situation. It also makes me realize that my quiet resentment might also come off to some like I wouldn't be a strong leader.

Shit.

My smile is timid. "Well, even if Minka is right and Heather is terrified of me, I still have to tread carefully. I wouldn't put it past her to put me in a compromising position on this retreat just to have a negative she can flash in front of the board members."

Gemma looks at me, bewilderment etched in the lines of her features. "You don't seem like someone who would let someone get in her way."

I open my mouth to refute her, but something Heather said this morning echoes in my ears. If you're the one leading, sometimes you have to hide your fears—or, in my case, my doubts—and simply *play the part*.

And by playing the part, I have one of two options. I can stoop to Heather's level and use my good standing with the board to bully her into giving the nod should I get offered the promotion. But that isn't me, and I don't want to be like her. My other option is to somehow prove to Heather I'm not a threat to her or her shiny title.

"So what are you going to do, Blakely?" Gemma asks.

I give her a knowing smile.

Maybe I came here already knowing what I was going to do, but it just took Gemma's prodding, the knowledge that I do have some of my coworkers behind me, and Slade's in-my-face commentary to make the idea that's been niggling in the back of my head to come to fruition.

Maybe this is just the push I need to own who the new Blakely is and howl at the moon.

THIRTY-ONE

Blakely

Nerves rattle through me as I make my way back to the cabin to take a quick break and grab a sweatshirt for the next activity.

And Slade.

At least, I hope I'm grabbing him to come along. After how he stormed out of here earlier, I'm not exactly sure how he feels about being anywhere near me right now.

When a branch breaks behind me, I whirl around, the thought of there being a damn bear there more than terrifying, but I breathe a huge sigh of relief when I see Slade. He's standing with his hands shoved in the pockets of his jeans, his shoulder is leaning against a tree to his right, and there is the most stoic expression on his face.

"Hey," he says.

"Hi." I offer a smile, not sure what to say.

"I owe you an apology." He takes a step toward me, eyes intent, and sigh heavy.

"Why apologize when all you said was the truth?" It's my turn to step toward him, to apologize. "I know—"

"I was out of line." A ghost of a smile turns up the corner of his lips and warms my heart. "You're under a lot of pressure, and the last thing I want to do is add to it, but damn it, Blakely, I want you to see who I see when I look at you. I want you to trust that same person too."

My eyes burn with tears because the sincerity in his tone and the emotion flooding his voice is enough to make my heart melt.

"Not everyone has the kind of confidence you have."

"I know." He nods and links his fingers with mine, creating a solid connection across a turbulent sea, and I'm so grateful he doesn't try to say more and just lets me have my own insecurities. That he still connects with me regardless. "I have something for you."

"For me?"

"*Mm-hmm.*" He tugs on my hand to follow him. I do so in silence as I try to figure out what it is I need to say. How I explain to him that sitting on a canoe in the middle of the lake, I decided that he's right and that my toes are back in the sand again.

"What is it?"

"It wouldn't be a surprise if I told you." He laughs and squeezes my hand. "But you need to close your eyes from here on out."

"Why?"

He looks at me like an impatient father would, and I smile in return. "I won't let you run into anything, but you have to promise to keep them closed."

I give him a defiant sigh to play along but close my eyes as he leads us through the forest. We walk over some uneven ground then up some stairs, and I assume we are at the cabin.

"Stand right there. Don't move," he says before letting go of my hand. I listen intently to his footfalls landing on the raised wooden floor of the cabin.

"Slade?"

"Patience," he scolds playfully. There is some more shuffling and then an odd creaking sound that has me angling my head. I jolt when his hands frame my hips and even more so when his lips find my ear. "Do you trust me, Blakely?"

The chuckle that falls from my lips tells him not exactly, but I nod.

"Open them."

When I do, the startled laugh that falls from my lips is simply a ruse to pretend that my heart didn't just tumble out of my chest and fall at his feet. "What is this?" I ask but can already see it plain as day.

Slade has jerry-rigged some kind of swing on the front porch of the cabin. It's two ropes attached to both ends of a large wooden slat. And on top of that, Slade is standing next to it, holding a red Solo cup out to me, and a bottle of wine rests on the window ledge beside him.

"Slade." I smile and shake my head slowly. I'm completely astonished by his thoughtfulness. "I'm speechless."

"And I'm sorry."

"You don't need to be," I say, and without thought, I step into him, run my hand over the scruff on his jaw, and brush the softest of kisses against his lips. "This is the sweetest thing anyone has ever done for me."

He holds the wine out to me while he takes a seat on one end of the wood plank. "Join me?"

"Will it hold both of us?" I ask.

"It's about two feet off the ground, so even if we fall, I promise you won't get hurt."

He made me a swing. He brought me wine. He tried to give me the one thing I told him was the only way I enjoyed the outdoors.

Funny enough, I've been enjoying it this whole time, simply because he is with me.

I take the hand he offers and hesitantly sit on the slat of wood, testing my weight bit by bit. There is a moment when I expect the roof to rip off or for the rope to snap, sending us both crashing to the ground.

"See?" he says, his grin widening.

"It's perfect," I murmur, still in a giddy daze over this silly swing that he went out of his way to try to make me happy.

We sit in silence for a few moments, the sounds of birds chirping and laughter from someone somewhere in the camp filtering through the trees. I have wine in my hand, a swing beneath me, a breeze on my face, and him beside me.

I don't care what happens with Heather because this—right here, right now—is all worth it.

"We all have fears, you know?" Slade says somberly.

"What is it, Slade?" I ask, linking my fingers with his.

"I talk a good game about you sucking it up and confronting Heather, but it's only fair to admit that we all have our own fears when it comes to our jobs. We all have our own insecurities when it comes to our actions. It was bullshit of me to call you out about yours when I haven't given you enough of me to do the same."

For the first time since meeting Slade, I see doubt or discord or something I can't quite read in his eyes. It's a vulnerability that is as attractive as it is surprising.

"You've given me more than enough." I smile, but thoughts of the phone call I interrupted the other day ghost through my mind, and I'm left wondering what exactly it is that Slade has to fear. Prisha mentioned he had been suspended, but she said it so nonchalantly, that I assumed it wasn't anything major. Maybe it was. Maybe there is so much more going on beneath the surface with Slade but he hides it under the guise of being so happy go lucky. How is that I've been so self-centered that I never even thought to ask him more about it? "Prisha told me you had been suspended." I'm not sure what I expect in reaction, but him nodding ever so slightly is not it. "Do you want to talk about it?"

He looks out at the lake in the distance, blows out a heavy sigh, and runs his fingers through his hair. "Her name is Ivy," he says, voice low and full of regret. "I was just coming off an emergency surgery I was called in for. Routine shit but urgent nonetheless. The ER was slammed that night—full moon or some shit—when she came in. I was walking through when an attending called out for help, saying he needed cardio STAT because they'd had to revive her in the ambulance on the way in." He pauses, and there is so much pain in his face that my stomach clenches over whatever it is he's going to say next. "She had been destroyed, Blakely." His voice breaks, and every part of me wants to reach out and hold him.

"I'm so sorry." It's stupid and does nothing to fix it, but it's all I can think to say.

"She was this little girl who had been beaten within an inch of her life, and I *froze*. All the years of training I went through flew out the window."

"You're human."

He emits a snort. "Yeah, well, when her dad came barreling in with his crisp dress shirt and expensive watch like some elite asshole, he claimed she fell down the stairs and demanded that I do my job and save his little girl. Shit, I took one look at the blood and bruises on his knuckles, and I *knew*. I knew he was the one who'd hurt her, and if I hadn't, her sudden cry when she saw him and the way she gripped my hand would have told me. And that gasp? God, Blakely, it will forever be etched in my mind. Total fear and helplessness and—shit. Just fucking brutal. But not more brutal than what he did to her."

"I don't even know what to say."

"Let's just say he didn't want her to say anything." He gives a laugh but it's self-deprecating at best. "I refused to leave her alone with that fucker. I told him he couldn't be in with her while I worked on her. And I swear when he leaned over to whisper something in her ear, he threatened her. Her eyes grew so huge and her chin quivered as she held back tears. I shoved him out of the room. I was busy fighting him to keep him away from his own daughter when she slipped into a coma." His voice is barely audible. "There I was, reacting to him and betraying the one principle I'm supposed to live by, do no harm."

"I don't understand. You were trying to make her safe."

"I was her doctor, and instead of checking her for a brain bleed like I should have been doing, I was busy provoking him."

"You can't blame yourself for a natural reaction."

"But that's my job, Blakely. That's the oath I took. I reacted to the outside when all I should have been focused on was the inside. I let my emotions get the better of me when I should have been one hundred percent focused on Ivy. I lost minutes to him, minutes that could have meant assessing her injuries and saving her from further damage."

I scoot closer to him and lean my head on his shoulder. "No one would blame you for your reaction, but I understand why you feel how you do." I press a kiss to his shoulder and then rest my chin there as I stare at his profile. The strong nose and thick lashes. The proud chin and stubble he's let grow during our time here. My heart swells. "So that's why you were suspended? Because you were dealing with him and not treating her? I don't understand."

"Let's just say I didn't exactly trust the fucker. After we got her stable and moved her to the ICU, I made my case to the cops that he may look like the doting single dad who never left her bedside, but I was and *still am* certain he was the one who hurt her. I wanted him nowhere near her."

"Understandably."

"Where my story fell short was that her injuries *could have been* caused by a fall down the stairs. But I saw the blood on his knuckles he'd washed off. I saw the terror in her eyes before she fell unconscious. It didn't matter how insistent I was because he had already convinced the police that he was some pillar of the fucking community who'd never hurt a soul. It's my word against his until Ivy wakes up and can give her account."

"I'm at a loss for words." I squeeze his hand tighter, hating this story, hating that he's reliving it just so I can hear it, but asking him to stop isn't something I can do. He's bleeding, so I won't let him bleed alone.

"Yeah, well, where they saw a doting father who sat by her bedside day in and day out, I saw a man willing to protect his reputation and life by any and all means. He'd hurt her that badly, who said he wasn't going to take it a step further? So I prohibited him from being in the ICU. I moved her to a different room when he got my superior involved. I then convinced a guard she was in danger and had him stand in her room whenever he was present. *That* is what got me suspended. He complained to someone he knows on the hospital board, and I was suspended from my residency program as well as blocked from her case pending review."

"And Ivy?"

"She's been in a coma since. Her other injuries have healed, but her brain, her cognitive function, is what we are waiting on. She needs to wake up. She needs to . . ." He lifts his free hand in defeat. "Can I tell you how much I hate saying I need her to wake up? It sounds fucking selfish. Her waking up and telling the truth will clear me from wrongdoing and put that fucker in jail. I'd get my job back, my life back. But that isn't what I mean when I say it. I just want her to wake up because she deserves a chance at knowing what life is like without a hand being raised to her."

He's amazing. The thought runs through my head over and over, but I don't voice it because I know he'd just refute it. He only sees a little girl he didn't help when he wouldn't have been able to prevent the situation in the first place.

"Is that who you were talking about on the phone yesterday?"

He nods but keeps his eyes straight ahead. "I was having John check on her status for me."

I slide my arm around him, and he slips his around me so I can snuggle in beside him and offer comfort. "No change?"

"No change."

"So, it's a waiting game then?"

"Pretty much. The reason I couldn't drive up here with you was because I had a meeting with the heads of the residency program. They were asking questions and reviewing my actions to discuss my suspension, but in the end, they want to hear from Ivy. If she says her dad abused her, then I look like a hero trying to protect her. If I'm wrong, then we shall see."

"And if you aren't reinstated in the program?" I ask.

"Then at least I was booted for a worthy cause."

The fact that he cares more about a little girl than his own career says so much more about the man he is than anything.

"I'm sorry you had to go through that."

He turns and looks at me finally. "Thank you for listening."

"Of course. Any time. Is there—"

Slade leans forward and kisses me—and not just a brush on the lips, either. It's the kind of kiss that makes my toes curl and insides furl and an ache splinter through every part of me.

But there is no urgency in the kiss, there is no endgame in his motions. There are just his hands framing my face and his tongue meeting mine in an intimate dance that takes hold of my emotions as much as it does my body.

It's a kiss purely to kiss, and I can't remember the last time I've done this.

Just kiss.

Just connect.

Just be in this space with a man who worships my mouth with an inexplicable reverence as if he's getting as much out of this as I am.

I love the feel of my fingers threading through his hair at the back of his neck. I memorize the soft sigh he makes when he deepens the kiss. I revel in the taste of his kiss on my tongue.

I push away the thoughts of how perfect this feels, how afraid I am of how much I like him, and simply allow myself to be pulled under the haze of Slade's kiss.

Every single second of it. The tug on my lower lip. The gentle pressure of his fingertips guiding my head. The adeptness of his lips.

When it ends, when his forehead is resting on mine and our hands are still on each other, right when I'm about to speak, the rope of the swing snaps, and we fall with a yelp and a thud.

Laughter.

It's all I hear. We laugh so hard that we're both on our backs with our hands on our stomachs and wine spilled on us. We laugh till our sides hurt and tears run down the corners of my eyes to my ears and then to the ground beneath.

"Oh my god. That was awesome," he says, the words coming out in huffs of laughter.

"'Trust me,' he said. 'It won't break,' he said." I can barely get the words out before we start giggling again.

And when he links his fingers with mine as we lie on the cabin porch with a broken swing under us and sticky wine coating us, I know for a fact this will be my most favorite moment of this trip.

THIRTY-TWO

Slade

"Who thought it was a good idea to make a group of women have a fishing contest?" Blakely asks as we gather the tackle boxes and poles the staff left out for us.

"Do you have something against fishing like you do against the outdoors?" I ask. "Because I could always make you a swing if it would make you feel better." She turns and looks at me, her eyes alive. "There's that smile again."

That damn swing was still my best epic fail ever.

"Gemma said Heather is dead serious about it too."

"She sounded that way during her instructions." Two hours. Designated fishing spots for each team. The guys can bait hooks if need be, but they aren't allowed to participate other than that. Biggest fish wins a one-on-one coaching session with none other than Heather herself. "So you want to fill me in on why you've spent this whole retreat trying to get as far away from Heather as possible and now, all of a sudden, you're telling me you have to *win* this contest? What am I missing here?"

"I can't hide forever from her, and frankly, it's about time she learned we're equals."

Well, hello there, Blakely. I do believe you've finally decided to come out and play.

"Don't look now, but I do believe you're preparing to howl at the moon, Blakely." I wink. "Good thing I have the inside scoop on just how to make this happen."

"Come again?" she asks.

"I'll tell you once we get to our spot."

Blakely doesn't know it, but she was just maneuvered into losing this competition, and I already have a plan for how to fix it.

"What do you mean you have the inside scoop?" Her eyes narrow.

"C'mon, control freak." I smack a loud kiss on her lips. "It's a good fifteen minutes to get to the spot. We need all the time we can get. Let's start walking."

"I have the drinks," she says and holds up the cooler.

"You know there are worms in there too, right?"

She sputters over a cough, and I die laughing. Definitely not a country girl . . . but I love that she's trying.

"You're serious?"

"I'm serious," I say with a nod. "And you're going to bait the hook with them yourself."

"Oh Jesus."

I pull her into my side and press a kiss to the side of her head. "It isn't a big deal. Then again, I'm not sure if it'll be worth it."

"What does that mean?"

"I'll tell you when you get there."

We trek to our designated spot on the far side of the lake. The one Heather assigned to Blakely. Not only is it the farthest possible location from the lodge but also there are no fish there.

I've asked.

On my morning runs, I've befriended some of the local fishermen . . . and I have a plan.

"We're almost there," I murmur as I look at the map, mind still processing what a bitch Heather is for teasing Blakely about her fear of bears. Blakely also told me how Heather admitted to trying to make her so miserable she would quit.

I have to say that I love that there's a lot more fire and defiance in

Blakely's resolve than before. Even better, she's working on a plan to put Heather promptly in her place.

I hate that she won't tell me.

I love that she wants to do this on her own.

"Hey, Slade?"

"Yeah?"

She isn't beside me anymore, and when I look back, I find her standing a few feet off the beaten path. Her lips are parted, and her eyes keep darting down to my dick and then back up to my eyes. "You're going to want to follow me."

"I am, am I?" I take a step toward her, my dick already twitching to life. "I thought we were supposed to be fishing." Another step. "Baiting the hook." Damn it to hell, she's sexy. "Competing for first place."

"We'll get to that soon enough." She runs her tongue over her lower lip before sinking her teeth into it, her eyes letting me know exactly what's on her mind.

Oh, I'm following, all right.

I step into the small clearing as a seductive smile tugs on those full lips of hers. "Drop the tackle box, Slade."

Our eyes hold for the briefest of seconds as I stare at the woman who has fucking rocked my world.

Then I drop the tackle box.

"Unbutton your pants," she demands.

I quirk an eyebrow and fight my own smile. "Bossy, bossy."

She takes a step toward me. "You told me earlier that, if I want something, I need to go after it."

"In so many words, yes." There's a slight tremble to her hands, her nerves flickering for a moment. I know this must be hard for her, but damn it if I'm not proud of her for stepping out of her comfort zone. I'm definitely not going to complain that she's stepping out of it with me. "What is it you want?"

She gives me a devil of a grin before she takes another step forward. "You."

Confidence looks so good on her.

"You trying to howl at the moon, Blake?"

She pushes me back against a tree and then drops to her knees. "You going to stop me?" I tense in anticipation when her hands find my zipper and our gazes meet. My smile is half-cocked and a guttural groan rumbles through me when those lips of hers wrap around my dick. She flutters those lashes at me and breaks her suction. "I dare you to tell me you don't want this."

I chuckle as my hand fists in her hair so she's forced to look at me when I say it. "Not on your goddamn life."

My moan settles through the trees as she takes me deep into her mouth with the first touch of her lips.

All thoughts vanish.

All cares are gone.

It's just me and her mouth and the warm, wet suction she uses that has my head falling back and my hand wrapping around strands of her ponytail, begging her to slow down so I don't come so fast and urging her to go harder so I can.

It's heaven and hell and fire and ice and every lustful tug between.

I see stars as her tongue slides over me and around my tip. She moans as her hand grabs my balls to play with them while her mouth suctions around me and takes me deep.

"Blake." My groan is guttural and raw and is exactly how she makes me feel.

She adds pressure with her hands, her fingers, her lips. Faster. Slower. Softer. Harder. I begin fucking her mouth as the pressure builds and the need swells.

My hands grip tighter. My muscles tense. My cock throbs. My growl cuts through the silence as she swallows every last drop I give her.

My head swims, and my body sings with endorphins.

It takes a few seconds to wade through the post-coming haze, but when I do, Blakely is standing before me. Her lips are swollen, her eyes are heavy with desire, and her hair a mess. She's never looked more beautiful.

"What?" I ask as she just stares.

"There. We're even."

"Even?" I laugh as I tuck my dick back into my pants.

"You surprised me last night. I surprised you today."

I take a step forward. "That's a dangerous game to start playing with a man who loves dares." I put my hand on the back of her neck and pull her into me so I can kiss her. It's brief but packs a punch, and when it ends, I keep her close so she can see my eyes when I speak. "There is no even in sex, Blakely. There's pleasure. There's wanting to make the person you're with fly. There's enjoying watching them soar and knowing you gave that to them. If sex is a contest you have to win, then you're doing it all wrong." Another kiss that, this time, begs me to fuck her. "I'll always get mine in the end . . . it's the journey to get you there that makes mine all that much more enjoyable."

"Oh."

My favorite sound of hers again.

But I love the way her throat moves as she swallows hard, how her eyes widen, how her breath hitches.

"Hey, Blake?" I pick up the tackle box and chuckle. "You can be bossy with me anytime."

THIRTY-THREE

Blakely

"Aren't you supposed to be helping me fish?" I ask as I glance to Slade, who is texting someone yet again.

He's been the most attentive man in the world this entire trip, but now that I need his help, he's on his phone.

"I thought that was against the rules?" He quirks a brow.

"Doesn't seem to me like you care too much about rules in the first place."

"Guilty as charged." He flashes me a grin that screams mischief. "And yes, I am in fact helping you as we speak."

"On your phone?"

"Yep."

"Do you care to explain because texting is not helping me."

"Yes it is." He tosses his cell onto the cooler and leans back on his hands. "You should be catching a fish in about ten minutes."

"What am I missing here?"

"I'll tell you if you tell me what you have planned for Heather?" he offers.

I'm not sure I like that trade.

"You'll know when it happens."

"Okay." He lifts the bottle of beer to his lips and takes a long sip of it. "Then I guess I can't tell you how you're going to win the fishing contest today."

I bark out a laugh. "Win? We've been sitting here for over an hour without a single bite on my line while we can hear others shriek in excitement when they catch one on whatever designated spot she gave them."

"Exactly. This whole contest was rigged, which is what I figured would happen after going drinking with the boys the other day. Horrible Heather's man was a little loose-lipped when he finally decided to join us. He kept talking about how she was picking everyone's fishing spots." He shrugs. "I may have done some reconnaissance on my morning jogs. I befriended a few locals who fish out here daily."

"So, you're saying . . ."

"I'm saying she gave you the one place in the entire lake where you have the worst chance of catching a fish. The waterbed here has some kind of algae in it the fish won't eat, so they don't bother with the area."

"That bitch."

"Yep." He nods. "And according to Dan, she knows which location is affected by it."

"It shouldn't surprise me."

"It shouldn't, but what I've done to fix it should." He looks over his shoulder. "And there he is. Right on time."

"Slade?" I say as I rise to my feet when I hear someone whistling on the path that leads to our little beach. "Who's that?"

"Impeccable timing," Slade says to the man as he stands and jogs toward where the cutest little old man appears. He has on a bucket hat covered in hooks and lures and tufts of his gray hair are peeking out beneath its rim. He's wearing dark green waders and is carrying a large bucket in one hand. "Ed. My man."

The two shake hands as water sloshes over the side of the bucket. I stare, my jaw slack with shock because it's easy enough to assume what's in that water.

"Perfect," Slade says and the two of them laugh over something before Slade pats him on the back and thanks him. Ed grants me a mischievous smile before giving me a mock salute and then turning to go back to wherever he came from.

"Slade Henderson. Who's Ed? What is that?"

He offers me a devilish grin. "Ed is Ed and this is your winning catch."

I look into the bucket and squeal at the fish swimming inside it. He's brown and fat and *huge* by my fishing standards.

"How? What? That's cheating!"

"Exactly." He presses a kiss to my lips before swinging the bucket a bit too close to me and making me jump back. "And a little cheating when the game is already rigged won't hurt anyone."

"How in the hell did you . . ." I'm dumbfounded. I point in the direction of where Ed just was. "One of the locals?"

"Yep." He looks into the bucket. "I may have stopped to chat a bit with him on my morning runs. We talked fishing. We discussed a mutual acquaintance we know at the hospital. And he was more than willing to help a nice guy like me to win a contest to impress a girl." He winks at me.

And if Ed knows Slade was trying to impress a girl, then that means he was talking about me.

With a random stranger.

"I told him a bit about what was going on. He told me a lot about how he may have done a few things to trick his wife into falling for him." He shakes his head as the cutest smile forms on his lips. "After that, he asked if he could help."

"*But why?*" I ask. Why would that man help Slade, and why would Slade do that for me?

"Because I didn't know if you were going to put Heather in her place or not—mind you, this was before I knew you had a secret plan— so I figured I'd help a little. Plus, he didn't come out of the deal empty handed."

"Care to explain?"

He smiles sheepishly. "I gave him some advice on a medical issue— he *really* loves his wife—"

"You prescribed him Viagra?" I sputter.

"No. That would be unprofessional of me, and I'm already in enough trouble in that department. But I gave him the name of a few specialists I know at the hospital who can most likely help him. In turn, he offered to give me the biggest fish he caught today, so long as I promised not to kill it and then release it after everyone sees it."

"You're serious, aren't you?"

"As a heart attack, and you know us cardio guys don't say that lightly." He chuckles and leans in. "Now, we just need to scream really loud so everyone knows you caught one."

"You're so bad."

"I know, and doesn't it feel good to be?" He leans forward and presses a chaste and unexpected kiss to my lips. "So let's scream and make some noise, then I'm going to pick this guy up so you can snap a photo of him—without the bucket in the background, of course—and then we'll throw him back to live another day."

"Are we really doing this?" I ask.

"Yes, Blakely, we are. She wouldn't hesitate to do it to you."

THIRTY-FOUR

Blakely

"**T**hat was cooler than cool. You have to know that."

Slade is leaning back in the lounge chair and hooks one of his legs under his other and angles his arm behind his head. Those light grayish-blue eyes of his just stare at me.

"What was?" I ask and take a sip of wine as the smell of meat on the barbecue on the other side of the lodge wafts our way. My stomach growls, but regardless of how hungry I am, I'm soaking in this silence with him.

"You telling the team that even though you won the contest, you wanted them to share in it too. The offer to take them to dinner will go a long way with them. It's something a leader does, and I think they'll remember in the future that it was your win, but you made it about them too. It was admirable of you."

"It's the least I could do considering I didn't win fair and square." I shrug. "Besides, we're a team. We're supposed to win together and lose together."

"And to think you still get a one-on-one mentorship meeting with Heather," he says sarcastically then snorts. "The look on her face was priceless when she realized you were the winner of her esteemed prize."

"It took everything I had not to burst out laughing."

Her stilted expression when the counselors posted the pictures on the projector screen and our, er, Ed's fish, was the biggest by far.

Her tight smile. Her fake enthusiasm. Her very crafted words as she had to concede her loss to me because, let's face it, the way she was talking before the proof was posted, you would have thought she had won.

But she didn't.

Score one for the good guys.

"I truly think she had every intention of winning the contest so the whole one-on-one thing with her for the winner was pure bullshit."

"I couldn't agree more." I raise my glass up to toast the tip of his bottle of beer. "Thank you. I mean it."

He smiles. It's soft and warm and makes me want to crawl into that small space beside him on his chair.

"I do believe I'm making progress towards winning our little side bet. She's coming around. The promotion is in sight."

"I don't know . . . I did tell you satisfaction was a hard thing to measure," I tease.

"Then I guess I'll have to try a little harder," he says before sitting up and pressing a kiss to my lips.

When he leans back, when those eyes of his dance with humor, I'm left wondering when exactly this charade we were putting on started feeling like more than just a sexy distraction.

Because no one was around for that kiss to be needed.

No one was there to pretend for.

It's just him and me and a whole lot of satisfaction left in the balance.

THIRTY-FIVE

Slade

She's gorgeous.

Dark hair fanned across the pillow, skin that's been kissed by the sun contrasting against the white sheets, dark eyelashes against her cheeks, lips that beg to be kissed.

It's a snapshot I want to memorize.

I think of last night. Of her sitting atop me with the moonlight coming through the open blinds. Of the arch of her back. Of the cry of my name. Of the pure exhaustion that tumbled us into sleep soon thereafter.

She stirs. Her chest rises and falls with each breath, the peaks of her nipples taunting me through the thin cotton covers.

When I'm with her, it's so easy to forget the shit going on in my life—the waiting, the wondering, the wanting. Yet, at the same time, if the shit hits the fan and goes against my favor, it would be that much easier because of her.

Christ.

She's a chick. Just a woman. One I've known for fewer than two weeks, so why am I thinking shit like that? Why am I wondering what will happen when life gets in the way and endless shifts call again?

"Good morning." Her sleep-drugged voice breaks through my thoughts.

That's why I'm wondering. That right here. Those green eyes fluttering open. That sleepy smile dragging across her lips. The urge to pull her close to me and just hold on.

"Morning."

"Please tell me you weren't watching me sleep."

"Of course not. You're a horrid sight to behold. Drooling and snoring and half-open eyes." I mock shiver. "And you're still absolutely gorgeous."

The flush of her cheeks from the simple comment validates all those thoughts I was just refuting.

I reach out and put a hand on her knee, which is bent up by my hip, and run my thumb back and forth over the cool fabric of the sheet.

Silence falls once again, sleep beginning to pull me back into its clutches when she speaks.

"You talked about fear yesterday." She clears her throat, and I open my eyes to meet hers, curious where she's going with this. I give a subtle nod for her to go on. "Before this trip . . . before you, really, I was petrified of losing my job."

"Understandable, but besides the obvious, may I ask why?" I squeeze her hip to reassure her. "You have a ton of experience. Any other company would be lucky to have you. You even said other companies have tried to recruit you before . . . so, why the fear?"

Her sigh is heavy. "Because as much as Paul and I separating was for the best, it still messed me up. He was part of my identity, and with him gone, I think maybe I was lost. My job was the one part of me that I knew without question. I don't have to fumble around to find Glam Blakely like I've been trying to find the *new* Blakely. My work is the me I understand, and so . . ." She averts her eyes, suddenly lost in that vulnerability I felt yesterday.

"It makes sense," I murmur.

And it does. It even brings to light her sudden insecurity when it comes to Heather. A woman about the same age as the woman her husband replaced her with. Both women are threatened by her in different ways, but only one of them can possibly take the one thing she wants— her promotion.

"Thank you," she says, her eyes finding mine again.

"For?"

"For being honest with me yesterday. It may not have been what I wanted to hear, but it's what I needed to hear. I mean, I've been so fixated on certain things that I kind of lost my way." She reaches out and runs a hand over my jawline. I turn my face into it and press a kiss to her palm.

"I meant what I said about what I see when I look at you, Blakely. You have a quiet strength you deny and a confidence you downplay. If you only realized how stunning you are . . . watch out world."

Her smile is soft, shy, and I slide my arm around her waist and pull her closer. I can't resist. Her cheek is against my chest, and my chin is on top of her head as we lie with our legs intertwined and assurances unspoken.

Our bodies fit perfectly together. It's weird how that happens.

"Shouldn't you be getting ready for your first set of meetings?"

"Yeah," she says, the heat of her breath hitting my chest, "but I think I'm going to shake some things up today."

"You are, are you?"

"Mm-hmm."

"A rebel now?" I press a kiss to the top of her head.

"What can I say? You inspire me."

THIRTY-SIX

Slade

"**D**r. Schultz. It's good to hear from you."

Breathe, Slade. Fucking, breathe.

"Thank you for coming in on Monday to answer our questions. The hospital review board needed to hear your voice and put a face to it."

"Agreed." I walk from one side of the shoreline to the other, my phone in hand as I wait for whatever it is that was so important he needed to call me, my goddamn future riding on his next few words.

"It doesn't change the outcome—that we still need to wait for her to wake up—but I think they needed to understand that you acted out of concern rather than because you had a God complex."

"Thank you for the opportunity, sir."

He clears his throat. "I know you've been prohibited from checking in on Ivy so I thought you might like an updated status on her condition."

His words take me back. "Yes, sir. Of course."

"She hasn't regained consciousness yet, but she is showing signs of improvement. Her vitals are stronger, and she's reacting to stimuli more so than before. Her doctor is optimistic. She's a fighter."

"That's good to know. Thank you for updating me." I run a hand through my hair and just stare out at the water.

"As the hospital advisor and program director, I must outwardly condemn what you did. In the same breath, I want you to know that your actions showed how human you are while the rest of us marvel at your extraordinary talents as a doctor."

"Thank you, sir. I'm not sure what else to say, but thank you."

I'm standing in the warm sunlight but chills blanket my skin.

"And if you tell anyone I said that, I'll deny it." He chuckles.

An awkward silence weighs on the line. I feel like he has more to say but isn't saying it, and I sure as hell don't want to stop him from voicing it.

"Okay then," he finally says.

"Why were you checking on her, sir?" It's the one thought that has been ghosting through my mind.

He falls quiet again, but I know he heard me because he hasn't ended the call. "Because of Kelly Flink, Gary Goodman, Andre Bastly, Dominic Gaffney . . . I can keep going with the names. Those are all my Ivy's, Slade. Those are all the patients who burrowed under my skin so deeply that after thirty years of practicing medicine, I still remember their names. I still have every detail of their case file memorized. All good doctors have those cases. All good doctors hold on too tightly at one time or another."

Emotion tightens my throat, and I have to take a second before I can manage to say, "Thank you, sir."

"For what?" He chuckles. "For reminding you that you're human? For letting you know that if a patient didn't get to you every now and again, I wouldn't want you as my doctor?" He pauses. "I'm impressed with your work so far. I know I'll be impressed with your work going forward when this matter clears itself up."

"Thank you, sir," I repeat before the call ends.

The shrieks of laughter break through the quiet of the trees. There are whoops and bursts of giggles.

Distracted, I find the owners of the voices right as the women come into view about a hundred feet in front of me. Fully clothed and led by none other than Blakely, they jog down the dock closest to our cabin and jump into the water. One after another. Cue more laughter and splashing.

The sight of them makes me smile.

Who am I kidding, Dr. Schultz's words are partially why I'm smiling, but everything about what I'm watching is too.

Even better, it was Blakely who led the charge.

I don't realize I've moved down the beach toward them until I hear someone clear their throat behind me. Turning, I find Heather standing there, arms over her chest, a look of disdain highlighting her face.

"Why aren't you joining them?" I ask.

"She literally just stood up near the end of the meeting and said, 'Do you know what we need? We need a water break!' and bolted out the door with everyone following. Literally, every single one of them."

"Except you."

Her eyes flicker over to me. "I'm the boss. I can't be doing that."

But she wants to. Oh, how she wants to. I can see it in her eyes. The need to be liked. The want to be adored. The desperation to be followed the same way Blakely just was.

I don't know how much younger Heather is than me, but she sure as hell missed the life lesson about leading by example. That, sometimes, it's okay to bend the rules and have fun. That respect and admiration can be won through kindness.

"Sure you can," I say. "Just because you're the boss doesn't make you any better than them, it just means you have more responsibility at times."

"You obviously don't know what I do." Her insecurity reigns in the comment. Her need to prove she's worthy of her position. Of her pay. Of their respect. I've watched it all week and don't know how no one else sees it.

Then again, maybe they do but can't exactly confront their boss about it.

But I can.

I'm not employed by Glam.

She emits a sound of disapproval as Blakely climbs up the side of the dock and then jumps in again like a little kid, cannonball and all.

"She doesn't want your job, you know."

"No one ever said she did," she snaps.

"But, in your mind, she's a threat to you when she really isn't."

"Why would I be threatened by *her*?"

"Because she's damn good at her job, and she has every board member on her side. If you were a team, if you supported her for this promotion, you know she'd have your back with them going forward. With someone else? Who knows what would happen. Plus—look at them." I motion to the women playing in the water like kids with her. "You have a team who looks up to her. They respect her because she respects them. If you do the same, they'll respect you too."

"They do respect me."

"Fear and respect aren't the same thing."

She snorts. It's her immature way of saying she isn't sure how to refute me but wants to do it on principle anyway.

"I'm sure you're every bit as talented and skilled in your own way, but having it and knowing how to use it to motivate people are two different things."

"You're out of line—"

"I beg to differ." I turn to look at her. "My telling you to figure out how to accept Blakely's experience is a whole hell of a lot better than letting you get sued for age discrimination and harassment after you force her out." My smile is quick and the shake of my head subtle. "I'm pretty sure I know who the board would side with on that one. I mean, they offered your job to her before you, right?"

If looks could kill, I'd be dead right now from the glare she's leveling at me, but I meet it with a half-cocked smirk.

"Slade!" Blakely is out of the water and walking toward us. Her clothes are clinging to her body, and she's leaving a trail of wet footprints behind her as she heads my way.

But it's the smile on her face that has me moving toward her without giving Heather and our conversation a second thought.

Because that smile is the most alive it's been since I've met her.

"Inciting a riot, I see?" I ask before picking her up, soaking clothes and all, and holding her against me.

Yep, her eyes are even better this close.

She laughs. "I was being spontaneous."

"Look out world, Blakely Foxx just might have found herself."

"And I'm not finished quite yet," she whispers.

"A full-fledged rebel." I press my lips to hers, not caring who's around to see the kiss I give her. "It's such a turn on," I murmur against her mouth.

"At your service."

I slowly let her slide down the length of my body, soaking my own clothes as she goes, but I don't care. I kiss her one more time as if we're the only two people here despite the sounds of laughter in the water.

"What's that for?" she asks.

"No reason," I say even though it's exactly what I needed after my call from Dr. Schultz.

A little bit of Blakely to kiss it and make it all better.

THIRTY-SEVEN

Exhaustion settles deep in my bones and all I want to do is snuggle with Slade back on the dock and enjoy the moment. I don't want to be here, about to do who knows what.

Sure, team bonding is why we are on this retreat, but my priorities have shifted a tad in the past few days.

He owns my mind. My body. And I'm not going to talk about the flutters I feel in my heart.

"Is this thing almost over yet," Gemma groans to my right.

"Almost." I slump back in my seat, close my eyes, and raise my face to the sun. At least the weather's nice. At least there's that.

"Christ," she mutters, "how much more can we do today? Relay races, which this body did *not* want to do, and then archery? I mean, if she wants us to go Hunger Games on each other, she better watch her back. And now we have to go off into the woods and conquer some obstacle courses? How 'bout I conquer a bottle of tequila behind the bar over there instead?"

I laugh loudly. "Just one more and then we're done with the team-building crap."

"Ah, you're forgetting the game of He Said, She Said we have slated for later tonight."

"Am I bad for wanting to say I'm sick so I can sneak away with Slade?" I ask teasingly when I'm very serious about it.

"Woman, I would have pretended to be sick this whole trip just for that man," she whispers back. "How much you want to bet that Heather has this partner thing predetermined for this next thing? She'll be partnered with Maddie because she's still pissed off over your little rebellion this morning and she'll have her bestie to vent to."

A slow smile slides onto my lips. "She *was* partnered with Maddie, but I may have switched some names around." I wink at her.

"You sly devil, you." She looks at me with wide eyes. "When did you do that?"

"She asked me to grab her things for her during the last meeting. I might have switched the cards in the envelopes and pulled out Maddie's."

"Who'd you pair Heather with?"

"Me."

"You what?" she asks, drawing looks of those around us. "Are you crazy?"

"It's time the two of us put this to bed, and what better way to do it than to force her to work with me."

"You're kind of amazing." She chuckles. "And I'll save that bottle of tequila for you. You're going to need it after being alone with her for the next few hours."

"This is bullshit," Heather mutters, quite the cheerful partner.

"You don't like these obstacle courses?" I ask innocently as I glance over to her.

"Can you tell me where the hell I'm supposed to go?" she demands, the black bandana wrapped around her eyes.

"You're doing just fine. Go straight like I said." I tsk. "And remember *your rules*—the person wearing the blindfold isn't allowed to talk."

She growls deep in her throat, and my smile is as wide as can be because she's at my mercy for the first time ever, and I love it.

Just like I loved the absolute shock on her face when she pulled out the envelopes that had the "random" pairings in them for teammates and saw she and I had been put together.

She had to have known it was me, but if she complained, then everyone would have known that she had handpicked to be partnered with Materialistic Maddie.

"Just stay the course. I'll let you know before you trip over a log or run into a tree," I say sweetly.

"Gee. Thanks."

"Uh. Uh. Uh," I warn. "Aren't we supposed to lead by example? I mean, if you say no talking and then someone hears your voice through the trees, then you'll have defeated the purpose of this whole exercise."

We walk a few feet.

"One step to your right. Good job." I glance over and can all but see her rolling her eyes through the blindfold. "So, now that I have your undivided attention, I'm going to ask the questions I think we both want to know the answers to. What is it with you, Heather? What exactly is the reason you hate me so much?" I touch her arm and pull her toward me so she avoids a rock. "Is it that you hate that I have experience? Is it that you hate anyone who challenges you to be better? Is it that you just want me gone so you can have your bestie from your last job get the promotion since you don't know everything you professed to know and you need her to hold your hand? I mean, we have the time right now, and I'd really love to know."

She's silent for a few moments, but I know she's stewing. Her silence won't last long. I give her a few minutes before she loses her cool and explodes.

When I was blindfolded, the only words she gave were directions. Short, sharp words, and nothing else.

I think she was hoping I'd do the same.

Not on her life.

"Slow down. You're going to step up in a few seconds. Okay. Right here."

We walk in silence, but her anger only seems to grow.

"With you around, no one will ever take me seriously," she spits out as if it's the most vile insult on the face of the earth.

Good thing she can't see my smile.

"And why would that be?"

"Like you don't know." She sighs.

"I don't. Because I get the feeling that you think I want your job." I stop in my tracks and watch her move slowly with her hands out in front of her like an idiot, and I shake my head in disbelief. "No, that can't be it since you already know I turned it down."

Her frustrated sigh overrides the quiet.

"It doesn't matter how many times I tell you this because you'd rather make me out to be the enemy. If I'm the enemy, then you have every reason to tell the board you can't work with me and therefore they should hire your friend for the position. What you don't get, Heather, is that you'd benefit far more from being my ally than my enemy. What do you think the board would do if you really pushed them on this? Do you think they would fire me because you don't get along with me, or do you think they would fire you because you can't get along with a valued team member who has consistently produced solid, money making ideas?" Her teeth are grinding at this point, but when I say, "Stop," she does and she pushes her hands out as if there is a tree right in front of her. "I think you're smart enough to know the answer even if you refuse to verbalize it. Still, I'm serious when I say I don't want your job. Our positions are supposed to complement each other, not be a rivalry."

"Complementing each other? Is that what you call taking every chance you get to publicly question my decisions so that everyone knows you have more experience than me? It's only a matter of time before the board sees that you are perfectly well-equipped to do both jobs and they'll merge the positions like they did in my old company and then I'll be shit out of luck."

Merge positions? Is that what happened in her old job? I always assumed she quit.

Her silence and her lips parted in a shocked O tell me she didn't mean for me to know this.

I stare at her and feel like so much makes sense now—her insecurity, her need to surround herself with people she trusts, her hostility—and yet, it doesn't excuse her refusal to accept the olive branch I keep extending. She just keeps repeating the same nonsense, and it makes me wonder if I sounded like that when I was making my excuses.

Just like they did with me, hers are coming from insecurity.

While I feel disregarded because I'm older, Heather feels like she has to prove everything because she's younger and lacks experience. Such similar scenarios, such different reactions.

"Can we walk and get this damn thing over with already?" she hisses the question and crosses her arms over her chest.

I move the few feet toward her. "Take the blindfold off."

"Why?" she asks.

"Because if you and I are going to figure this out, it isn't going to look like a hostage situation." She stands there like a petulant child. "Take it off," I order.

She rips the blindfold off and glares at me as she clenches her jaw. "Happy?"

"Look. We can either work together or apart, but I'll be damned if you think you're going to run me out of a company I've worked at for over half my life. I'll say it one more time: I don't *want* your job. Selling isn't my thing, but I love figuring out how to put a bow on the damn package to make it pretty for you so you can sell it. When I do well, you do well. So, what you need to ask yourself is how you're going to suck it up and work with me. It's either that or find a new job. Got it?"

Heather stands there like a guppy opening and closing her mouth. Without her squad at her flanks, she doesn't seem to have the balls to respond. The quick barbs are nonexistent, which is just further proof that her age and immaturity are part of the problem.

"I just don't think that's going to work."

"Why?" I take another step toward her, determined to leave this retreat with whatever this is between us solved. "Because you refuse to compromise? Or because you choose to see me as a threat instead of a resource or ally?"

Our eyes meet, hold, and she's just about to say something when there is a loud noise about a hundred feet to our left. Part shuffling, part branches breaking, and I say the first thing that comes to mind. "*Bear.*"

"Bear!" Heather screams at the top of her lungs like a petrified child.

Be quiet.

Stay still.

I'm sure it isn't a bear.

All three run through my mind but before I can say anything, Heather emits

a piercing scream seconds before lunging toward me in sheer terror.

It takes me a second to process that Heather's clinging on to me for dear life. The same Heather who mocked me for being afraid of bears and told me I should fake it and lead by example is now trembling uncontrollably and babbling incoherently. Even weirder, I'm surprisingly calm.

"It's okay. *Shh.* You need to stay calm," I tell her as I look every which way I can to see if it was actually a bear that made the noise.

But while I can't see anything, I can hear everything.

The shouts from the men as they barge through the woods toward us, their hero capes flying.

"Blake? Heather?" They shouted over and over.

"Over here," I shout back.

"Bear!" Heather screams again before suddenly pushing off me a second before the men come into view.

"Are you guys okay?" Testosterone Ted reaches us first, but Slade is right behind him with Harley Hal and one of the activity directors from the lodge. They all look around cautiously, the activity director holding a can of bear spray up toward the trees around us in defense.

"Whatever it was is gone," Heather says, her hands now shoved into her pockets to keep everyone from seeing how badly they are shaking.

"The way you screamed, I could have sworn it was eating one of you," Hal says, huffing from the run to us.

There is more thrashing through the foliage, and we all spin around to see Maddie and Gemma jog to a stop.

"Who's the one with those ear-splitting lungs?" Maddie asks, her gaze immediately landing on me.

For a split second, I stare at Heather, at her wide eyes and her suddenly composed demeanor, and I know it would be so easy to out her. I could let everyone know the catty woman who made fun of me for being scared of bears is actually the one who was terrified when it came down to it.

I could use the moment to make her look just as bad as she has made me look time and again, but I don't. I refuse to be her. I choose to lead by example.

Yes, I'm the older of the two of us.

Yes, I'll be the mature one.

Yes, I'll show her that we aren't in competition, and that, at times, yes, I'll take one for the good of our partnership.

"It was me," I say with a laugh and a bashful raise of my hand. "You know how much I fear bears."

And out of the corner of my eye, I see Heather stutter in motion, lips falling lax, eyes blinking rapidly.

Yes, I just covered for you. Now it's time for you to grow up and do the same, I say with the look I give her.

"Thank god it was just a scare," Gemma says as Slade slides a hand around my waist and presses a kiss to my temple.

"Let's get out of here," the activity director says. "Just in case it was one."

He turns to lead the way out of the woods, but Slade tugs on my hand, his head dipping down so he can look straight in my eyes.

"You okay?" he murmurs quietly.

"Fine." My smile is quick, strained.

When I go to walk, he keeps me in place.

"What?" I ask.

"That wasn't you who screamed, was it?"

"I don't know what you're talking about."

"I've heard you scream my name plenty on this trip"—his grin is lightning quick—"and that wasn't you."

I shrug coyly, and then we both jump when there is loud rustling at our backs. Slade pushes me behind him for safety as we turn so that when he throws his head back and laughs, I have no idea why.

I step out from behind to see what's so funny.

And there with his green waders on, fishing pole in one hand, and bucket hat loaded with hooks sitting atop his head, stands Heather's bear, Ed. His grin is huge and his eyes are mischievous.

"*Ed?*" Slade chuckles as he moves toward him. "What in the hell are you doing out here?"

"Hey, guys." He holds up his free hand in greeting. "Just taking a short-cut here over to a new hot spot I found when I guess I scared the bejesus out of that girl you were talking there with." He lifts his chin in the direction of where Heather and the rest of them went.

"You let us think you were a bear," I say around a laugh.

"Yeah, well, she wasn't being too nice to you, so I figured she deserved a little scare to knock some sense into her." He shrugs. "A little fear never hurt no one."

"Ed," Slade says and laughs, shaking his head in disbelief, "the world needs more men like you."

"Maybe so," he says, "but this one needs to get some fishing in before the sun moves behind the hills." He starts shuffling his feet. "You two have a good rest of the day now."

"Thanks. Good luck," Slade says.

"Don't need it, but thanks." His laughter filters back through as we both stand and stare at the direction he went.

"Did that really just happen?" I ask.

"Yes, it did." He snorts. "Fucking, Ed."

"I'm glad to know there really wasn't a bear, but I'm happy to know I didn't act like an idiot either."

"True." Slade reaches out and links his fingers with mine. "Does Heather understand you just took the hit so she can save face?"

"I think she does."

"Why would you do that after everything she's done to you?"

"Sometimes, you have to be the bigger person to spark the change, and other times, you simply have to play the game."

He shakes his head and laughs. "Is that right?"

"There's more than one way to howl at the moon, Henderson." I take a step away from him but don't drop his hand. "Someone pretty awesome taught me that."

THIRTY-EIGHT

Blakely

"**Y**ou cold?"

"No."

This is right where I want to be—on the dock, toes in the water, Slade's arm wrapped around me, and with the moon high above.

"I still can't believe we won that stupid game." He laughs and shakes his head.

"How did we guess all of those things right about each other?" I think of the silly questions tonight in our Glam version of the old game show testing contestants' knowledge about their newly married spouse.

What's your ideal date night?

What do you wear to bed?

What food do you hate?

"We're the ones pretending, and we beat everyone who wasn't."

I laugh softly at his words while they sting at the same time. Because he's right, we are pretending.

Or maybe we were pretending, and I forgot about that. I got caught up in how so damn easy everything is between us—the talking, the playing, the sex—that I forgot we were, in fact, faking it.

I did exactly what Prisha warned me not to do. I let the ease of Slade and how he treats me mess with my head.

Sure, the sex is fantastic, but there can be sex without long-term emotions.

And I let those grow when I knew I shouldn't have.

I made the mistake of thinking this is more.

Deep breath, Blakely.

He's a rebound.

Don't ruin the last night together.

You forgot that's what this was.

Tuck your thoughts away.

It's what you needed so you took it.

Enjoy the time.

He's just a rebound.

"Tell me, when you're reinstated at work—"

"When?"

"Yes, *when*. Just like *when I get the promotion*. What's next for you?" I ask. "Will it be hard to step back into your rounds at the hospital after being gone for so long?"

"It shouldn't be too hard. I'm sure my inbox will be loaded with cases the minute I'm allowed to return." He knocks his knee against mine. "What about you? Do you think your bear sacrifice will pay off with Heather?"

"I'm not too sure." I shrug. "But I know I'm leaving here in a much better place with her than I was when we arrived. Not only do the rest of my colleagues see me in a different light but also, I confronted Heather. I attempted to clear the air with her, and I tried to be the bigger person. If she can't accept that olive branch, then at least I know I tried and have a leg to stand on with the board."

"I'm so damn proud of you, Blakely."

Those seven simple words have emotions clogging my throat. So much so that I close my eyes to try to let it abate while I memorize everything about the moment. His warmth beside me, the way he makes me feel, the sound of the water lapping against the dock, the scent of his cologne, the complete and utter adoration I have for him, all cement themselves into my mind's eye.

"You're quiet," he says, pulling me back to the present.

"I'm just enjoying this." I rest my head against him.

"Did you just say you're enjoying this? Outdoors. Nature. Not hanging out on a broken porch swing?"

"Yes. I do believe I am enjoying this."

He pulls me in tight against him and gives me a bear hug before pressing a kiss to the top of my head. "Look at all this personal growth. Who knew?" His chuckle rumbles through his chest and into me.

"Hey, Slade?"

"*Hmm?*"

I tilt my head back to look at the moon, let everything I've learned about myself on this trip run through my mind, open my mouth, and let out the best attempt I can at a howl.

It's lame and cheesy and ends in me laughing and burying my face in my hands, but at least I tried.

"That's my girl!" Slade says as he joins in with a howl of his own before laying me back on the dock and kissing me.

Then undressing me.

Then making love to me.

One last time.

THIRTY-NINE

Blakely

"I do believe this is yours."

I shut my car door behind me as Slade holds out the napkin. I bite my bottom lip and then smile when I look down at it.

Blade's To-Do List:

~~Make Paul regret he ever let you go~~

~~Figure out our history, when we met, how long your legs really are, pet peeves, etc~~

~~Make Horrible Heather see you differently~~

~~Win your co-workers over by being fucking awesome~~

~~Convince everyone we are madly in love and meant to be~~

Get the promotion

~~Find the real Blakely again~~

Fall hopelessly in love

"I think we did pretty damn good, don't you?" he asks as my eyes slide down and stumble over the last line item. Taking it in my hand, I keep my gaze focused on it as I try to shove down my feelings that are tumbling out of control.

The last thing I want him to see swimming in my eyes is that I somehow forgot that last task was a joke.

It takes me a second to feel in enough control of my emotions before I can meet that blue-gray gaze of his. "We did, didn't we?"

"We make a good team, you and me." He reaches out to link his fingers with mine as I lean my back against my car. "There's more to be done though."

"Oh?" I say, forgetting the promotion line item and letting my hopes get the better of me.

"Yep. I do believe we have a bet we can't determine the winner of yet. Apparently, satisfaction is measured in terms of a promotion when it comes to you." He winks. "And since that's yet to be determined, should we say that we're in a holding pattern?"

"Yes. Agreed." I swallow over the relief that I'll get to see him again. "To be determined."

He knocks his knuckles on the top of my car. "I'm sorry we had to take two cars up here, but I'm sure you're probably sick of me and can't wait to have some peace and quiet."

"Don't be ridiculous." They're the only words I trust myself to say as another pang of sadness hits me.

"You sure you're okay to make the drive?"

"Yes. Of course." I bite my cheek and laugh nervously. How silly was I not to heed Prisha's advice not to fall for him? How ridiculous was I to allow myself to think that last item on the list was a real thing?

"You sure?"

My smile is forced as I set my purse and the napkin inside my car. "So, what dastardly deed should I commit to break us up?" It's stupid, and I shouldn't have said it, but being nervous and keeping my mouth shut don't work well together.

"Nah. Blame it on me." His smile is soft, voice quiet. "Say my residency was too much and I couldn't commit to giving you everything you deserve."

"That isn't something I'd say—"

"Anyone who knows me would agree with that statement, so it isn't exactly a lie." Another reticent smile that I read as an unspoken apology. "You deserve the world, Blake. Don't you ever forget that."

I stare at him, wondering if this is his way of telling me we'd never work. His eyes and his words aren't matching up, but hell if I'm going to call him on it. Shouldn't I just be happy that I got this time with him, that I was able to experience all there is about Slade Henderson and his eternal optimism, and not complain?

But I want to complain. I want to fist my hand in his shirt, yank him close so his mouth meets mine, and pour every ounce of emotion into the kiss so that when we part ways, he knows exactly how I feel.

Fear of rejection has me rooted in place and rocking on my heels in lost chances.

"Thanks. I guess." Awkwardness consumes me.

"No need to thank me. It's just the truth." Slade reaches out and tucks a piece of hair behind my ear, the heel of his hand lingering on the line of my jaw. Our eyes hold, and I swear I see everything that's roiling around in me reflected back in his eyes. If that's the case, then why doesn't *he* say something? Why don't *I* say something?

"Okay, then," he murmurs. "Thank you for letting me come and play pretend with you."

"No need to thank me either." I brave a smile that's one hundred percent bittersweet.

He leans forward and gives me the simplest but most tender of kisses I've ever been given before in my life. My heart jumps into my throat, and tears spring into my eyes. I'm grateful that he rests his forehead against mine, his hand still on the curve of my neck so I have a moment to recover.

"It was my pleasure watching you find yourself, Blakely. Don't ever forget how you felt this week. Don't ever forget who she is. We'll talk soon."

When he leans back to meet my gaze again, I have a reason for the tears welling in my eyes—one that he can understand, at least—his words.

But when he opens my car door for me and then shuts it, I know the tears are for so much more.

They're for who I found.

Who I fear I've lost.

Didn't Slade say the heart is where everything begins and ends?

I've never thought those words to be more true than now as I leave a piece of mine behind with him.

FORTY

With my hand on the steering wheel and my thumb thumping to an unknown beat, I watch until her taillights fade around the first bend.

Then I lean my head back against the seat of my car and wonder what that sudden empty feeling is inside me.

You were just dumped.

I chuckle, but it doesn't make it any easier to swallow.

"Get back to your life, Slade." I blow out a breath.

A life that's consumed by endless hours of work.

That isn't conducive to anything more than casual whatever I was doing.

But that was before a chance encounter with Blakely Foxx.

That was before this retreat.

That was just before.

FORTY-ONE

Blakely

"So there was the hot sex, the belly-aching laughs, the long talks in the moonlight, and the comfortable silence on the docks," Kelsie says, "and you guys haven't talked since then? Are you freaking crazy?" She bats at my thigh. "I mean all the signs are there!"

"Signs?" I chortle. "Signs of what?"

"That there was something more there." Her voice ratchets in volume with each word.

I turn to look at her laying atop my comforter beside me. "No, there was getting caught up in the moment is all. Two people thrown together reality show style—you know, forced to live together type of thing." It's so much easier to lie to myself than to believe Slade and I could have had something real.

"See! I told you he would be the perfect rebound for you. There's nothing like some earth-shattering sex at the hand of a younger, virile man who has a nice smile to make you get over your asshole ex."

"Virile?" I laugh through the ache of missing him that radiates through me.

"That was my code for humungous, adept cock."

I choke on my next breath and cough through the laughter. "Jesus, Kels."

"Are you going to dispute it?"

"I plead the fifth." I hold my hands up in surrender.

"But that's all there was, Blake?"

"What do you mean?"

"You didn't develop feelings for him? I mean . . . it's only normal to—rebound fling or not."

"It doesn't matter whether I did or didn't, it only matters if it's mutual."

"Well? Did you ask him how he felt about you?" she asks and laughs in disbelief. "Of course you didn't."

"I believe his words were something along the lines of, 'It's been fun pretending with you.' And then he went on to say how everyone would believe if we broke up because he doesn't commit to anyone. I don't know about you, but it doesn't get more subliminally clear than that."

"And your point is what? Sometimes we say things we think the other person wants to hear even when they aren't exactly the truth."

I smile and shake my head. "It isn't the same."

"He kissed you good-bye, right? I mean, you don't kiss your fake girlfriend good-bye when no one else is looking."

I close my eyes and let the tears burn there. The ones riddled with disbelief that Slade feels the same way. It took me less than a week to feel like this for him, so why has it taken the same amount of days to doubt every single second of it?

"Let's face it, he was a rebound. Just like you said he was. Perfect for the moment—for what I needed to get over everything with Paul, but not for reality."

"I call bullshit."

"You can call it whatever you want, but it is what it is." I close my eyes and sigh.

"What it is, is you being a chickenshit who's afraid to put yourself out there."

"You forget. I did put myself out there. And it isn't as if we haven't talked since. We've texted, and I've asked him if there was anything new about Ivy. He asked me if I'd heard about the promotion yet. There were no words about having a great time or about missing each other. There was no, maybe we should try this thing between us. It was causal. It was easy." Just like Prisha warned me it would be. He has no clue how much I've fallen for him because, simply put, he is just that much of a nice guy. "That's it."

"Text. Text. Text. Thanks for joining the twenty-first century, but you need to pick up the phone and call him. I mean, you're head over heels for this guy."

Isn't that the problem though?

How can I be head over heels in love with a guy in this short amount of time? How do I admit that without sounding like a crazy woman who is supposed to be convincing herself that he is a rebound? Has to be.

No one falls that quickly unless they are emotionally unstable after a huge breakup. No one falls that quickly without ruining themselves when the other person realizes they're a rebound and moves on.

"He's way too good to be true. It's probably best to leave it as it is." I plaster a smile on my lips that I hope she believes and try to own my comment. It feels like I've been doing that a lot lately.

"If you say so," she says as I look toward the ceiling to avert my eyes because I don't want her looking too closely. If she does, she'll see the truth. She nudges me with her elbow. "Look at you all hitting-it-and-quitting-it. I never knew you had that in you." She pats a hand over her heart, and sighs affectionately. "I'm so proud of how far you've come in such a short time."

"You're such a drama queen."

"Always. All I have to say is, *damn*, can I get a rebound like that? I know my divorce was years ago, but Momma needs some of that." She adds a nod for emphasis, and I take the chance to segue the conversation away from Slade and the ache in my chest every time she mentions his name.

"Besides, the last thing I need right now is to be distracted by a man when I have my big interview to prepare for."

"That's right!" Kelsie reaches out, grabs my hand, and squeezes. "But I don't think you need much preparation. I can feel it in my bones that you're going to nail it. It's your time to shine, and I can't wait to put my sunglasses on so I can watch you glow."

I squeeze her hand in return, letting the comfortable silence of two best friends settle in the space between us.

I'm more than certain she sees how nervous I am about my impending interview this week.

And I let her.

Little does she know I'm nursing a broken heart and am too ashamed to admit it to her. Even worse, I'm too much of a coward to think I deserve what it is I really want.

Reciprocation of that last task on the to-do list.

That, and one Slade Henderson.

FORTY-TWO

Slade

"**D**esk duty looks good on you, Henderson."

I look over the piles of binders stacked on the desk in front of me and glare at Prisha. We're in the bowels of the hospital, a windowless room with white walls and not much else other than paperwork, an ancient laptop, and more paperwork.

"I'm starting to regret offering to help Dr. Schultz log all of these test results from his study, but I was going out of my mind waiting." I lean back in my chair and scrub a hand over my bleary eyes.

"It has to be a good sign that he's letting you back in the hospital, right?" She leans a hip on the desk opposite of mine and stifles a yawn. "I mean, if he was going to kick you out of the program, one could assume he wouldn't let you touch all of his beloved data."

"That was my thought when he called, but now?" I point to the endless stacks of statistics to be logged. "Now, I'm not so sure."

Prisha cocks her head to the side and eyes me for a beat. "You haven't mentioned her, you know. You've been here five days, and we text all the time, but you haven't brought her up other than to redirect the conversation."

"That's bullshit," I argue but know she's right.

"You've moved on just like that?"

I rub my bleary eyes before looking over to Prisha.

"Moved on?" I ask.

"Yeah. You played mountain man with Blakely and then you washed your hands of her? Such a classic Henderson move. Should I assume you're actively looking for a new project to fix?"

I chuckle as much of a laugh as I can muster. "I didn't wash my hands of her, Prish. I'm just elbow deep in this shit and trying to get my life back."

"And?"

"And being on the outside, watching you guys run from one place to another, exhausted, scarfing down a meal when you can, and sneaking moments to sleep—"

"You miss every second of it."

"Hell yes, I do. Desperately. But stepping back and seeing the dedication and sacrifice of it all right in front of me was a blatant reminder of why nothing ever stuck for me before with a woman. I don't have the time or the bandwidth to manage that and do this."

"Plenty of us do."

"Good for you."

"Lots of excuses and not much action. If that's the case, she's probably good to be rid of you." She sighs before rolling her shoulders and then stretching her arms up.

"Very funny," I murmur and toss my pen onto the desk.

"I'm serious. I liked her . . . and I think part of your misery is because you like her, too, but you aren't quite sure what to do about it."

"Thanks for the psych eval, but I'm good."

But I'm not. I'm far from it. I fucking miss her. Her smile. The scent of her skin. The sound of her laugh. The sparkle in her eyes.

Fucking sap.

"I think part of Slade's problem is he's going through sex withdrawals," John says as he walks in. "What is this? Party in the basement?"

"Something like that," I mutter and fist bump John.

"You're crazy, Prish, if you think Blakely was anything more than a little side fun for Slade. We all know how he plays."

"Fuck off," I joke as he winks at me.

"You ready for rounds?" John asks Prisha, who nods. "Later, lover boy," he throws over his shoulder as they head down the hall. I'd give anything to be going with them.

My groan fills the room as I slump in my chair.

Is John right? Am I not at the point yet in my life where I can involve someone in my day to day? Where I can ask her to deal with the burden of my residency?

I close my eyes and wonder how I can justify asking Blakely to do this with me. She just ended a relationship where she wasn't taken care of, so how can I ask her to have one with me when I'm gone more than I'm around. And in normal times, even when I am around, all I want to do is crawl into bed and sleep.

She deserves so much better than that.

We were in a fantasy situation on the retreat. It wasn't real life.

Not to mention, I don't even know how to have a relationship.

First world problems, I know.

But how do I invite her into this life when I'm hanging on by a thread most days?

I'm dragging ass. Big time. Missing her doesn't make it any better either.

I pick up my phone to text her—something, anything to talk to her—but then second-guess myself.

Maybe I am wrong.

Maybe I am the one who developed feelings for her but she was just enjoying a little freedom sex after getting divorced.

Then again, when Testosterone Ted texted me the other day, he seemed to think we were still together. So, has she not publicly broken up with me in her office?

Not sure how to read that one.

I pick up my phone to call her, confront her . . . hear her voice, and just when I do, I'm called over the PA system.

Maybe there's news about Ivy. Maybe Dr. Schultz has good news for me. Maybe I'll finally get my life back.

I look at the blinking cursor on my blank text and then shove my phone into the pocket of my lab coat.

I'll text her. I will.

It'll just have to wait until after this shift.

FORTY-THREE

Blakely

"The four of us will have to go out and celebrate," Gemma says as she rounds my desk.

I smile through the exhaustion of the day. "We will. We definitely will."

"Congrats, Veep." She gives me a wide smile and wiggle of a dance.

"Thank you. It's late. I appreciate all your help, but I'm sure Ted is wondering where the hell you are."

"I told him I was working late. Helping you get settled and officially move offices. He sends his congrats."

"Thank you, again." I look around my mess of an office I haven't been alone in all day long. "I think I'm just going to sit here in silence for a bit and let it all sink in."

"You sure I can't stay and help?"

"Nah. You've already helped plenty."

"Good night then."

"Good night."

I sit in my chair and sigh into the empty space. I'm torn between closing my eyes and soaking it all in and staring out the window to the lights of the city below. In the distance, I see the red light blinking from the helicopter pad of Memorial General and smile.

Slade.

I need to call him—at least now I have a valid excuse to.

I pick up my phone from where it sits atop the congratulatory card from the flowers that Heather bought me earlier. Its sincerity is still in question, but it's the first in a long line of many steps for her, so I'm taking it for what it's worth.

It's been nine days since Slade and I parted ways. Nine days of wanting to call him and being worried about doing so because I have no real reason to do so other than to hear his voice. It's been nine days of missing him and feeling silly for missing him all in the same breath. It's been nine days of second-guessing everything I feel for him and if it's real.

I type out the text, "Give me a call when you have a minute," and then hit send.

It only takes a second before my phone rings. Butterflies take flight in my stomach but I can't answer fast enough . . . but then the minute I do, nerves reverberate through me.

"Hello?"

"You can always call me, you know." His voice. *That voice.* Hearing it is a salve that soothes all those worries away and brings me back to him and the dock and the moonlight across his face.

"I know you're probably busy and—"

"And if I can't answer when you call, then I'll call you back when I can talk."

"Okay."

Silence falls over the line, and I hate this feeling of unease when we've never had it between us before.

"You been okay?" he asks, the PA system in the background calling something out.

"Yes. Great actually." I pause. "I got the promotion."

"What? *You did?* I knew you would." I can picture the smile on his lips as clearly as I can hear it in his tone. "Congrats. God, Blake, I'm so proud of you."

And in those few words, I'm back on that dock with my heart swelling, my emotions surging, and hope mounting.

But I can't be—this can't be—or else we would already be. I'm old enough to know I can't wish something into existence.

"Thanks. I—I couldn't have done it without you."

"That's bullshit, and you know it. You were doing it without me all along. You just needed a little encouragement, is all."

"I've been meaning to call. I wanted to hear your voice." It isn't what I meant to say, but it's the truth. His voice. *Him.* That's all I've been looking forward to all day and here we are and I'm stumbling over my words.

"I miss you, Blakely." His voice is a deep rumble and has me catching my breath.

"Things have been crazy. It's just been . . . I don't know."

"I've felt the same way. This real-life thing is . . ."

"Yeah. I know. It kind of gets in the way," I say, thinking of the breakup excuse he gave me that I've yet to use.

I guess I'm still holding out hope.

So, what now? I want to ask. Why are we both saying we miss each other but neither of us is asking the question? Are we trying to feel each other out? Is that why we're being so cautious? Or is his hesitancy because he's being the Slade that Prisha warned me about? A man who doesn't realize he's easy to fall for? A man who now realizes I actually have tumbled head over heels for him and is now trying to let me down slowly so my feelings aren't hurt?

Slade isn't the type to mince words, so the fact that he is now tells me all I need to know. This—us—is too much for him, too real, when all he's used to is casual dating, so now he's trying to figure out how to move on. Exactly like Prisha said would happen.

Christ. This is why marriage was easier. You just knew to expect disappointment and disregard. You didn't have to wonder and read into the silence.

"Heather is better to you now?" he asks, shifting the conversation away from our train wreck of a topic and toward something less treacherous.

"I still don't trust her as far as I can throw her, but baby steps." I laugh softly. "And you? Are you back to work? How's Ivy doing?"

"I'm not officially back yet," he says, his lack of answer about Ivy has me reading between the lines. "The person who oversees the program took pity on me and is letting me do some data analysis entry on a study he's doing, but as for seeing patients, I'm still suspended."

"I'm sorry. I was hoping you would have been back in the swing of things by now." And, of course, my head goes there. To the place that overthinks how he hasn't been exhausted from working twenty-four-hour shifts and discredits the excuses I made for why he hasn't called me—that he's been too busy getting back into the swing of things—now hold no weight.

"Me too. But I've been working nonstop trying to gain some favor by doing this. The good news is Ivy is slowly showing more signs of coming to: eyes fluttering open for minutes at a time, reaching for a drink before falling back under, that kind of thing. So fingers crossed she'll wake up soon and will have weathered the storm without any long-term damage—physically, of course—and then we can all put this behind us."

I think that, for him, it is going to be an empty win simply because getting confirmation that the girl was abused might validate his actions, but it won't make him feel any better.

"That's good though, right?" I ask, desperate to keep talking to him. I'm alone in this tower of an office building but he makes me feel a little less so. "That she's responding. That she's having moments of consciousness."

"Only time will tell," he murmurs. "You haven't broken up with me yet. Why?"

His question throws me and I chuckle a nervous laugh. "I couldn't . . . I didn't want to."

"Why's that?"

Do or die time, Blakely.

I take a deep breath and close my eyes. "I feel like there is so much unfinished business between us. The to-do list. The . . . and I . . ."

"Me too."

"You too?" I ask. What does that mean? What is he saying? "So, what do we do about it?"

"Well, I did win the bet, so isn't there the last of our unfinished business to tend to? Like you owing me dinner?" The smile in his voice eases the vise gripping my chest until I realize that there is more to tend to than just the bet—like the last task on that damn napkin.

It was in jest. He said it from the beginning. And yet here I am, a ridiculous female still thinking I want it to be true and hurt that it isn't.

My smile is bittersweet, and when I speak, my voice doesn't reflect any of the turmoil that is roiling around inside of me. "Are you assuming you won? That I'm satisfied, Slade?"

His chuckle rumbles through the line. "You did get the promotion."

"Maybe I need other things to feel satisfied."

"Are you implying I didn't deliver? We howled at the moon, Foxx," he teases.

"Maybe I need to try out the goods again to be sure."

This. This is what I need. The sexy banter. The playful flirting. This is what makes me feel like us again . . . not that there is an us, but it's normal for us.

"How about Friday night? Does that work for you?"

I close my eyes and smile to the empty room. "Yes. Friday sounds good."

"Should we meet up after you get off work? We could go to Metta's and actually eat there or—"

"After work is fine."

"I'm sorry." His chuckle rumbles across the connection. "I'm taking over when this is supposed to be your date. Tell me what you want to do and I'll make sure it happens. Hell, you're the new take-charge Blakely, so I'll let you take charge and shut my mouth."

"No. It's fine. I don't mind. How about we meet at Metta's, have a couple of drinks, and then I'll figure out somewhere to go after that?"

"So, you're going to surprise me?"

"Something like that," I say. "How about seven o'clock? Is that too late?"

"It's perfect."

"Okay, then."

Silence clings to the line because I don't want the call to end. There's something about him on the line that makes the day all that much better.

"I'm looking forward to seeing you, Blakely."

"Me too."

"Until then."

And when the call ends, when the quiet of the empty office building settles around me, there is a smile on my lips and a pocket full of hope building within that maybe . . . just maybe, Slade and I can try our hand at whatever this is.

Still, I feel like a fraud because the new take-charge Blakely would have just told him how much I want there to be more than just a celebratory dinner.

She would have told him she wants that last task on the to-do list.

She would have laid it all on the line.

There's always Friday night.

FORTY-FOUR

Blakely

"**H**uge bouquet of flowers for one Miss Foxx," Minka says as she carries a vase filled with peonies into my office.

"Huh," I say as I move over to them and pluck the card out of its holder.

"Who are they from?" She all but dances on her toes.

"No idea." But I do know. At least the giddy female part of me thinks I do. I open the card, and my heart sighs as it swoons.

> To Blakely,
> Keep howling at the moon.
> You deserve every bit of this.
> —Slade

"Slade?" Minka asks.

I nod and read it again. "Yeah."

"God, you're so lucky. I wish Jared looked at me the way Slade looks at you."

The lump in my throat grows even bigger.

I look up and smile at her. "I'm a lucky girl." But the words sound a little shakier than I intend them to sound.

Because it hits me how damn much I care for Slade.

Not care for, who am I kidding? *Love.*

I bite the bullet and admit it to myself.

I think I've gone and fallen for Slade.

Jesus, even I know how stupid that sounds.

If he knew, he would run the other way.

It's the kind of emotion that people will tell me I'm crazy for feeling so quickly.

But it's true.

I pick up my phone and call him, but he doesn't pick up. Within seconds my phone alerts a text.

Slade: Everything ok? I can't pick up.

Me: Yes. I'm fine. Thank you for my flowers. They're gorgeous.

Slade: You deserve them.

Me: How did you know peonies were my favorite? I love them.

Slade: They are? Good guess then. But isn't that just how things are with us?

Me: Strangely yes. See you Friday.

Slade: I'll be there with bells on.

I laugh because I don't put it past him to actually wear bells. Staring at our texts, all I can think is how right his comment is about knowing peonies are my favorite.

It's just how things are with us.

FORTY-FIVE

Slade

"I'm confused," I say when I open the front door, bleary-eyed and craving my bed more than my half-eaten pasta sitting on the counter. "I thought you were here and then left already, swearing to never come back."

My mom's smile widens as she steps inside and presses a kiss to my cheek. "You look exhausted," she says and breezes past me like she owns the place. "How come you look like you're working when you're still not working?"

"Um . . . what are you doing here?" I ask as I stand at the door and stare after her. I still have my scrub pants on, but my shirt off, and I have a half-drank beer in my hand.

"I told you I had to come back for Aunt Millie's surgery. Don't worry"—she looks over her shoulder—"I'm not staying here." She stops in her tracks and looks down the hallway and then back to me, eyes wide, and mouth open in shock. "I'm not interrupting anything am I?"

It takes me a second to get her gist. "No. God. Mom." I sigh her name out. "The only thing you're interrupting is my five precious hours of sleep. I'm so tired I couldn't even do _that_ if I tried."

"_Do that?_" She giggles as she rounds the countertop and looks in my bowl before heading to the fridge. "It's called sex, honey, and I'm more than aware you have it."

"This conversation is wrong on so many levels." I sink down into my seat and resume eating. It's cold now, but I don't have the energy to make anything different.

But when I look up, my mom is already cutting up lettuce and tomatoes and making a salad. "You need veggies," she says. "All those carbs aren't healthy."

"Thanks for the nutrition lesson," I grumble.

"Would you rather we chat about why you've been avoiding my calls?" she asks as if she's Mary Freaking Poppins.

"I've been working. I'm not back on call yet, but like I told you, I'm helping Schultz out—trying to get in his good graces—and you know how much I love doing mindless bullshit."

"Mindless, yes, but at least you aren't pulling twenty-four-hour shifts."

"I kind of am, though, trying to get my body back in the swing of things on the off chance I get reinstated soon."

"It must be why you're a bowl full of sunshine."

I glare at her. "Why are you here?"

"You're avoiding me."

She's right. I am.

"No, I'm not."

"You never ignore my texts." I give her one of those you-have-to-be-kidding-me looks. "Well, you ignore them but not this way."

"And what way is that?" I ask around a bite of pasta.

"In the way where you don't give me an inkling of how your camping trip went."

"Is that why you're here?" I laugh. "You want to get in my business?" Christ.

"That Glam girl you went with. What's her name again?"

My eyes flash up. Narrow. "What do you mean Glam girl?"

"I was checking your Instagram and saw someone tag you from your retreat. It said something about it being Glam and all kinds of those weird pound sign things after it."

"Hashtags."

"Yes. Those. I always forget their new name."

"That's beside the point. Your stalking, meddling . . . annoying abilities really need to take a back seat."

"I wasn't stalking. I just happened to see it." She waves a hand at me. "What was her name again?"

"Who? You mean, Blakely?"

"Yes. Such a pretty name. And talk about beautiful. Classic and sophisticated looking all at the same time."

My mother is stalking my love life through Instagram. It doesn't get any worse than this.

"Yes, she's something else."

And hell if that isn't the goddamn truth.

"Well, Lane said—"

"Lane?" I bark out my cousin's name. I'm going to kill the fucker as soon as I remember what I actually told him. I've been in my head so much these past two weeks that I'm kind of foggy on what I said and what I simply thought. "Please, tell me what you and Lane discussed." I cross my arms across my chest and lean back in my chair.

"He just said you really had a good time. That you really liked her."

"Uh-huh." I draw the word out as I take a sip from my bottle of beer. "And your point?"

"My point is nothing. It just isn't like you not to at least say *something* to me about a woman you go out with."

"Yeah. Normally, I just say some shit to push your buttons."

"Exactly, but this time, you've said absolutely nothing."

"Mom, I'm tired. Can you just stop beating around the bush and get to why you stopped by here because I know it's more than just to say hi and fix me a salad."

She slides the salad across the counter and then grabs some salad dressing from the fridge for me.

"Thanks," I mumble.

"You know." She sighs and leans her hips against the counter opposite of me. "You reach this time in your life where you realize you're growing up. That what you thought was enough before, isn't enough any longer."

"And?"

"And I'm just wondering if you really like this Blakely but can't understand why this time is different, why she's different, and so you're fighting yourself on admitting it."

I look up from my food and meet her eyes. There's so much kindness and love looking back at me that my defenses crumble just a little. "All of the above and then some."

The startle of her head tells me she's shocked I just opened up to her. I am too.

"Then what's the problem? If you like her, and she likes you, why are you so grumpy? Love is supposed to make you happy."

"Let's slow down there with the L-word, 'kay?"

"Why does it scare you?"

And fuck does it scare me.

"It isn't me who's scared, all right?"

A slow smile slides onto her lips as she cocks her head to the side. Did I really just admit to my mom that I've fallen for Blakely? Did I really just admit that to myself?

"Tell me about her," she says softly.

I fight my innate urge to deflect questions related to my dating life, and it doesn't seem too hard because I miss Blakely like crazy and at the same time wonder how in the hell this happened.

I don't fight the smile that comes. "She's . . . something else. She's confident and intelligent, and she has a great laugh." I look at where my hands are clasped around my beer bottle and shake my head. "We just click. That's the only way I can put it. I went on that stupid trip to try to help her out and left wondering what in the hell happened to me."

My chuckle is slightly self-deprecating, but my mom's smile is sincere.

"You know what's funny, Slade? If I were to ask you that question about anyone else you've dated, your response is how she has great eyes or killer legs. It's always about looks. With this Blakely, you didn't make a single comment about her appearance and we both know she's gorgeous . . . so, I don't know about you, but to me, that says a lot."

"I don't know how this happened." I rise from my seat and grab another beer I don't really need.

"I know. It's hard to believe someone actually loves you and your pushiness and kind heart," she teases.

"Ha. Let's not go that far." The crack of the bottle cap fills the kitchen.

"Does she know how you feel?"

"I'm not even sure how I feel." I chuckle and sit back down.

"Yes you do," she murmurs as she runs a sponge over the counter. "It's in your eyes when you talk about her. It's in your tone. Why haven't you told her?"

"For a lot of reasons." I yawn.

"Try me."

"Her last relationship was a marriage." I quirk an eyebrow, waiting for judgment from my mom but there is none. Just patient eyes waiting for me to explain. "I'm thinking since her husband left her for a younger woman, the last thing she's ready to hear or wants to hear is that I've fallen for her."

And that's the crux isn't it? Sure, falling in love in this short amount of time is crazy, but admitting it and then being rejected is ten times worse.

"How do you know unless you tell her?"

"What if she spooks? Where exactly does that leave me?"

"And what if she's feeling the same way you are and is afraid to voice it?" I start to speak, but she cuts me off. "You're the guy who says what he feels at all times. You're spontaneous and in-your-face and encourage people to live their lives without looking back. You're the one who doesn't hold back, so why are you doing it now when you need not to the most?"

Blakely's expression in the lodge's parking lot flashes in my mind. The emotion hiding in her eyes. The tenderness in her kiss. The quiver in her laugh.

Then I think of the space I've subconsciously given myself, hoping this ache in my chest would go away or dissipate. It isn't supposed to be burning brighter. I think of the distance I've given her to see if she'll just move on, use me as her rebound, and realize she doesn't want a man right now.

And I think of how goddamn miserable I've been doing all of this— being without her.

"You really like her, don't you?"

I sigh. "I do, Mom. I do when I shouldn't. I do, and I can't explain why."

"Oh Slade, honey, that's the best kind." She takes a seat beside me, turning her chair so her feet are on the lower rungs of mine. "You know, fear makes people do stupid things sometimes."

Like falling in love with someone after only a few short weeks.

"That's profound." I don't look up from my salad.

"*Fear.* Of being loved. Of being rejected. Of being hurt," she continues as if I didn't speak. "Sometimes it makes people do stupid things."

"Like?"

"Like push people away because it's too good to believe it's true."

"I'm seeing her in three days. I'll let you know how your theory pans out," I deadpan, unofficially letting her know this little heart-to-heart is over.

She leans over and presses a kiss to my temple. I slide my arms around her waist for a hug. She stands there and runs her fingers through my hair. "Maybe we can do dinner before I head back home again?"

I snort. "That's just another excuse for you to meddle."

"Get some sleep," she murmurs.

I'll take that as a yes.

FORTY-SIX

I stop momentarily to look at myself in the tall window storefront to my right.

The dress I bought for tonight—burgundy with a deep V neckline, and a cut that clings down to my waist and then flares a bit at the legs—is the perfect choice. It says I'm not trying too hard but is still subtly sexy in all the right ways.

My shoes, on the other hand? The black peep-toe heels that add four inches to my height say I want him to take the dress off me and demand that I leave *only* the shoes on.

Nerves rattle in my stomach as I bring a hand to my hair to tuck an errant strand behind my ear. I'm excited and anxious and worried and everything under the sun for whatever is to happen tonight.

That's a lie.

I know what's going to happen tonight. I'm going to be the new Blakely who takes what she wants. The one who was MIA the last time I saw Slade when we were standing in the parking lot at the lodge and was too chickenshit to tell him what I wanted—*him*.

I can do this.

I got the job, and now I want the man too.

Taking a left at the street corner, I halt in my tracks when I come face-to-face with Paul. Déja vu hits me. But this time Paul is alone.

There's no Barbie to distract him or flaunt like a trophy. It's just me and him and a world full of baggage that I want to throw into a dumpster, light on fire, and never look at again.

"Blakely." His eyes roam up and down the length of me, and if there were such a thing as buyer's remorse, his expression would be the trademark for it.

Not going to lie and say I don't enjoy seeing it.

"Paul. What a surprise." When he leans in to give me a kiss on the cheek, I take a step back. "What are you doing?"

"Just saying hi. Since when is it such a big deal for me to kiss you on the cheek?"

"Since you left me. Since we're divorced. Since I no longer have any desire to try to make things cordial with you . . . you lost the right to assume anything about me."

His expression freezes, and he blinks his eyes several times as he tries to adjust to this new me. The one who speaks up instead of swallowing the comments as to not make a scene.

"Wow. Okay." He nods as that smarmy smile graces his lips. "I wasn't aware it was a crime to be cordial."

"It isn't. But cordial is all you ever were to me. There was no passion, no spark, no anything other than constantly trying to satisfy that overgrown ego of yours, and now that I'm no longer married to you, I don't have to pretend anymore." I glance to my right where someone laughs loudly. "If you'll excuse me, Slade's waiting for me."

Proud of myself, I skirt around him, but then he grabs my arm. It takes everything I have not to give him the satisfaction of yanking my arm back. Instead, I look him straight in the eyes and raise an eyebrow in question.

"Where was this Blakely when we were married?" he asks.

"She was always here. You were too preoccupied with yourself to notice her."

And without another word, I take off down the sidewalk toward Metta's with an extra swing to my hips and the hope that he's watching me and seeing what he gave up.

By the time I walk into Metta's and request a table, I realize that I don't care if Paul was watching. In fact, the best part about that whole interaction was its little boost to my confidence and the reinforcement that the new Blakely is here to stay.

Sliding into a booth in the back corner, I know for certain that I wasn't off in reading Slade's cues. I realize that Prisha's advice was just that—advice—and that I should heed it but use my own interactions with him to form my own opinion.

And my opinion is that there is something between us.

With each passing minute, I'm more and more certain of it, more and more high on the anticipation of seeing him again and falling right back into whatever it is we can be together.

I jump when my phone rings and scramble to answer when I see Slade's name on the screen.

"Hi. Everything okay?" I ask, realizing he was supposed to have been here fifteen minutes ago.

"It's fine. I'm not going to make it."

I shake my head as if I didn't hear him correctly. "Slade?"

"Something came up," he says as I hear a woman laughing in the background and déja vu hits me for the second time tonight.

It's still of Paul, but this time it's of the calls he'd answer but was always in a hurry to end. The ones where a throaty laugh could be heard just before he disconnected. The laughs I now know belonged to Barbie.

"Slade?"

"I have to go. I just—I'm sorry."

Without another word, the connection goes dead.

And every ounce of confidence that I was just soaring on comes crashing down around me.

By the time I get home in my brand-new dress and sky-high heels, I've worked myself up into a tizzy. My lone text to him remains unanswered, and every excuse I've fabricated as to why I was basically stood up, I've systematically debunked.

One by freaking one.

The woman's voice in the background doesn't help my overactive imagination from reliving everything with Paul all while taking Prisha's damn advice and twisting it to fit its narrative.

To put it mildly, I'm hurt and more than mad at myself for believing that this could be real.

That a good guy like Slade Henderson could really like an almost forty-year-old divorcée.

Then again, maybe there aren't any good guys left after all.

FORTY-SEVEN

Slade

My pulse pounds like a freight train in my ears as I wait for Dr. Schultz to go through the chart in his hand.

This isn't how I expected tonight to happen. A phone call when I'm standing in the middle of the florist shop and then rushing to get to the hospital as soon as possible. A command from my mentor to grab my lab coat out of my locker, throw it on, and meet him in the pediatric unit ASAP.

Putting on that lab coat is the closest thing I've felt to being a doctor in a long time. It's a good thing.

I think.

"She's asking for you." His voice is a somber hush as his eyes flicker to the closed doorway to our right before meeting mine. Ivy is in that room speaking with the police psychologist.

"For me?" I ask, surprised Ivy would even remember me. The poor little girl has been through hell and back, I should be the last thing she remembers.

He nods. "She's been stirring for the past week, signs here and there, but she woke late this morning. She was confused and agitated, but once she understood what happened, she calmed some."

I hate that I'm just finding out about this now and thankful I'm finding out about it at all.

It had to be a big, scary place to wake up in when the last time you were conscious you were bleeding and hurting while people were shouting orders and things were being poked and prodded into your body.

"Is it really the best idea for the police to be in there questioning her so soon?" I ask in that same hushed murmur.

"Shouldn't that make you happy, Slade? Her answers to their questions are what might get you back in that coat permanently."

"Of course that's important to me, but her well-being is what's paramount."

He nods as he stares at me, those dark eyes of his studying me intently. "By looking at the notes in her chart, she seems to be doing as well as can be expected after being out for a month. She's apt to be a little fuzzy on some things, stiff muscles, you know the drill"—he waves his hand in my direction—"but she's young, and her arm still having to be in a cast, her body has healed during the time. For the most part, it seems all signs are hinting that she's going to make a full recovery."

A similar sense of relief to the one I felt when I'd heard she'd woken up floods me. She's talking, her vitals are strong, and it seems as if there's no long-term damage. Thank god.

"That's great news, sir. The outcome could have been so much worse." A silence settles between us as a nurse walks by, and he steps backward into a small alcove off the main floor. I follow. "Is there something else?"

"Ivy is busy telling the police about how her father did this to her. And not just this once, but numerous times. For a little girl, she has quite an incredible memory."

My stomach churns, but this isn't news to me. I knew it in my gut the minute that son of a bitch strolled in here that night with his arrogant attitude, indifference to his own child, and the blood caked on his knuckles.

I nod. It's all I can do because it's taking me a minute to process everything. The bastard father. The sweet, battered little girl. That I was in the right—and sure, I always knew I was in the right, but there were moments in the middle of the night when I wondered if I was wrong. If

I had overstepped when I prevented her father from being in the room with her. If I had ruined my career.

"I don't know what to say," I finally murmur and run a hand through my hair. "I'm at a loss."

"This isn't my department," he says, "but I'm here because of the consequences and how they might affect one of my most talented residents." He shakes his head with a drawn-out sigh. "She asked for you because she said she remembered you telling her she was safe with you." When he looks back to me, his eyes have tears welling in them just as mine do. We both blink them away, and he clears his throat. "While I can't condone what you did and how you went about doing it, I can tell you that it definitely made its mark. That's something we all strive to do and often fail. Congratulations, Dr. Henderson, not only on being reinstated but also on being the type of doctor we need more of. One who cares about the patient's well-being more than they do their own self."

"Thank you, sir," I manage to say around the emotion clogging my throat.

"And let's make sure it doesn't happen again," he adds with a chuckle before patting me on the back. "You're cleared to go in and see her when the police come out."

"What happens next?" I ask, the question broad.

"The father rots in jail—hopefully, she goes on to live a gloriously happy life, and you become a highly regarded cardiothoracic surgeon." He shrugs as if it's without question.

"Nothing's ever that easy."

"Let's hope this was your difficult part and from here on out is smooth sailing."

"Yes, sir."

"Call me when you're done and let me know what happens. I have to get back to my patients."

"Will do," I say as I pat my pocket and realize my phone isn't there. My mind and emotions are on overload, so who knows where I left it.

And, honestly, who cares? This moment is so much greater than anything I've done thus far in my career. I've been reinstated. She's awake.

As much as it feels as if a huge burden has just been lifted off my shoulders, the weight of the moment is still crushing.

Ivy is in there, giving the police information to put her dad away for a long time.

She asked for me. She said I made her feel safe.

Blowing out a breath, I lean back against the wall and pat for my phone again. My first instinct is to tell Blakely. Not my parents or John, Prisha, and Leigh . . . but Blakely.

The door beside me swings open, and a woman walks out. She's slight in stature, her hair is a light grayish-white and is pulled up in one of those clip-things, and reading glasses are hanging from the V of her shirt.

Our eyes meet, and she smiles warmly. "Dr. Henderson, I presume?"

"Yes. How is she?"

"I'm Felice Philemon, child psychologist. I work with the police department when it comes to minors."

"Nice to meet you. Slade Henderson." We shake hands as her expression softens. "I'm not at liberty to talk about what we discussed, but I think you can imagine what was said considering the lengths at which you went to protect her at the expense of your career." She shakes her head ever so slightly. "That's one incredible little girl who I have no doubt will thrive after she's given some time to heal."

"What happens now? I mean if her dad . . ."

"When and if what happens should happen with her father, she'll live with family members. Several have stepped forward and offered to be her guardian. CPS will vet them, see who is committed to getting her the counseling she'll need, and ask her who she feels most comfortable with—that type of thing. She'll be taken care of."

"If you were waiting for her to wake up to press charges, why have people already stepped forward?" I ask. "I mean, that implies you knew all along what had happened and—"

"I don't have the answer to that, but from what I gather, her father is well-known in many important circles that have a lot of influence. Perhaps the district attorney wanted to make sure she had all the tools she needed to ensure he couldn't weasel out of the charges. With Ivy's statements and my assessments, I think she'll have all she needs. But, of course, this is all supposition as I'm not at liberty to discuss any of this with anyone."

"Of course. Strictly supposition," I say. "I don't understand why she asked for me." It isn't what I'd planned on saying, but it's out and I can't take it back.

"When you're suffering in the dark, it's amazing how much you cling to the one person who brings you a glimmer of light." She pats my arm and lifts her chin toward the door. "You should go in."

I stare at her for a beat longer before looking at the door I need to walk through. Nerves rattle with an anxious anticipation and hesitation.

Taking a deep breath, I push it open and enter.

I haven't seen Ivy in weeks. Not without her head wrapped, bruises marring her olive complexion, or without machines attached and monitoring her vital signs.

Her eyes meet mine. They're a jarring blue, the color of sapphires, and I realize I didn't remember that. Possibly because the subconjunctival hemorrhages in both eyes made it impossible for me to see her eye color.

But now they're blue and they're staring right at me as if she's memorizing every single thing about me.

I stare, too, because she's tiny. The hospital bed that dwarfs her little body, the sheets tucked under her arms, and the two braids her sandy blonde hair has been put in for manageability rest over her shoulders.

Her smile is timid, tentative, as it should be for a little girl who is waking up to an all new world for herself.

"Hi," I say softly as I look back at Felice, who's stepped into the room behind me, before taking a few cautious steps toward the side of the bed opposite Ivy's casted arm. "I'm Dr. Henderson."

"You're him. *Your voice.* You're the one from that night."

My chest constricts as I fight back the emotion that those simple words evoke in me. "I am." I nod. "I can't tell you how happy I am to meet you, Ivy."

"Sorry. I forgot my manners. I'm Ivy."

"I know." I chuckle and marvel at her all at the same time. "I heard you wanted to see me."

She nods, her eyes flickering over to Felice before coming back to mine. "Is it okay—can you just sit and hold my hand for a little bit like you did that night?"

I blink back my tears, the ones I'm not supposed to show as a doctor, but fuck, I'm human. How can I not be overwhelmed in the moment by this incredible little girl?

"Of course." I pull the chair toward the side of the bed and take a seat as I slide her tiny little hand into mine. Someone painted her fingernails pink while she'd been unconscious. I'm not sure why that gets to me, but it does. Such a tiny gesture that says she is loved by someone. "I can sit here all night if you want me to," I murmur.

She smiles again, but I can see the exhaustion in the smudges beneath her eyes and in the way her eyelids are so slow to lift back up when she blinks. "Thank you." Another heavy-lidded blink. "Just thank you."

FORTY-EIGHT

Blakely

"I'm sorry for tonight." Slade's voice is a deep rumble that I'm not actually certain I want to hear. "I can explain."

"Don't bother." The woman's laugh echoes in my ear. The bottle-plus-some-more of wine I drank doesn't help to dampen the stubborn hurt that has festered inside of me with every ticking minute of the night that had passed. "It doesn't matter." I try to sound nonchalant but the bite to my tone says I'm hurt.

"Blakely—"

"No. Really. I get it. You had more important things to do—"

"That isn't what happ—"

"Do you know how much I wanted to see you? Do you even understand—"

"Iv—"

"I have to go."

"Iv—"

I end the call with his last word unfinished and clutch the damn phone in my hand as I try to fight back the ridiculous amount of hurt radiating in my chest. Hurt? Maybe it's more like dying hope.

I told myself I'd never let a man treat me how Paul did, and I'm sticking to it.

My cell rings again and I push the call to voicemail.

This is for the better. It's too soon to get involved with a man. I need to just be me for a while. I need to settle in these new shoes. What was I thinking when I thought Slade was into me?

This is for the better.

At least that's what I repeat to myself as I shove the tears off my cheeks determined to remain unfazed.

Or to want to call him back.

Within seconds the phone dings an alert.

Don't look.

Don't look.

I look.

And my heart falls to my feet.

Slade: Ivy woke tonight. I was called to the hospital STAT. I accidentally left my phone in my locker so I couldn't reply to your text. This whole ordeal is over. I've been reinstated, but more importantly, she asked to see me. She wanted me to sit with her and hold her hand. That's where I've been. Do you really think I would have canceled for something that wasn't important?

I reread the text a dozen times as dread and embarrassment filters through every fiber of my being. My hands start to tremble as the gamut of emotions I've been through this evening take their toll. The most prominent one being shame.

Here I am, the whole night thinking about me, me, me. Not once did I stop to consider that Slade wasn't screwing me over. Not a single time did I think that maybe Ivy had woken or there was some kind of emergency he had to tend to.

All I could focus on was the woman's laugh and him canceling on me.

Talk about being a selfish bitch.

I'm still staring at his text, wondering how exactly I should answer when his next text comes through.

Slade: I love that you're being the new, strong Blakely, but can't you cut a guy some slack? I promise to make it up to you.

I should be the one saying that. I should be the one texting frantically to ask for his forgiveness because I'd assumed the worst when I should have given him the benefit of the doubt.

Slade: I can give you proof that I was where I said I was if that's what you need.

And that statement is like a dagger in my chest. It solidifies my chickenshit train of thought that I'm not ready for a relationship. At least not one with a man as deserving as Slade Henderson. I'm nowhere near where I need to be emotionally to do this. I'm the one who's almost forty. I'm supposed to be the mature one. And here he is, looking after my needs and assuming I need proof because of what Paul did to me.

I'm the jealous psycho, and he's the freaking saint.

He deserves so much better than that. *Than me.*

I struggle with what to text back. With what to say.

An apology would be what he deserves, but how do I tell him I'm sorry for assuming he was with another woman when there isn't even an us to begin with? How do I explain that I'm obviously not one hundred percent over the hurt Paul caused when I clearly thought I was? How do I say that I'm not exactly sure how I'd go about accepting all of the date nights, special events, and family moments in our lives that he would undoubtedly miss time and again because of someone else's medical emergency? I'd never want him to be feel like he has to choose between his love for his work and upsetting me or letting me down.

On top of all that, when one of those medical emergencies happened, would I be left wondering if he is in fact telling the truth?

Didn't I just prove I can't handle it?

Didn't I just validate how much I need to work on me so that I don't bring others down?

I type and delete and type and delete a million things but none of them express any of the jumbled and confused emotions owning me.

So, I don't type an apology. I don't even address the issue. Who's the mature one now?

Not me.

Me: Congratulations on both fronts. I'm glad she is awake.

Slade: When can I make it up to you?

Me: No need to. You deserve so much better than me. Thank you for everything.

Slade: What is that supposed to mean?

Me: Congratulations again.

I turn my phone on do not disturb and toss it on my dresser before falling face down onto my bed, knowing I just pushed the best thing that ever happened to me away because I'm not the best thing that could ever be for him.

And I want to be. *God how I want to be.*

But my reaction tonight tells me I don't deserve him or his kindness and huge heart.

I need some time to think.

To sort my own emotions out.

To figure out if I can be the woman he deserves when I full well know he deserves the whole freaking world.

FORTY-NINE

Slade

"**Y**ou on again tonight, man?"

I look up from the chart I'm reviewing at the nurse's station and over to John. I'm so exhausted my bones are tired. "This is my second thirty-hour shift in a row," I murmur before taking a sip of scalding hot coffee. "So, yes. The answer would be yes."

"Ahh, your body forgot what it was like to be pulling these kinds of hours, didn't it?"

"You could say that." I scrub a hand over my face and stifle a yawn.

"What's up with What's-Her-Face? Blakely. How was dinner?"

I give a partial chuckle. "We didn't go. It was the night Ivy came to."

"Oh shit."

"You can say that again."

"Oh shit," he repeats with a smart-ass grin.

"Funny."

"You going to make it up to her?" he asks just as a nurse from across the floor calls his name. He takes a step back. "I mean, if you don't fall asleep during the middle of it."

I flip him off but shake my head.

That's the big question, isn't it? Am I going to make it up to her?

How can I when I can't get her to answer my calls or texts?

If I knew where she lived, I'd try to get her to answer the door, but I don't. So, short of sitting outside of Glam like a stalker to get her to talk to me, I'm not sure what to do.

God do I fucking miss her, but hell if I have a goddamn clue what happened.

Work. Residency. Getting matched to the right hospital. That's what matters. The right here and the right now and not fucking up after everything that has happened.

That's what I need to be focusing on, not a new relationship when I'm diving head-first back into work.

Relationship?

Did I really just use the R-word? When did I start thinking of Blakely in those terms? And how is that even possible when we haven't seen each other since the parking lot at the lodge?

I need to keep my head straight.

Then why do I keep looking at my phone every chance I get, hoping she's called or texted?

It's the exhaustion.

It has to be.

FIFTY

Blakely

"You doing all right?"

I look up to see Gemma standing with her shoulder leaning against the doorjamb. "Yeah. Sure. Why?"

She shrugs. "I don't know. Just checking." She moves into my office and perches her ass on the edge of one of my chairs. "Tom said he's been texting with Slade. He asked maybe if we could all go out for drinks, but Slade said you've been so busy he's not sure if you'd be able to go."

The pang that hits me is real and raw, and I nod to buy time to find my words to respond. "He's right. I've just been trying to catch up to speed on everything," I lie.

Don't say too much.

Don't look her in the eye.

She'll see right through you.

"You sure everything is okay with you two? You know I'm here if you need to talk."

I plaster a smile on my lips and look up to meet her eyes and away from today's daily text Slade left me. The one asking if we could talk.

"Yes. Of course. I'm fine. We're fine."

FIFTY-ONE

I stare at the ceiling of my bedroom.

My body and mind tired but thoughts running wild with the one thing I can't stop thinking about even through the exhaustion.

Blakely.

My goddamn heart jumps out of my chest every time I so much as think her name.

It all begins and ends with the heart.

The irony.

She'll come around. She'll pick up the phone. She'll . . . I don't know what.

She has to.

This broken heart shit is for the birds.

FIFTY-TWO

Blakely

"**Y**ou're shitting me," Kelsie says as she looks into my living room where I'm sitting on my newly plumped and fluffed pillows.

"What?"

"This is what he texts you?"

I jolt in awareness, and then shove the misery I'm trying to hide back down. "It's no big deal."

"C'mon, Blakely. I'm not going to give up until you talk to me. How long are you going to stay mad?" she says, reading his text aloud to me. "I mean, that sounds all kinds of sweet to me."

"You call it sweet, I call it stalkerish," I lie and give her a tight smile before taking a sip of my wine. The texts are getting harder and harder to resist, but his sweet-hearted nature only proves why I don't deserve him. "Isn't there some kind of rule somewhere that says don't fall in love with your rebound?" I shrug. "And I didn't, so sue me."

She walks around the island and leans her butt against it as she studies me, the expression on her face one I know from years of friendship. It says she's not buying it, and I'm not in the mood for a Kelsie lecture. Not when I've been miserable for the past seven days with a heartache that I keep trying to convince myself is because I'm doing the right thing for once.

And not for myself, but for him.

I can be unselfish.

That's what I'm being.

And if I keep telling myself that, then maybe I'll start to believe it. *Maybe.*

"So sue you?" She chuckles. "What are you, ten years old?"

I lean my head on the back of the couch and look to the ceiling. It's way easier to study the drywall than it is to meet her eyes and let her see how miserable I am.

"You don't understand."

"Huh." She remains silent until I look at her. "What I don't understand is why you won't just save face, tell him your imagination went a little wild, that you overreacted, and apologize. You know, *the truth.*"

"The truth is I read too much into everything. I mistook the fun, no-strings-attached retreat, and made it more in my mind because he was the first man who made me feel good again since Paul . . . so, of course, it was easy to mistake feeling good for having feelings."

"It is, and that was a whole mouthful of words where you mentioned the word 'feel' three times just to prove you don't have feelings. If we're going to talk like ten-year-olds, then here's mine: 'I spy a lie.'"

"Whatever."

"Oh, there's another juvenile response. We can do this all night, the back and forth, or you can tell me why you're suddenly running away from one of the best things that's happened to you like he has the plague."

"I am not," I assert.

"You are too." She takes a sip of her wine as my phone beeps the second alert on the text. "And the only thing I can figure out is that you really, *really* like him and now that you realize it, you're scared to death."

"Aren't you the one who was applauding me for hitting it and quitting it?"

"I was wrong."

I do a double take, coughing on my sip of wine. "What was that?"

"I was wrong," she says it so matter-of-factly that all I can do is laugh.

Kelsie is never wrong. Ever. Just ask her. She'll tell you.

"Have some more wine. It'll make you realize the error in your ways and comment."

"No error." She shrugs. "It's the truth. I was wrong Blake. You really do like him, don't you?"

Her stare is unrelenting, and tears well in my eyes under its intensity. All I can do is nod. "I just need time to think."

"About what? About how you're going to call him up, apologize for being irrational, and set a time to go have that date where you're going to confess to him that the few nights in the middle of the woods wasn't enough? That you want more? Him and his kit and caboodle?"

She offers me a half-assed smile with a waggle of her eyebrows, but it doesn't help with the sudden panic clawing its way up my throat.

"Any man who makes me this kind of crazy, jealous bitch . . . I mean, do I want that? Do I want to be that person?"

"Maybe that means he's worth it."

"You're just arguing to fit your narrative," I say while secretly clinging to her words.

"Think what you will."

But there's a nonchalance to Kelsie's words and demeanor that almost makes me want to fight to prove her wrong. If anything, my best friend is never blasé. She's passionate and in-your-face and this change of demeanor has me digging my heels in strictly to make a point.

Or make myself believe my own lies.

"So, what?" I set my glass down and cross my arms over my chest. "You're telling me I should boil bunnies and go crazy over him, and you wouldn't be worried?"

Her sigh is slow and frustrated. "That isn't what I'm saying *Ms. Dramatic*. What I'm saying is with everything that's happened, cut yourself some slack. Being scared is normal."

"Look, I was married to a man who always put work first . . . do I really want to go that route again? I mean—"

"That's the lamest excuse I've ever heard. What's your next one because I have all night to debunk every excuse you're going to throw my way." She plops down on the couch across from me. "You like the guy. You want to explore what else there could be. It's okay to admit it, to want it, while also being a bit overwhelmed by it."

"You aren't supposed to be encouraging me. You're supposed to be telling me I hit it, I quit it, and now I need to move on."

"I've never seen you like this before. Defensive when you want to believe what I'm saying." With a shake of my head, I start to reject her words when she holds up her hand to stop me. "I've never seen you so miserable. You've been moping around all week. You're angry and cynical when you're typically not. You refuse to talk about *The Bachelor* with me because you say love is stupid and can't be felt that quickly."

"It's true."

"You're living proof that's a lie."

"For Christ's sake, Kels—"

"He made you happy. He made you come alive. Why would you throw that chance away because of some stupid notion that you aren't good enough for him because you had one minor meltdown over him having to break a date with you?"

"He's supposed to be a rebound," I whisper, the fight I was putting up now nonexistent with her words.

"Oh, Blakely. Who am I to say he was just a rebound when it seems without him you fall flat?"

"You know more than anything that a man should not make or break the person you are. I let Paul do that to me. Never again."

"But Slade's not Paul and you're fighting against him as if he is. Slade doesn't have to make or break you as a woman, but he sure as hell can help you shine." She moves to sit next to me, her smile soft and knowing as she places a hand on my knee and squeezes. "Slade helped you shine. He made you see yourself in the same light I see you in but could never get you to believe was *and is* real."

"I've made a royal mess of this, haven't I?"

"Kind of." She scrunches her nose as I flop back on the cushions.

"Great. I'm supposed to be this strong, new Blakely, and instead I'm the old one: whiny, indecisive, insecure, and *lonely*."

"You're going to slip sometimes. That's to be expected."

"But I slipped with someone I care about."

"There's a surefire way to fix it," she says as she rises from the couch, walks over to where my phone is, and tosses it onto the couch beside me. "I'm gonna get going. I think there's a call you need to make."

FIFTY-THREE

Slade

"Hello?"

Her voice. That voice. It has relief flickering through me.

"Hey. How are you?"

"Good. Terrible." She laughs, and I love the nervous edge to it because, for some reason, I can relate to the sound of it.

"Well, those two things shouldn't be mutually exclusive so should we break each one down?" I ask.

"Why do you do that? Why do you try to make me feel at ease when I'm the one who should be apologizing to you?"

I chuckle. "Come again?"

"There's something about you, Slade, that immediately makes a bad situation feel so much better. It's maddening."

"I'd think it's a good thing," I say.

"It's maddening only because I wish I could do the same. But I'm stalling. I'm focusing on that instead of why I called."

"It's good to hear your voice."

"See?" She laughs, and it's a little lighter this time. "There you go again, trying to put things at ease when I'm the one who needs to be doing that."

She's adorable when she's flustered. I know I can't see her through the line, but damn it, she's adorable.

And I miss her.

"Then by all means, Ms. Foxx, the floor is yours."

Silence blankets the line followed by an audible inhale. "I screwed up. It's hard for me to say that, but I screwed up, and I made all kinds of excuses to myself why my screw up was justified, but in the end, they were all stupid. I'm sorry."

That's three screwed's.

I smile. It's the most honest smile I've had in the last ten days because it reminds me of the night we met—her diatribe and what happened afterward.

And I know this—whatever this is—is going to be okay.

"We all screw up."

"Yes, but I pushed you out. You called to cancel, and I understand why, but in my head, I made it out to be more than it was and then, of course, I felt like an idiot when you told me the real reason. I was too embarrassed to admit I was being selfish and . . . I'll stop myself now."

"Please. Continue." I settle back into my couch. "I like hearing you talk."

"Slade."

Christ. Her voice. *My name.*

"I apologize that I didn't give you more. I was flustered and left my phone in my locker. You deserved an explanation."

"You don't need to apologize for anything. It's my fault. Totally my fault. I'm supposed to be the new Blakely, but when I heard a woman laugh in the background, I immediately—"

"I'm not Paul. Far fucking from it." And the truth comes out. How did I not see that before? She thought I was making excuses, which I can understand given her history. Understandably she's insecure and maybe drew the conclusion that I had moved on. Doesn't she get I don't think I could move on? Hell, I'm having a hard enough time just trying to get through an hour without looking at my phone hoping she'll call.

"I know you aren't."

"And the lady who laughed was the florist who I was buying flowers for you from."

"Oh." There's that sound I love that she makes. "I don't want flowers—I mean, I like them, but I don't need flowers."

"Unless they are peonies?"

Her laugh is quiet before she says, "Except peonies."

Even though she doesn't say anything else, I can hear her smile over the silence.

"What is it that you *do want*, Blakely?"

"*You.*" She makes a strangled sound. "I mean to see you. Like so I can fulfill my end of the deal we made."

You.

Her first response was the right one.

It's the same goddamn one I have.

Question is, what does that mean in the scheme of things?

"I think I can manage that," I say playfully. "In fact, it would be the highlight of my week."

"Really?"

"*Mmm-hmm.* Meet me where we first met. Seven o'clock. This Friday night."

"I'll be there with bells on."

I end the call, toss my cell onto the couch beside me, and close my eyes.

I'm fucking exhausted, but hell if that didn't just make everything all better.

She called.

Thank fuck for that.

FIFTY-FOUR

Blakely

My breath catches when I see him sitting there. He has on the same black T-shirt and dark jeans that he was wearing the first time we met.

I put a hand to my stomach where butterflies take flight and know it's now or never.

With my other hand on my purse and the napkin inside, I make my way to the bar and slide onto the barstool beside him, smiling when I notice the whiskey the bartender sets in front of me.

He remembered.

I want to look at him, just drink him in and make up for all the lost time, but instead, I keep looking straight ahead as I take a sip, my heart beating a million miles a minute.

"Now that's a drink," Slade says beside me. "I would have pegged you for a red wine type of girl." His knee bumps against mine. "Or is that whiskey?"

"*Mm-hmm,*" I murmur.

"Rough day, then."

"Rough week, actually."

It's taking everything I have not to turn to him and see those eyes and that smile of his.

"What happened? Did your boss piss you off?"

"I am the boss now."

"Impressive," he murmurs. "Your car break down?"

"Nope." I take another sip. "I told my ex off the other day. That was a bright spot in the week."

I feel his body jolt beside me, but I keep looking ahead, keep playing this game because there is so much I need to say to him, but I know the minute I turn to him all that's going to come out is I've fallen in love with him . . . and he deserves to hear it all.

"He probably deserved it."

"He did, but he isn't worth wasting my breath on."

"Smart lady." He hangs his head and chuckles. I see him in my periphery, and my fingers itch to reach out and touch him. "So, it isn't the job or the car or the ex . . . may I ask what it is that made your week so rough?"

"You see, I met this guy." I finally turn to face him, and what I thought would happen, happens. My words slip away—hell, the world slips away—when our eyes meet just like that first night. Back then, my loss of words was because he was strikingly handsome and I wondered why in the hell he was talking to me. Now I know there is so much more to him than his looks, and I don't want him to stop talking to me.

He offers me a lopsided smile. "Lucky guy."

"That depends how you look at it," I murmur, afraid to look away and miss one more second of everything about him.

"Meaning?"

"Meaning I met this guy. He was pushy and handsome and so goddamn nice that I couldn't say no to him when he insisted he spend time with me. He was unexpected and not even on my radar. He brought out sides of me I never knew I had, and . . . and now, I'm not sure what to do about him."

"What's there to worry about if you like him?" He angles his head to the side as he braces his hand on the back of my barstool. His thumb rubs up and down over my bare shoulder, sending electric currents through my every nerve.

"There's everything to worry about." I chuckle when all I want to do is reach out and touch him in turn.

"Like?"

"Like how I tell him I like him more than I should. Like how I keep thinking about him and how much fun we have and wondering if that's what it would always be like. Then I worry if our connection was so strong simply because we were removed from reality and now that we're back, it wouldn't be the same." I suck in a breath of air and continue before I lose my nerve. "Then there's the fact that he's such a genuinely good guy that I wonder every day if I deserve to have someone like him—I mean if he were to want to have me, that is. Add to that he makes me boil-bunny crazy with how much I want him, but I'm afraid to tell him or put my heart on the line because I've been told in the past he doesn't typically stay with one woman for very long—"

And before I can finish the litany of things I want to say, Slade's lips are on mine. I try to keep talking, to keep explaining, to plead with him, but he just puts his hands on both sides of my face and slips his tongue between my lips to stop me.

I've never been told to shut up so perfectly.

I don't care that we're in the middle of this trendy bar where people are probably thinking how tacky we are because they don't matter. Not a single person or any of their opinions do. The only thing that matters is him and this moment and the hope that is surging through me.

He ends the kiss with a brush of his lips and then pulls back ever so slightly with his hands still framing my face. "Boil-bunny crazy?" He quirks an eyebrow. "Something tells me that should concern me."

"Okay, Ted Bundy."

His grin is as wide as mine as we stare at each other like teenagers, drinking in the moment.

"Touché." His thumb runs over my bottom lip. "So, about this guy?"

I laugh. It's loud and rich and carefree and feels so damn good after the stress of the past week.

"I think maybe my fear was preventing me from accepting how I felt about him and I think he felt about me." Hope resonates through my voice and the little boy look on his face has me melting.

"Love is sometimes hard to accept," he says.

"And sometimes it's so effortless it's scary."

"Maybe that's when you know it's right." He brushes his lips against mine again.

"Wait. Love?" I ask trying to pull back, but he holds me in place as his lips smile against mine.

"Yes, *love.*"

This time he leans back, our eyes locked as our hearts beat in synch.

"Whew." I look around the bar. "I sure hope he shows up tonight."

It's Slade's turn to throw his head back and laugh, drawing the stares of those around us.

"Why's that?" he asks over the rim of his glass, playing along.

"Because I have something important to give him."

"His walking papers?"

"Nah." I slide the Blade's To-Do list across the bar top so it sits in front of him. "This."

"What's this?" he asks as he looks down, the soft chuckle on his lips falling silent when he sees it.

"A little something I crossed off tonight before I came here. It may have been a tad presumptuous, but there was no way in hell I was leaving anything to chance this time around."

"A woman who takes charge. I kind of like it."

"Someone taught me confidence was attractive."

"It is. Howling at the moon is even sexier."

"I believe I may have done that a time or two."

"Don't ever stop."

The smile toys with the corner of his mouth as his fingers slide down and link with mine.

"This true?" he asks of the napkin, eyes intense, voice thick with emotion.

"Is it crazy if I say yes?" I whisper. "I never believed in love at first sight, but, Slade . . . I think you owned a little piece of my heart that first night when I walked out of here."

"You've owned me since your first rant."

Lovely. But isn't that so perfectly us?

"I'll make mistakes, but I'll try to fix them."

"I appreciate that." He leans forward and kisses me. The kind of kiss that makes the ache begin to burn and the need begin to beg. "You know what I appreciate even more?"

"*Hmm.*"

"A completed To-Do list."

I throw my head back and laugh. "Is that all you needed?" I tease. "Is that all it takes to turn you on?"

"No. You're all I need, Blakely. You're who I'd pick every time. Hands down." Our lips meet again. "*Just you.*"

EPILOGUE

Blakely

Eighteen Months Later . . .

"Uneventful is good, right?"

"Uneventful is great, but while I admit that I'll welcome the extra sleep next month when my residency ends, I'll definitely miss that thrill of it all."

"I'm sure you will," I say as I look at the trees towering above us as we drive down the stretch of country road.

He asked if I wanted to go for a Saturday drive—somewhere out of the city, off the beaten path. Maybe grab a bite to eat at some unknown hole-in-the-wall or sit and watch the sunset at one of the many lakes not too far from the city.

Country-nature-y stuff I used to roll my eyes at but now realize is one of the ways Slade decompressed after a long week of saving and losing patients.

He squeezes my knee. "Everything going good with the party planning?"

"So far so good."

"I'd tell you again that my mom is willing to fly in early to help, but that means she'd want to stay at my house, and my house means her being nosy, and her being nosy means no sex when you stay over so—"

"So no inviting her to help then." I laugh and tilt my face up and close my eyes, enjoying the cool wind and warm sun coming in the open window. I love his mom. She's everything I never had in a mother and more than anyone wants. God love her, her twenty questions, and her endless meddling.

I had considered trying to involve her in the planning stages of Slade and his friends' graduation-type party for completing their residency and passing their boards, but the no sex thing made that a nonstarter. "Can you believe you're almost an official attending? Long coat here you come."

"It's surreal," he murmurs as he pulls off the main road, causing me to turn and stare at him.

"What are you doing?"

"Don't worry, bunny boiler. I'm still not a Bundy."

"Funny." I look around at our surroundings on the narrow one lane road weaving itself through the trees. "But seriously. The sun is setting soon, I don't want to get lost out here in the dark."

"I wanted to check out this place that Ed told me about."

"Ed?" I laugh his name out with affection woven into it, while shaking my head at the odd friendship the two of them fostered the past eighteen months. It's definitely a strange pairing, but they text every once in a while, and Slade's even gone fishing with him a time or two.

"Yeah. He has a friend who is selling a cabin up here. He told me to come check it out for him because it's supposed to have a lake loaded with fish."

"Is he planning on buying it?"

"Who knows," he murmurs as the trees open to a clearing.

"How cute is that?" I say more to myself than to him. The small house has light gray clapboard siding with white shutters on its windows. A covered patio bends around the front with a raised deck to match. The steps leading up to the front door are worn in their centers and make me think of how many people have probably enjoyed this house over the years. There is a large patch of vibrant green grass next to where we park, but it's the lake at the house's back that catches my attention.

Peaceful.

That's the first word that comes to mind.

"What are you—"

"It's for sale," Slade says without letting me ask the question as he slides out of the car. "Ed's ankle is still tender from his fall, so he asked if I'd check it out for him."

"So, you're just going to go in?" I climb out of the car as he strides toward the front door like a man on a mission.

He turns around, holds his hands out, and gives me a roguish grin. "A little breaking and entering never hurt anyone." He laughs as I stare wide-eyed at him. "Relax, Foxx. I have the code to the lockbox. Come on, check it out with me."

I hurry after him, marveling at how much he's made me step out of my comfort zone over the past year and a half: skinny dipping in the moonlight, making love during a roadside pitstop, singing at the top of my lungs during karaoke night. I thought I had been living before Slade Henderson, and now I know I had no clue what living really was.

Every day is definitely an adventure with him.

"It's quaint, huh?" he asks as he jiggles the key in the lock as I walk up behind him and press a kiss to his shoulder.

"Sure."

"I'll make you love nature one of these days," he teases.

"Hey." I swat his ass. "I've gotten better and—oh." I draw the word out as I step inside the cabin that looks nothing like I expected. The floors look like rustic barn wood with warm touches of grays and blues, but it's the wall of windows that showcases the lake beyond that steals the show.

I walk toward it, my eyes drawn to the shadows of the trees falling over the lake and the colors the setting sun is slowly painting the sky. I'm mesmerized by the beauty and how serene it all looks and feels.

"Gorgeous, isn't it?"

"The cabin or the view?" I ask.

"All three."

"Three?" I turn to look at him.

"The cabin, the view, and you standing there."

Swoon.

I stand there and blush as he peeks his head into the door off the great room. "Good-size master bedroom. En-suite bath." He moves toward the windows and takes a right into what looks like a newly remodeled kitchen. "Nice appliances. Granite countertops."

"No stairs except for the front ones. Do you think Ed could manage those all right?"

"Probably," he says as he jiggles the handle of the door off the kitchen that leads to the back deck. "Let's check out back."

"Slade." His name is an exasperated sigh.

"Humor me."

"Fine." I stroll over to where he is. I don't dare say this out loud, but if I were to ever want to buy a cabin, this would definitely be one I could wrap my head around.

It's when I clear the back door that I falter in my tracks. Sure, the lake is beautiful, but Slade is standing next to what looks like a brand-new white porch swing with a ghost of a smile on his lips and a glass of wine held out to me.

"What is this?" I ask, a little taken back.

"I wanted to do something nice for you." He shrugs sheepishly. "I rented it for a night, complete with the white porch swing and glass of wine that I owe you and will now have finally delivered on."

"Slade." My heart swells as I take the glass of wine from his hand before stepping forward and pressing a kiss to his lips. "All of this for me?"

"I can give you more if you keep that kiss coming."

And I do as he puts his hand on the small of my back and pulls me against him. Our tongues meet and our soft sighs fill the twilight around us as we kiss.

I lean back and look at him, my brow raised as I look at the swing and then back at him. "Should I trust that this one isn't going to fall?"

"I'm pretty sure this one is a little more solid than the one I rigged at the lodge." He chuckles. "But you won't catch me complaining about the outcome."

It creaks when we sit on it, but it doesn't fall. I snuggle into him and he wraps his arm around me and pulls me close much like he did that first night at the bonfire we still attend on a monthly basis with his colleagues.

"How the hell did we get here, huh?" he asks and presses a kiss to the top of my head. I close my eyes and revel in everything he makes me feel: safe, loved, cared for, respected, and *whole*.

"I don't know, but I sure as hell wouldn't change a thing."

"There was something about you that first night, you know?" he says, his voice thick with emotion that has me looking up at him. "It was like I walked in and saw this gorgeous woman drinking a whiskey, and I was intrigued. Then you had the gall to ignore me."

"I was making you work for it," I tease, remembering how pissed I was that he didn't leave me be.

Thank god he didn't.

"The funny part is this has been the most effortless thing I've ever had to work at in my life. It just *is* with you, Blakely," he says as I press a kiss to the underside of his jaw. "Before you, I thought there would have to be a trade-off—either a woman or my job. It is a demanding one, and I didn't think I could give one hundred percent to both . . . but I was dead wrong. What I didn't realize is that having you beside me makes work even better because I have someone to come home to at night. I have someone to share things with."

"Where is all of this coming from?" I murmur as lights in the grass between where we're sitting and the lake start to flicker to life.

"I don't know." He shakes his head. "Maybe I'm just realizing how grateful I am that you put up with my crazy, spontaneous ideas like taking a ride to the mountains when I know you hate them. Maybe it's knowing that something I did put a smile on your face or feeling your kiss on my shoulder when you wake up and slide out of bed to let me get a few more hours of sleep."

I repeat the same thing I tell myself all the time when it comes to Slade: he's too good to be true.

And he is.

Thank god he's mine.

"You know," I say as more solar lights illuminate, "if you want to get in a tit-for-tat conversation about all the ways you've made me happy, I'd be more than willing to go there, but I think we'd be out here all night."

"Perfect. The porch swing. Wine. A—"

"Mosquitos," I say, and we both chuckle as a cricket to the right of us begins to chirp. "We could make a list then. Compare notes. You know, typical date-night behavior."

"Ah, a woman after my own heart, offering up list making as a romantic pastime."

"What can I say, you've converted me."

He clears his throat. "There's only one thing left on my list right now."

"Oh really? What's that? Sex on the patio with the crickets watching?"

His smile pulls up one corner of his mouth. "Not a bad idea, but not the one I had forefront in my mind."

"You're turning down sex? Geez. Eighteen months and the spontaneity and passion are gone," I tease.

"Not gone." He chuckles softly. "They're only just beginning, Blakely."

"What?" I turn to look at him. There's emotion welling in his eyes, and I see he's holding something out to me. "What is . . ." but the words fade as my fingers hold the worn and tattered napkin from Metta's all those months ago.

And I choke over a surprised sob when I see the last line item.

Blade's To-Do List:
~~Make Paul regret he ever let you go~~
~~Figure out our history—when we met, how long your legs really are, pet peeves, etc.~~
~~Make Horrible Heather see you differently~~
~~Win your co-workers over by being fucking awesome~~
~~Convince everyone we are madly in love and meant to be~~
~~Get the promotion~~
~~Find the real Blakely again~~
~~Fall hopelessly in love~~

Ask Blakely to marry you

"Slade?" I ask when my eyes are very capable of reading what he's written.

"I mean it. You're it for me, Blakely. The beginning, the end, and every breath and moment between. Sometimes it's hard to fathom that it doesn't get any better than this, but when it comes to us, I truly believe it doesn't. I fall more in love with you every single day, and I know that we've never really talked about if you want to get married again, and if you don't, I understand, but that doesn't mean I don't want you to know I still want to spend the rest of our lives together in whatever capacity that might be. And—"

"Will you stop talking?" I laugh the words out as I thread my fingers through the hair at the nape of his neck and pull him toward me for a kiss, much the same way he did me that night we decided there was an *us*.

This time, there is something a little sweeter about our kiss, something a bit more poignant in the moment. This time, it tastes like tomorrows and forevers and all the things you want to share with someone. This time I know it's real.

"Blakely—"

"Will you stop trying to convince me when I already know how I feel. When I already know—"

"Don't you need a ring to—"

"I don't care about a ring. I only care about you. About us. And— oh my god, it's gorgeous." I stare at the diamond sparkling in the rising moonlight as tears well in my eyes. "It's . . . Slade." I look up to him while I'm at a total loss for words and see tears glistening in his eyes too. "Yes. The answer is always a million times over, *yes*, when it comes to you."

Our lips meet through our smiles and the taste of tears on our tongues, my heart irrevocably his. And our kiss turns into laughter that echoes all around us as if the forest around us is joining in our happiness too.

"Thank god you said yes. You know how I like my task lists completed."

"Oh *geez*." I roll my eyes.

"I guess this would be a good time to tell you I bought this cabin too."

"You what?" I shriek.

And, this time, when I launch myself at him, we fall clumsily into the grass.

Our kisses turn to sighs.

Our sighs turn into moans.

And we make love for the first time with so much promise before us. With a future we can't wait to fully live out.

Slade Henderson asked me to marry him.

Me.

I guess forty isn't so bad after all.

EPILOGUE 2

Blakely

Blade's To-Do List:

~~Make Paul regret he ever let you go.~~

~~Figure out our history: when we met, how long your legs really are, pet peeves, etc.~~

~~Make Horrible Heather see you differently.~~

~~Win your co-workers over by being fucking awesome.~~

~~Convince everyone we are madly in love and meant to be.~~

~~Get the promotion.~~

~~Find the real Blakely again.~~

~~Fall hopelessly in love.~~

~~Ask Blakely to marry you.~~

~~Live Happily Ever After.~~

COMING SOON

I hope you enjoyed Slade and Blakely's story in *Flirting with 40*. Up next I have the continuation of my Play Hard series. Four books about four different sisters trying to help their dad save their family sports management agency. You can check out the books in there series here:

Hard to Handle—Out Now

Hard to Hold—Out December 1, 2020—Available to Preorder

Hard to Score—Out February 16, 2021—Availableto Preorder

Hard to Lose—Out March 17, 2021—Available to Preorder

ACKNOWLEDGMENTS

I'd like to thank *my crew*. The women I've met along this journey, who I've chosen to surround myself with. Some are fellow authors, some are readers, some are professionals, but all are now considered friends. It's not often you get to do a job you love . . . and these ladies only add to the experience.

ABOUT THE AUTHOR

New York Times Bestselling author K. Bromberg writes contemporary romance novels that contain a mixture of sweet, emotional, a whole lot of sexy, and a little bit of real. She likes to write strong heroines and damaged heroes who we love to hate but can't help to love.

A mom of three, she plots her novels in between school runs and soccer practices, more often than not with her laptop in tow and her mind scattered in too many different directions.

Since publishing her first book on a whim in 2013, Kristy has sold over one and a half million copies of her books across twenty different countries and has landed on the *New York Times*, *USA Today*, and *Wall Street Journal* Bestsellers lists over thirty times. Her Driven trilogy (*Driven*, *Fueled*, and *Crashed*) is currently being adapted for film by the streaming platform, Passionflix, with the first movie (Driven) out now.

With her imagination always in overdrive, she is currently scheming, plotting, and swooning over her latest hero. You can find out more about him or chat with Kristy on any of her social media accounts. The easiest way to stay up to date on new releases and upcoming novels is to sign up for her newsletter or follow her on Bookbub.

Made in the USA
Monee, IL
12 February 2021